D0422120

SHIRKER

SHIRKER

A NOVEL

CHAD TAYLOR

Walker & Company
New York

The author gratefully acknowledges the assistance of
the Authors' Fund of the Arts Council of
New Zealand Toi Aotearoa.

First published in Great Britain in 2000 by Canongate
Crime; first published in the United States of America in
2000 by Walker Publishing Company, Inc.

Published simultaneously in Canada by
Fitzhenry and Whiteside,
Markham, Ontario L3R 4T8

Library of Congress Cataloging-in-Publication Data
Taylor, Chad.
    Shirker: a novel / Chad Taylor.
      p.   cm.
    ISBN 0-8027-3350-6 (hardcover)
    1. City and town life—Fiction.   2. Drug addicts—
Fiction.   3. New Zealand—Fiction.

PR9639.3 T32 S57   2000
823'.914—dc21   00-060023

Printed in the United States of America
2   4   6   8   10   9   7   5   3   1

For Debra

I was born beneath a bigger sky. The year of Our Lord eighteen hundred and seventy-four — for years were the Lord's then, and He was ours. Planets circled undiscovered. Neptune was a 28-year-old, Mars lined with fresh canals. The sparkling blackness between the gas-lamps: your sky is so much smaller, bereft of distance and mystery. You look up to it and wonder a little less.

I admit to a similar transformation. I too have been reduced in the interim: an epic shrunk to a cartoon. I am foolhardy and laughable, now, and this story, when it ends, will be the toast of children and the empty-headed. To this fate, however, I remain indifferent — where children and the empty-headed stand in the new order is hardly clear. To me it seems they are astride you all. Their wants have become giant. They rule you, crowding all with their shiny, multi-coloured toys, their music pounding at the walls. I am tired of your appetite for colour: skin, hair, clothes, buildings, homes, wrappings — everything is vermilion now, the variety frenetic. The bed-ridden Matisse worked on paper so bright the doctors feared it would blind him. He died before that could happen: it is you who have fallen sightless, scalded by your contemplation of brilliant things.

Forgive me. My mind wanders. My sinuses, blocked by the usual city allergies, smell lacquer and wood polish; my cataracts discern the most minute details. I have spent so much time becoming old, you understand, letting go of the things which youthful senses take for granted, that recollections when they appear are clear and vivid. An echo pretending to be a reprise.

I arrived carrying a cardboard suitcase and a brown paper bag filled with notes, coins, jewellery. The everyday amassed, a sum of things far greater than their worth. I can report no pattern to this increase in value: one decade it is china, another it is machines, and another it is buttons. Whatever: circumstances have required me to maintain such a collection. A lonely man draws many things up round himself for warmth.

I think I am hungry. The food is over-elaborate. Nobody comes. I speak to *a box. In the weeks I have lain here I have come to love its mechanism. It sits patiently by my bed: it is one of your better creations. When it is listening — which is always, the moment I open my mouth — it purrs, its record light candy-red. I awake in the dark and test it: I cough or clear my throat. And it burns, faithfully. It waits in attendance.*

The days are uniform. A series of pillows, plastic cups, cramped motions, pains.

Uniform.

1

The younger of the two policemen crouched to unstrap the watch from my unmoving wrist. He held it up and read out the time from its stopped, dangling face. 'Five-fifteen,' he said, wincing. 'Guess that's when he bought it.'

Broken glass fanned out from my body in a white flower, testimony to the force with which my 160 lbs had passed through the top-storey window and fallen to strike the street below.

'So what do we call that?' he asked his friend, sealing my watch in a plastic bag and putting it in his pocket. 'Time of impact or something?' He looked down at my feet. 'Nice shoes,' he said.

So that's what it came down to, my life of thirty-something years. That's where it starts and that's where it ends: nice shoes, and the steps I have taken in them, the places I have been, the premises I have entered. I could blame the whole thing on a pair of brown Oxford wing-tips, not too much tooling, with their new laces courtesy of the local hotel. They have been resoled twice, now, their toes shod with curved steel tap-plates. They were made for me by a man named Bob Cleft. I had always promised myself I would have my shoes hand-made. Growing up, you wear such terrible shoes. Things your brothers wore, handed down. They don't fit. Your stride suffers.

Bob I found in a workroom in one of the corridor alleys running through the central city – a long time ago, before they started tearing up all the buildings in central Auckland and planting empty glass towers. The street was damp, its stone walls and moss recalling the prison and execution yard that stood there even longer ago, before I was born. The door was heavy and patched with clipped tin, and inside smelled of sawdust and machine oil. The shelves and cutting benches were dirty white pine stacked high with leather and cardboard patterns. A black iron sewing machine stood in the back room, and between it and the workroom the wall was divided into nicotine-stained shelves filled with feet, the lasts from his many clients over the years. Some pairs were wrapped in yellowed linen, others linked with parched black tape. The children's feet were snug in crumpled newspaper. The remainder lay bare, their soles brushed with sawdust and dry leather clippings.

Bob wore half-framed bifocals with thick lenses and pursed his lips round a moistened rollie when he was concentrating. He asked me to leave my socks on and sit on his work stool, and then he squatted and cupped my foot in his leather apron, wrapping the measuring tape round it five or six different ways. He wrote the figures with a carpenter's pencil on a blue-lined index card and told me to come back the following week. When I returned he had made my feet in wood. They were lying on the workbench. The wood was younger and they were marked with my name in waxen capitals, but when he was finished he would store them on the rack alongside the others, turn their soles to face the light of the weak yellow bulb.

On the first fitting he poured us both tea from a decorated aluminium pot while I tried on the shoes. I stood up, and he rested his cup and saucer on the window sill and bent down to chalk the leather. Then he had me take them off again so he could confirm his measurements, holding each shoe like some hollow ornament, the thumb and forefinger of his right on the heel, the tip of his left forefinger on the toe. And then abruptly he said, 'I'll give you a call when they're ready.' I had to come back a second time, for a second pot of tea. Every pair equalled two visits, two cups of tea, two helpings of macaroons. I remember Bob's voice above the soft, drizzle-hushed patter of traffic passing the window, a lower pane frosted with the steam from his stained china cup. People don't look after shoes nowadays, he was fond of telling me; we used to unscrew the studs from football boots and wear them for work; I had a box camera with a perfect lens; learned to drive when I was 14 years old.

The first pair of shoes he made me were black and buckled. He put a special welt between their soles and uppers and lined them with new leather. The pair I'm wearing now he cut in brown calfskin and reinforced the eyes for the laces. For my correspondent shoes he chose green suede, and into my black calfskin semi-brogues he inserted steel-caps. They weren't intended for violent ends: the steel acted as a permanent last, preserving the shape of the toe.

On the final fitting I would lace his work and admiringly turn my feet as Bob stood back with one arm across his chest. Then I would hop down from the bench and feel the sole press up into the arch of my foot, the lining cup my heel. My repaired posture disclosed its marring. I would locate a pain in my shoulders, a crack in my lower back. I would cross the workroom floor and revel in the evenness of my step. I would feel certain again. Bob would finish his tea with a loud slurping noise and swill the leaves around in the bottom of the cup and say, 'Well, I won't be keeping you.' And it would be time to pay him and leave.

I paid him in cash instalments, $500 a pair. He made good money. I asked him about rent, once. Bob shrugged, three tacks between his lips, hammering a sole with a circular motion. He knew the workroom, like other buildings in the area, was marked for demolition, or at least for energetic renovation. Maybe, handing over the wad of notes and not worrying about the change, I'd unconsciously treated each job as the last. Either way, it shouldn't have surprised me as much as it did when I arrived at the workshop door one day to find the sign saying CLOSED. I pressed my face against the window. The rooms had been emptied. The workbench was on its back, legs in the air, the departed forms of every client marked by gaps in the sawdust on the empty shelves.

I stood on the stone steps pretending I hadn't seen it coming but of course I had. Each time I visited the street traffic was thicker, more congested, and all the shops nearby were gradually being replaced, a slow-business restaurant here, an empty car park there. I knew the current would catch him eventually.

Since then I've crossed hundreds of streets in his shoes, claiming them as mine by the distances I have covered. I have walked yards and metres, miles and kilometres, stood waiting in the rain, stomped on the accelerator pedal and, despite a promise to the contrary, kicked ribs and shins. They have always held their shape. My arches haven't fallen and my back doesn't ache. I have stood through bad times. And in good times, I've put them on and walked out.

Good shoes make every step a sure one. Children may trip themselves up but the pavement hardens as you get older. You don't get up as easily. How many times I have learned this, I've lost count. But I do keep track of the other details. Bob Cleft, for instance, I think of all the time.

I thought about him as my feet were clawing the air and the turbulence of my falling form saw them rise, first level with my face and then, gradually, above my head. I stared at my shoes as I plummeted head first, trying to right myself, trying to think what would be the best way to fall, to survive. As the ground rushed up, the city stretched out to embrace me, to reclaim me as its own. The realities of my life were returning as sure and as hard as the ground beneath. Falling, I could see everything as it really was. Instead of being an industrious man engaged in vital tasks, I had ignored everything that was important until it was too late. Falling to my death, I was granted this wisdom of hindsight. The actual drop took only seconds: the decisions I had made – my true fall – commenced much earlier.

It started in the morning, in the dark place behind my office I call a bedroom. I coughed and fumbled for my watch. Three o'clock: it was getting worse. I lay there for a long time and then got up and made a pot of tea. I drank it staring out the window. I watched the night. I counted the colours and the cars passing by; people stopping at the pie cart below. I tracked the cleaners making their way through the office block at the opposite corner. They set out on the top floor and worked down in steps. There were three of them; one with the mop trolley, two with bags. The baggers moved like an advance party, emptying wastepaper baskets, scoping out new offices. The mopper followed more slowly. They met on one of the lower levels and ate sandwiches on the boardroom table. They spoke softly while they ate, made jokes, swapped sections of the newspaper. Every night, twenty floors, mops and buckets and a packed lunch. Cleaning the building looked like the real work. All people did during the day was come in and make a mess.

Thinking at that time of night is good, normally. The silence permits words and ideas and the phone doesn't ring: you're left alone to sort things out. You can flick through an album of people you won't see again or places you'll never go, the acclaim you'll never receive: the second quarter of the clock can be a reassuring place. I made another pot of tea and sliced some blue cheese, the crumbling segments sticking to the blade. The hour was so quiet I didn't hear it coming. I was wiping my hands when I realised dawn was upon me.

I looked around. Sepia had washed over the room. The shadows were long and dark and without detail, the highlights burnished. The furniture could have been chosen by another person: the papers, the battered office equipment; things had altered since I'd examined them last. The place suddenly resembled a stage set. I experienced the abrupt sensation of waking up in a movie theatre, halfway through a film. That's how it felt and, blessed and hindered by a dead man's hindsight, I believe that's how it actually was. With that sunrise, the world changed.

I got up and pushed back the chair. I showered and put on my good suit. I was due for a morning appointment with a vice-pinstripe at Brands, a glass tower firm with lavender doors, at which I was going to tell him what to do with all their money. I deal in futures – ironically, when you think about it. I plan investments, calculate returns, recommend new ventures on the experimental, freemarket roller coaster that New Zealand has become: I make guesses, in other words, and hope they turn out good. Intuition is my speciality, which goes some way to explain the shapes I can see when I squint at these scenes from the corner of one eye. But for now let's just leave it for the boring job that it is, the thing that I don't really do that takes up a great deal of my time and other people's trust.

As the minute hand of my watch passed eight I was walking along the street. The city was settling down to work, swapping stories about the weekend and trying to work out its schedule. Office windows flickered with the static of white shirts and work-space dividers, rubber plants and undelivered memoranda. Every corner and hoarding was covered with posters advertising Mardi Gras. The parade was less than a week away: Mardi Gras, spring celebration. Sponsor-paid TV spots apologised for any disruption to traffic. Pale blue banners hung from the street lamps, transparent in the early sun. Mardi Gras, parade, Mardi Gras. Everyone was going to the parade.

The parking lots had been filled by the morning commuters. The drivers left queuing outside had cut their engines and buried themselves in their newspapers, wound down the window and listened to the radio, raked back the seat to stare up at the vinyl. They watched me walk by, wondering if I was anything to do with the police cars they had glimpsed earlier, but I wasn't. I still had an hour for breakfast and I was planning to kill it at the Apollo.

The Apollo was a tiny wood-grain and chrome café in Vulcan Lane, two blocks from Brands. Every summer its business spilled out into the street, blocking the pedestrian traffic with tables and chairs, the doors held open by a blackboard saying BREAKFAST LUNCH JUICE. There was an arcade game in the corner. I tried playing it once, punched in 20 cents to pilot an arrowhead blip rolling backwards and forwards along the bottom of the screen and firing – sadly, pathetically – at phalanx after agile phalanx of pucks, counters and napkin rings. I had four lives and they lasted less than a minute. I was thinking maybe this morning I would do better. The Apollo was run by Lee, who wore thick-rimmed spectacles and a tattoo on his shoulder. Lee surfed, and I was wondering what would happen to the morning menu when summer came.

I was also thinking how my trousers draped softly with each step and that my breath didn't taste good. My chest was tight. Something was congested, deep down. If you had asked me I would have attributed my condition to the change of season but the seasons were always changing. You might have suggested my earlier wakefulness had been caused by transmissions in the ether from the man whose body I was about to find but, like my congestion and spring, it seemed more likely to me that they were simply things that happened at the same time. Walking that morning, I didn't know he had been dead five hours and I didn't know his name. I didn't even know he was there until I turned the corner and saw the crowd.

The only noise was the whine of an empty bus as it passed and footsteps and my disordered, soon to be irrelevant thoughts. There was no high window, no poisonous umbrella tip or shot being fired. All I saw was a street and a crowd. And that was my mistake. Right there, in the faces of strangers and expressions I only now realise were knowing: that was where my fall began.

II

2

The crowd was standing at the entrance to Insurance Alley, a seven-foot-wide service corridor running between two big Shortland Street office blocks. The walls on either side are windowless and five storeys high, the space a ziggurat of fire escapes falling to bitumen paved with trash. The entrance is illuminated at night by an insurance company neon and the far end, opening on to Shortland, is blocked by a waste-glass disposal bin. Entering after sundown a body is rendered invisible, making it a haven for a pre-pub joint or a $25 unit of sexual relief. This morning's crowd weren't in the market for either. There were over a dozen of them, mostly commuters, and they were huddled before a uniformed policeman who addressed them with an outstretched hand. The entrance itself was crossed with plastic tape babbling the words POLICE LINE DO NOT CROSS.

I slowed as I passed and then stopped, listening to the cop telling everyone in a steady voice over and over again that they should all get on to work, to their jobs, or to somewhere else if they didn't have jobs because there was nothing to see, or certainly nothing anybody would want to look at. He wore the same fixed expression as the drivers queuing for the parking lot.

Trying to get a better look, I stepped between some of the people and, glancing down, saw something between their feet: a black square. A wallet. Someone had dropped it in the gutter. I picked the wallet up and shook it – it was damp. I held it up and called for everyone's attention. 'Excuse me,' I said, and moved towards the policeman, holding out the wallet.

'Morning,' he smiled grimly, and lifted the tape with his thumb.

His reaction was so automatic that I had stepped over the line before realising his mistake. 'Thanks,' I said, moving forward, and then I was standing in the alley. Past the crowd now, I could see the Shortland Street end and the blue and red lights of the police cars that had drawn everyone's attention. They must have been there for some time: walking through town, I hadn't heard them pass. The cop patted the adhesive tape back in position and faced the crowd again.

If I was going to tell the policeman he'd got it wrong I'd have to tap him on the shoulder and make a fool of myself in front of everybody. I hesitated, choosing my words, but he picked his first.

'Word's getting round,' he said, as if that was how it always was. 'Sooner you guys move him, the better.'

'How long's he been here?'

Now he turned his head, the sun outlining his profile, and spoke to me as if I'd forgotten something. 'Since three a.m.'

'Three a.m.,' I said. 'It was a nice morning at three a.m.'

'Wasn't up,' he said, not letting the uncertainty creep into his voice. 'You're from Central, right?'

The easiest thing was to keep walking to the other end of the alleyway, maybe by waving the wallet a second time. Besides, I could catch a glimpse of what was going on. I was interested.

'That's right,' I said, pocketing the wallet. I turned and started walking. 'Thanks for your help.'

The alley was cool, and smelt of piss and lichen. The contrast between the ground and the sliver of morning sky meant I had to shade my eyes in order to see anything. I cupped my hands to my face and immediately drew my elbows in tight to avoid bumping any of the figures I now saw standing like sentinels in the darkness. I counted six, maybe seven, uniformed policemen standing along the alley and another four out by the cars. No-one spoke. Radios crackled unanswered. Everyone was waiting, out of their depth.

At the end of the alley two uniformed officers stood facing each other on opposite sides of the big steel bin. As I drew closer I could hear them arguing and stopped, pretending to be interested in something on the wall.

They were arguing about opening the bin. The cop in the alley was waving a black security torch and saying no, you can't do it that way, we have to wait for it to be photographed first, and besides it's city property. The cop on the Shortland Street side had his hands on his hips and was shouting about standard procedure and police authority. Every time the cop on the Shortland Street side issued an instruction his opposite in the alleyway stubbornly vetoed it. The cop on the street appeared to have more authority but the cops in the alley seemed, by virtue of their doing 'the dirty work', to carry some special weight which the street cop wouldn't override. The dialogue was hostile but it was also energetic and complex and the men were devoted to its ritual. They were stalling, and I couldn't work out why until I realised that each officer was arguing that the *other* should take responsibility for opening the bin. I turned and looked at it more closely. The alley cop was saying definitely no, no way, not without a written order. Exasperated, the street cop glared and raised his hands to the sky, turning and looking at his colleagues for support. The alley cop slapped the torch against his leg. The container stood in greasy silence.

I crouched closer to the rust and the lichen's slick. Down one vertical edge of the bin where daylight caught the metal ran a moist, red line. Something inside me fluttered.

The stalemate was broken by a low, mechanical rumble that grew as it advanced down the street and broke with a hiss of hydraulics and brake pads. I straightened up, light-headed, to see a yellow *Recycle Now!* truck arriving, its driver peering nervously from the cab. The policemen greeted it with nods and mutterings. 'Finally,' said the alley cop. He thwacked the torch into his hand like a baseball bat. 'Hope he brought his fucking spanner.'

'Or the key,' I said, trying to move the taste in my throat.

'He won't have one for that, mate.' He shined the torch on the lid. The lid was wired shut, closed with countless nervous bindings of electrical cable. When I reached out he flicked the beam away and stopped me with the casing: 'Prints, mate.'

The street cop had called the truck driver over in order to explain something. The driver's head bobbed nervously as he listened.

'How long can it fucking take?' the alley cop said. He didn't take his eyes off the two men until the driver went back to his cab and opened the door and drew out a pair of long, blue steel bolt-cutters. 'Good,' the cop said, and his relief spread out behind us. I could hear movement along the alley and new footsteps drawing near. I tried to look busy, to wrap myself in the mistake that had got me this far.

The truck driver held the bolt-cutters above his head as he climbed through the narrow gap between the bin and the wall, sucking in the gut of his overalls, standing on tip-toe in his work boots. The cop pointed away from the bin. 'Okay, back, guys,' he ordered, but everyone was moving closer to see. The end of the alley was crowding with uniforms. The truck driver finished his examination of the wiring and said no problem and grunted as he jerked open the handles of the bolt-cutters to a full arm's width, testing the cable with their parrot beak.

'Move, I said!' the alley cop called again and I, being the only civilian, was the only one to move. I backed into a dark grey suit who put his hand on my shoulder and pulled me down slightly to talk into my ear.

'My name's Tangiers,' he said, 'And I'm from Central.' He turned me a little into the line of his stare, running his tongue round his teeth. 'Guy at the front said you're from Central.'

I spoke quietly: 'He made a mistake.'

The bolt-cutters closed with a snap and the wiring bloomed and fell to the ground. Tangiers kept his grip but looked past me, now. The alley cop was still telling the other policemen to get out of the way. A man wearing a parka pushed past and squatted in front of the fallen lock, tugging on rubber gloves. Someone else started taking photos with a flash-gun. On the street side a group of cops were lifting the lid. It took three of them to raise it, hands above their heads, stepping in front of each other until they were touching nothing and the lid swung down on its hinges with a crash.

Dust and flies jumped in the sun, then settled into a swirl, rising in sympathy with the sweet, rotten smell that was now seeping into the alley. There was a pause and then the flash-gun resumed its popping. Everyone was looking at the shape daubed across the inside of the lid in huge, red smears – blood. The driver tipped his head, trying to read what it said before the alley cop asked him to move away.

The alley cop took off his cap and leaned over the edge of the bin, leaning into the sunlight. He quickly raised his hand to his mouth and looked up at the sky. When he made himself look again he turned his head to the left, then to the right, wrinkling his nose. He wiped his eyes and stood back from the bin and turned to one side. Then he threw up, his vomit splattering on the sidewalk.

Suddenly there was no tension any more, as if he had lost his nerve on behalf of everyone else. Disembarrassed, the crowd broke up. There wasn't so much hurry now. Over the next few minutes a routine quickly established itself around the bin: photographs, measuring, the taking of notes. And whatever they were doing, everyone was checking it with Tangiers, and double-checking, bringing their questions and forms up to him, standing alongside without bothering to look at me. I waited it out, knowing I couldn't leave without his permission. The longer I gave it, the more routine things would become and the less exceptional my intrusion would seem. I hoped. Tangiers was either very reasonable or very busy. He had let go of my shoulder. He put his fingers to his chin to listen to questions and pointed them like a gun to answer. I maintained the most neutral pose I could.

Sir, the police received an anonymous call. The call said to look in the bin. Was it was a hoax call? The call was very specific. Anything else? There was a report of a mugging in the park. The park was adjacent to the scene. Someone seen running across the parking lot. The parking lot was also adjacent to the scene. Where was that report? Sir, we'll get you that report. Identification? No, sir. Identifying marks? No identifying marks. When can we move it? Soon, we think. Where's the coroner? Someone called him. Should be here soon.

'What's soon?' Tangiers barked. 'How long is soon?'

Nobody knew.

I was staring at the marks on the lid. Tangiers followed my gaze.

'What did you say your name was?' he asked, remembering.

It came out weakly: 'Ellerslie Penrose.'

'Penrose,' he said. He swivelled his body round without shifting his feet, referring us both to the upturned lid. 'Any idea what those marks are?'

I shrugged. 'No.'

Tangiers pointed at the bloody swirl. 'They look like letters to me. A single letter, repeated.' He traced his reading with a black-nailed finger. 'That could be a P. You reckon?' He stared at the bloody initial. 'Like P for Penrose.' Then he pushed back the flaps of his jacket and put his hand back in his pocket. He looked at me. 'It'd be a bit much to ask for, wouldn't it?'

'It would.'

'So, P – Penrose, how do you explain that?'

'I guess . . .' I looked at the bin, the red stain running beneath. 'If you think about it, everything is happening all at once anyway.'

He waited.

'So naturally, some things are going to happen at the same time. Some things will be the same. Others will be different. There might be a pattern in that, but a pattern isn't necessarily causal.'

'You're saying it's a coincidence.'

'Yes.'

A cop wearing heavy rubber gloves put down his walkie-talkie and hooked his thumb. 'We found his clothes,' he said.

'Any ID?' Tangiers asked.

'The wallet's missing.'

I froze.

Impersonating a police officer. Trespass. Interfering with evidence, withholding evidence. My name begins with a bloody P.

Tangiers turned to me. His saliva made a popping noise as he parted his lips to smile.

'So,' he said. 'Shall we take a look?'

I didn't say anything.

'This is part of my job,' he went on. 'If you want to do it, you should find out about it a little more.'

I tried to stop my voice shaking. 'I don't want your job.'

'You like telling people you're a cop?'

'I didn't say that. The policeman at the top of the alley let me in. He made a mistake. I don't impersonate cops.' Tangiers poked out his bottom lip and raised his eyebrows, furrowing his brow like a big dog. 'He let me in without asking who I was. I thought the alley was clear. I was taking a short cut. Actually, I'm going to breakfast. I have breakfast at the Apollo most mornings. I don't know anything about what's going on here. If someone made a mistake, it wasn't me. One of your cops made a mistake. I can't help it if he can't do his job.'

He popped another smile. 'Come and have a look, anyway.'

'What?'

He tipped his head at the bin, eyes sly. 'Don't have to.'

'I want to,' I said.

'Why?'

'Curiosity.'

He gave me another face full of How About That. 'You're a curious person.'

'You're trying to annoy me.'

'What makes you say that?'

'It won't work.'

'I can see that. You're a lot smarter than me. And I think—'

When I started walking away in the middle of his sentence, he did look surprised. I walked fast up to the bin, keeping my eyes straight and ignoring the smell. When my chest was almost touching the rim it was so bad my eyes had started to water. I inhaled deeply, making myself take in every part of the smell. Shit and oil and piss and rotten meat. Warm plastic from the flash-guns. Sweat and nylon jackets, aftershave. And then I made myself look inside.

It wasn't so bad because at first I couldn't tell what I was seeing. There were a thousand parts to it, without priority, and the thin ray of sun cast it in gleam and shadow. But slowly, as I looked it up and down – mimicking, I realised, the alley cop's gesture – the segments drew together and from the initially random pattern emerged the sensation that I was intended to see what was now before me. Like the circumstances of the morning, it had merely been waiting for its cue to become clear.

Inside was a naked man who, though he had died a long time ago, was still doing his best to sit up. The broken bottles and shards of glass had sliced him open and bled him blue. His struggles had only multiplied the countless slashes and cuts: in his dying moments he had flayed himself alive. Muscles were severed, bared to the bone. The soft pink skin of his stomach was a razored tramway bulging with deep red offal. The stiffer muscles of his chest and shoulders were slotted with thicker, more chiselled fragments. There must have been a point when exhaustion and unimaginable pain had told him to sit still, but he had thrashed until death set in and his exhausted body sank, slipping downwards on its transparent bed of a hundred scalpels.

The top of his head was segmented like an orange. Long grey hair sprouted from pie-segment islands of scalp and yellowy fat. His eyes were shut and his face was tipped upwards, open-mouthed. Rigor mortis had preserved the last desperate shapes of the muscles. A possum caught in a trap will gnaw off the captured leg; a man will attempt to climb from a glass-disposal bin even though the movement of doing so slashes him further. His body was contorted, a signature of a wretched, animal death. His hands were reaching, palms uppermost, for the lid. To press against it, wipe it. With his own blood.

The smell was still fresh. Garbage, meat and liquor. I followed the alley cop's steps backwards and crouched to press my head against the wall, stepping over his bile. I was drooling saliva. I spat and steadied myself. I was determined to not be sick. I stooped, stood straight, felt dizzy, sucked in air. I was shaking.

'Christ,' Tangiers said, still looking inside the bin. 'What a horrible mess.' He shook his head, trying to loosen the vision. 'That what you came to see?'

I was wet-eyed. I said nothing.

'The worst part is moving it,' he said. 'Turning it over. The hands and the feet . . .'

'Oh fuck,' I said. Everything whirled. 'Please.'

'I'm just saying – what you feel now, I always feel that. Every time.' Someone was debating loudly about the best way to remove the corpse. 'But you have to look. Everyone has to look. All the incidents I've attended, I've seen the same thing happen. No-one wants to look and everyone does. They do what you do. You know why? Because they have to be sure. They have to be sure the person is really dead so they don't bury anyone by mistake. And they have to be sure that it isn't them.'

I turned, finally, breathing through my mouth. Tangiers waited, patient. 'That's my theory, anyway.' His mouth stretched into another smile. 'You okay?'

'Yeah.'

'What interested you? What made you come down here?'

'Someone said he died at three.'

'That's correct, we think the person did die at three. An officer shouldn't be giving out that sort of information.'

'I woke up at three this morning. As if maybe I heard something.' I coughed. 'I was too far away to hear anything. But you know what I mean. You know?'

He took that in. 'You live around here?'

'Close by.'

'You live close to here.'

'The Dilworth building.'

'That's only a short walk from here.'

I nodded. 'Corner of Fort and Customs.'

'You live in the Dilworth?'

'It's my office address. It's not residential.'

'That's right. It's illegal to live at an office address.' He was pleased to discover something else I'd done wrong.

He looked at me hard. 'Do you know anything about this incident?'

The wallet in my pocket. 'No.'

'See anything? Hear anything at all?'

The leather banging against my chest. 'Nothing.'

He was nodding. 'You just came and looked.'

'Because I was awake at the time, yes.' I echoed his nod but he was looking away, pointing me out to one of the uniforms.

'Take this guy's details.' The uniform nodded and stepped towards us. Tangiers looked at me again. 'Hell of a coincidence about that letter,' he said flatly.

'I don't know anything about it,' I said.

He didn't seem convinced either way. He stared at me until gradually he became occupied with a different, unvoiced thought. The uniformed cop stood next to me with his open notebook and looked back at Tangiers and asked if there was anything else. Tangiers pulled his hands out of his pockets and did up his jacket button.

'Escort Mr Penrose from the scene.' He swivelled on his heel.

'Thanks,' I called back, but the uniformed policeman was already leading me away. I followed him to the barrier and stepped out into the street and kept on walking.

My breakfast was waiting uncooked at the Apollo and my appointment was still good at Brands. The work they had for me was part of an ongoing contract – easy money, which I needed. But I didn't stop to eat and I didn't make my 10 o'clock. I did walk to the Brands building in case I was being followed, but when I reached the lavender doors I hung out in the lobby for a few minutes, checked the street and then walked outside again, every inch of my skin cold and wet in the sun.

3

I headed towards my office unable to believe what I had done. Removing such a vital item from a murder scene was plainly the wrong thing to do. Pocketing the wallet was inexcusable, and every second I held on to it increased the gravity of my situation. Leaving the alley with it was a conscious wrongdoing. By the time I was ten minutes down the road, I had committed a major crime. I couldn't believe I had got this far. I kept expecting to hear running feet and Tangiers shouting and hailers blaring my guilt. When I heard the police helicopter approaching in a slow circle, my stomach turned with it. I hid beneath an awning while the sound was loudest and moved out the second it began to fade. I was walking so fast I nearly went under a truck. It was making a grocery delivery to one of the Chinese restaurants, cabbage and lettuce scraps trailing from its pallet. Smiling as I started, the grocer waved thanks. I stared back, thinking of the corpse's stiff, bloody hands. As soon as the truck had backed halfway into the loading bay I stepped round the front of it, ignoring the oncoming traffic.

My building was now only a street away. The Dilworth stood six storeys high and was undergoing endless repairs. Wind whipped the sacking hanging from the scaffolding, flashing the tide-line of graffiti between the gaps. Its ground floor was a dim, green-tiled arcade. Its only tenants were a travel agency staffed by two chain-smokers and a yellowing PC, and a second-hand book store. The doors were clear. I would be safe once I was inside.

The elevator was open when I got there, waiting. I got in and closed it and pressed the button for six. The winch came alive and replaced my breathing with the reassuring silence of empty floors dropping away beneath the cage.

Their numbers passed on a mother-of-pearl clock face. The Dilworth was laced with art deco extras. It had been all offices once, in some newsreel yesterday, but in the decades since then business had moved uptown. Now the first floor was vacant and the second and third were leased out for legal storage. Behind the wooden doors with their frosted-glass windows and stencilled announcements of offices and workers within, stood only rows and rows of fireproof filing cabinets, silently collecting dust. After two years I knew the lessees of floors two and three better than they did; second: Feckle and Minister; Bounce, Doppel, Roman; Gentry and Lang; and Phillips Heat Brangwyn; third: Feckle and Minister (commercial transactions); Phillips Heat Brangwyn; Brite & Self.

Occasionally you'd bump into a temp or a holiday law clerk wandering amazed through the corridors and pretending to be lost. Likewise some of the long, empty rooms of the fourth and fifth became party venues around university graduation time, attracting their own peculiar crowds, but on the sixth floor where I kept my offices the only people I was likely to meet were a deadbeat teenage couple I called Franny and Zoë who lived on the west side of the block.

The elevator squeaked to a stop. I listened for a second before pulling open the cage and stepping into the reception area. The worn strip of carpet stretched into the distance, slipping round a corner. I was in the central core of the building, high above the city and the morning heat. The hallway smelled of floor polish and dust. When I found nothing waiting for me in the low electric light I shut the cage and sent the elevator down again.

Everything was deserted. The Dilworth was always closed but business today was even slower than usual.

My office door was unlocked. I'd learned soon after moving in that anyone who wanted to get through it could. I shut it and took out the wallet and slapped it on the desk. More slowly, I took off my jacket. Its armpits were dark and wet. I stood there holding it, breathing through my nose. Everything was much too close.

26

I pulled the chair out and turned it round and sat with my arms resting on the back, cradling my chin.

The wallet's black leather was smooth, its once-pebbled texture worn to a shine. Its curve betrayed the owner's habit of tucking it into his back pocket. I used the nail of my little finger to flip it open. There was no plastic window: its contents were hidden behind the leather. I wiped my palms and, with my fingertips, lifted it like a broad, delicate pair of binoculars. Then I turned it upside down and shook everything it contained on to the desk.

There was no money, although a receipt from an automatic banking machine showed $100 had been withdrawn three days before. There were five copies of an antiques dealer's business card – Ash Antiques – and because they were all new and suitable for presentation it seemed likely that the owner of the wallet worked there. There were also cards for a upholsterer's, a second-hand book store, a tariff and freight forwarder and an 'editorial consultant'. All were worn, and the back of the tariff card bore two phone numbers. There was a folded newspaper clipping torn from the For Sale section: garage sales, second-hand. 'Junk man,' I said aloud. 'You're a junk man.'

I found a small black metal disc inscribed with two vertical silver stripes and one angled line: the label for a car's choke. A photograph, trimmed with scissors to wallet size, of a black cat hunched beneath a coffee table. Some stamps. The inside top left corner of a foreign postcard. A latch key. A raffle ticket, its folds coloured dark grey. And a trading card: *Star Trek: The Next Generation* (card 106, Lieutenant Commander Data).

I flicked back to the card for Ash Antiques. Only the store name and number, no address. The choke tag could mean his car was falling apart. Three till receipts from the same coffee house in the 246 shopping arcade: he'd probably taken morning tea there, when he was alive.

I picked up the phone and dialled the numbers on the business cards. At the second-hand book store I got a fax. There was no reply at the upholsterer's – probably out chasing up ads in the *Trade and Exchange*. I tried the other numbers. The editorial consultant's opened with a squealing fax, suddenly interrupted by someone picking up the phone. He sounded impatient. I transferred the receiver to my other hand. I didn't know where to start.

'Hello?' he asked a second time. 'This is Veale.'

'I'm calling for Mr Ash,' I said.

'Yes?' He was sounding more businesslike. I shook out the Sapporo can full of pens on my desk and found a ballpoint.

'It's about – the matter we were discussing,' I lied.

'Yes,' he said, and waited. I was taking a new lined exercise book from the desk drawer and opening it, folding the cover back at the spine, pressing the pages flat on the desk top. On the first page I wrote: VEALE?

'You do remember Ash Antiques?' I asked.

'I do. You're an associate of Tad's, I gather.'

'Tad Ash?' I guessed.

'Yes.' Veale was thinking, now. I was writing the words TAD ASH. 'And your name was . . . ?' he wondered.

I ignored the question, groping for something safe. 'I'm calling to ask if there's been any – progress.'

'Well, I would have thought that rather obvious. I can scarcely do any more until Mr Ash delivers on his part of the bargain.'

'Right.'

'You'll excuse me, but I must ask your name.'

'Of course. Tad was wanting a verification.' I underlined the name TAD ASH three times. There was some sort of business arrangement between Veale and the murdered man. Already I had something.

'I can't imagine why.' Veale sounded suspicious now, and slightly alarmed. 'Who is this, please? What is your name?'

I took a deep breath. I was about to an invent a reason for anyone who'd heard of Tad Ash to call me. I'm an old friend, I work for him, I'm trying to track him down, I've never heard of him, I don't know what he looks like, I saw that he was dead. That he'd been taken to the alley, stripped and thrown into the bin. By someone who wanted to cut him with glass and stop him forever. The phone waited faithfully, hissing through the receiver. I covered the dark little holes with my hand and tried to find the energy to speak.

The outer office wall was a strip of ceiling-high window panes that encircled the entire sixth floor. In the adjoining room where I kept my bed I had painted them over, but here and in the bathroom they were bare. Someone could be watching from the hotel opposite or the bus stop or even the church, craning their neck to look up. Here, at my desk, I was well back from the glass. But someone could still be looking. I'd considered that when I moved here, but never again since. Everything around me seemed new but very, very old and familiar. Maybe it was nothing more than the sunlight drawing my attention. I had a habit of rocking forward on the chair while using the phone. Carefully I put its feet on the floor.

'Who is this, please?' he asked again. Fidgeting, while I sat so calm.

I have worked in many offices in my life: small with the odour of air freshener; large and breezy turning cold in winter; refurbished villas with a brick fireplace in the reception area and thundering plumbing. I have taken back-rooms and shared kitchen duties with a typesetter, a betting shop, a pattern cutter and a student photographer. Four years ago I bit the bullet and signed a lease for three linked office spaces at commercial rates and built shelves for everything. I put my red-lined map of the city on the wall and my filing cabinets on either side of the door. The full sets of the *Encyclopaedia Britannica* for the years between 1978 and 1983, which Louise helped to complete, stacked outside the bathroom. My notebooks, my scrapbooks, my record collection. My stereo sat in pride of place, the position of the speakers an acoustic ideal. All I had to do was fix the turntable, which had broken before I moved in. I'd been too busy to get on to it. I'd had filing to do.

I even bought a computer with the intention of slowing the near-exponential growth of paper in my life but after a month the task had lost its urgency. Now it sat on the desk by the phone, slowly turning obsolete. Its digital tongue was spoken less, now. When it needed repairs parts had to be soldered and cannibalised. I got Zoë from down the hall to look after it. Some nights I had to walk across and ask them to turn down the music, and I'd seen a computer there the night they'd passed out and I had to break to do so myself. Zoë had rigged my machine with a stolen modem and software for something called the Internet, which she promised me would be big someday. I said I could wait. Mechanisms rarely agreed with me. I had to run my hands over paper in order to think. I liked touching the words as I read them. The monitor was fogged with fingerprints, a trail of my double-checking, my hesitations and queries.

It wasn't always like this. My cares were once less solitary. I liked living by myself. But sometimes I felt as if there was someone else in the room, a nameless observer, watching my actions, listening to every thought.

I shook my head clear and I took my hand away from the phone and tried to ask about a complete stranger, a hypothesis, a horror-show spectacle who had roiled my stomach and made me proud to have not thrown up. I would cover the fact that I'd ransacked his belongings and invent a persona which allowed me to remain anonymous, and then I would poke around his corpse.

'Who is this?' Veale demanded, agitated now. 'Who are you?'

I couldn't believe what I was doing. 'Nobody,' I said, embarrassed. 'Nobody at all.'

I put down the phone.

I wiped my face. I closed the exercise book and put it back in the drawer. I picked up the cards and everything else and put them back inside the wallet. When it was safe I would go back to the alley and drop it in the car park, say, or some other place nearby – somewhere that could plausibly have been overlooked. I should never have picked it up. It contained so much that was important, and opening it up, making those calls – I had probably complicated things enough.

Now the sun felt hot. I stood up and crossed to the window, raking my fingers through my hair. I opened the filing cabinet by the door, found a handle and cranked open the louvre windows. Their creaking threads upset the seagulls crouched on the ledge outside. Then I unlocked the refrigerator and made myself a pitcher of ice water and gulped half of it before it had time to cool.

I pulled off my shirt and threw it in the laundry basket, then took off my shoes and socks and walked to the bathroom barefoot. My piss was a light brown stream. My back ached. I sat with another glass of water at the kitchen bench and looked out the window. The seagulls were coming back, picking their spots in the sun. The church had shrunk over the years. It was a white clinker-brick chantry, one of the last in the inner city, its door guarded by a long neon sign: EKALE OTOPO A I E U. I had no translation. My bare toes touched the lead window-frames thick with white paint. The breeze from the open louvres stroked my hair. The bench top was still cool.

I took a shower and scrubbed myself clean of all smells, real or imagined. Afterwards I opened the bathroom windows and watched the steam tip up to the sky.

My bedroom was on the opposite side of the office, divided from the rest of the space by a ceiling-high bookcase filled with art texts, dictionaries of biological species, scrapbooks, medical guides and manila folders containing things I had yet to place in the filing cabinets. The layout of the bedroom was identical to that of the office except for the black-painted windows. I hung my towel on the end of the bed and chose a bottle of cologne from the bedside table, the only other piece of furniture in the room. I splashed it on my neck and under my arms and the soles of my feet. I lay back and counted the scratches of sunlight that gleamed through the snicks in the masked glass.

I shook out more cologne, rubbed it on my shoulders. Then I capped the bottle and lay back on the sheets to feel the alcohol evaporate and the hours since 3 a.m. catch up, my body warm with tension and fatigue.

I woke to find the other rooms coloured richly in the afternoon light. I got up and dressed in front of the mirror, put on my Coney Island cufflinks and my watch and picked up my wallet to check how many dollars I had.

There is a photograph on my bedroom wall, a single Polaroid. I don't remember who took it but I do still have the memory of its being taken, the music of the piano and the chatter of the bar. I stood close and looked it over again. It showed me standing in the foreground, lost in glare but beyond that, just short of a grainy

4

My first instinct was to shut the door again, fast. But he blocked it, stepping into the room before I could move, strolling past my desk with his hands in his pockets. His plainclothes extra stayed in the hallway, a hand from the shadows securing the door. 'Having a night out?' Tangiers asked, 'After such a busy day? Who're you gonna meet?' He swivelled, cracking his fast little smile. 'You'll dine out on this morning, yeah? Stories to tell.'

'I've been telling people already,' I said. Trying to play it tough, to match him.

'Really?' He turned back to the desk, eyeing the papers and the envelopes and the broken-down computer. 'Know a lot of people?'

'Yes.'

'They come here?'

'Yes.'

'How many?'

'What?'

'In the last week, how many times?'

'Well, none, but—'

'Last fortnight?'

I looked around. 'Maybe—'

'What about the last month? How many people?'

'I can't remember.'

'Your girlfriend stay over?'

Chewing my tongue. 'I'm not with anyone, currently.'

'Huh.' He stood by the desk looking at the map pinned above it, and I looked at the wallet. He was standing right over it, leaning forward to inspect the drawing pins. 'What are these?' He tapped their red plastic heads. 'What do they indicate?'

'Real estate.'

'Thought you were in finance.'

'Companies with finance invest in real estate.' I talked fast, trying to keep his attention, willing him not to look down. 'The areas indicated by the pins have, or will probably, attract speculators.'

'The areas indicated by the pins . . .' He nodded. 'You speak very precisely. You speak like a cop, possibly a lawyer.'

'I trained as a lawyer.'

'You a lawyer?'

'My degree's in business.'

'So why not a lawyer?'

'I'm too nice.'

He smiled at that. 'Ha. Very good. It's funny and it's like-able.' He scrutinised the filing cabinets. 'You understand why I'm here, right?'

'To ask more questions?'

He turned to face me; I was relieved. 'That's part of it.' He nodded over my shoulder. At the signal the extra stepped forward, took the handle and closed the door on himself, leaving us alone in the room. 'It's a personal call. I know you won't mind. You were pretty frank this morning: this is your address, as it turns out. Most people lie.'

I looked as interested as I could. 'Really?'

'They give their parents' address, or a work number.'

'My parents are dead.'

'And you work from here? It looks more like a home.'

I breathed slowly: 'Sometimes I sleep over. I eat lunch here – that's why I have the kitchen set up. The work I do means keeping strange hours – I have to keep track of the markets overseas. So if it looks slightly lived-in, that's why.'

He nodded. 'I don't know anything about the terms of your lease, Mr Ellerslie Penrose. You've been to law school, you probably know more about it than me anyway.'

'I didn't go to law school, I did a few papers.'

'In what?'

I blinked. 'Commerce. History.'

'One's ideas must be as broad as Nature if they are to interpret Nature,' he declared. '*Study in Scarlet*.'

'Ah.'

'I know what you're thinking. Sherlock Holmes. Basil Rathbone. Curly pipe, little hat.'

'I guess.'

'There's more to it.'

'Yes.'

'Holmes is an inspiration.'

'To you?'

'To all engaged in law enforcement.' He turned away from the desk and sat against it, his square arse a dough-roll away from the leather. 'Did you know Sherlock Holmes was the first to use plaster of Paris for taking impressions of footprints and other evidence at the scene of a crime? The first. He was the first to examine the dust on clothes as a means of identification. He analysed the ashes of different tobaccos – no-one had paid attention to that before he did. He was the first to develop a scientific process exclusive to criminal investigation. The cases of Sherlock Holmes were used as official training manuals by the Chinese and the Egyptian police. When Edgar Hoover was chief of the FBI he stated that the bureau had incorporated Holmes's methods to the full. The Sûreté's criminal laboratory at Lyon is named after Conan Doyle, in honour of his creation.

'Holmes's method of deduction – of eliminating all possible explanations for a crime until that which remained, however improbable, had to be the truth – that process is the template for modern police investigation. Deduction. That's why I'm here. Would you mind?'

He approached me with three quick steps until his quick little smile was inches away from my face. He took me by the left wrist. Suddenly he tightened his grip and turned to the right, forcibly extending my arm across his chest while jamming his left elbow into my neck. I swore and twisted but remained caught, my arm helplessly extended: any pressure I exerted would only invert the joint. 'Hey!' I said, uselessly, and found myself having to lie flat on the desk to avoid the arm being broken. Tangiers was fiddling with my cufflink. He undid my shirt sleeve and rolled it up, shoving the jacket fabric until it bunched. He turned my arm in the light, unapologetically twisting my shoulder to examine the flesh and swollen veins. Then, just as abruptly, he released me. 'Spotless!' he declared.

I took back my arm and sat up, dazed. But instead of backing away he now clapped both hands on my face and turned it to the light, lifting my eyelids with his thumbs. Again he maintained a warning grip, pressure enough to keep me from struggling but a steadiness intended to reassure. I stood bent over as he peered into my eyes. 'Clean!' he barked, and released me for the second time. 'You're not a needle user.'

'No, I'm not.' I stepped back. My sleeve was bunched so tight I had to shake it loose, and my face was reddening. 'I could have told you,' I spat.

'Insurance Alley is an area known for drug activity. The man we found today was an addict. His body was run through with holes.'

I was panting. I was out of breath. 'Yeah?' I said. My arm hurt.

'Yep. Needle tracks up to here. I think the old man was there to score. Possibly, I thought, from you. But then we checked and you have a legitimate income. Then I thought maybe you also were a junkie. But I see you're not. So. Watson.' He cracked his little smile. 'I deduct these scenarios from those I consider possible.'

'Really? That's great.' My tone was carelessly sharp. I'd been afraid when he first walked in but now I was losing my temper. 'That's why you're here? To storm in and assault me?'

'Assault?' He raised his eyebrows but kept his smile.

'You grabbed me, you put in me in a lock—'

'I wouldn't call that assault. I'm following up my investigation with some questions. I looked at your arm. It's true I touched you, but . . . it's a grey area. At best.'

'A grey area.'

'Like I said.'

'Fuck you.'

'See, in a court of law, that's insulting a police officer. That's an offence. But am I going to arrest you for that? Of course not. Telling me to go fuck myself is a reasonable response in this situation. You've

36

got to look at the circumstances, be realistic.' He raised a finger, nominating an unspoken point. 'Not unlike this,' he said, and then pointed the finger at the wallet lying on the desk.

I said nothing.

'A wallet, a dead man's wallet. Evidence from the scene of a crime. Which begs questions. How it came into your possession. Why it's here.' He picked it up. 'We discovered his clothes rolled up at the other end of the alley. Shoes, underwear, crucifix, fountain pen – but no wallet. Theft, we decided. So what do we have to do? Look for fingerprints, footprints, threads of fabric. Dust. We've been on our knees. We scraped his fingernails. Scraped up little bits of shit into plastic bags. Degrading work, dull. And all the time we're doing it I'm thinking, boy, if only we had that missing wallet, we'd have something to go on. What a vital piece of evidence. And look here. Look at what we have found.

'Now, I'm not saying you did it with malicious intent. Maybe you found it nearby. Maybe you were going to call us. Maybe you even picked it up by mistake. I'm going to be realistic, Ellerslie. I'm going to look at the circumstances. Why did you do it?'

I didn't answer.

'Play it your way,' he said, opening the wallet. 'Now I'll have to make it official, take you down to the station, and all that.'

He stopped, staring inside the wallet. His brow furrowed. He stabbed his paw into the leather, riffling through its contents. He was looking increasingly perturbed. He found a business card and pulled it out. He threw that on the desk and went through the rest of the contents. He started to throw them on the ground. The papers and dockets dropped around the toes of his shoes like hair on a barber's floor. I tipped my head and looked at the card. Ellerslie Penrose, it said.

When I had taken as much time as I could smoothing my sleeve I cleared my throat. 'Officer. Detective, whatever; could I have my wallet back, please?'

He looked at me. He had sucked in his fast little smile. He rocked back on his heels, raising his chin, aiming it at me. 'This is your wallet.' He said it as if he didn't believe it. I know I didn't. I had picked up the wrong wallet on my way out. I crunched my fingers in my sweaty palms. He let out his breath. 'Damn,' he said. 'Shit and damn.'

He was trembling with the effort of controlling himself. He sucked air through his nose, nostrils flaring. I reached out and took the wallet from his hands: he didn't resist. I crouched and started picking up my things. And then, moving again with his sudden speed, he caught my hand under the sole of his shoe, pressing it hard into the boards. 'You know what's wrong?' he said. 'Can you spot the error?'

I gritted my teeth.

'It is a capital mistake to theorise before one has data,' he said, stepping down on my hand just a little bit harder. '*Scandal in Bohemia*.'

I almost yelped as he stepped off it. At the door he stopped and turned towards me. 'I'm watching you,' he said. 'Remember that.' He continued walking out backwards, and the door swung shut.

5

The more I thought about it, the angrier I became but it was too late to reply now, too late to do anything except walk out carrying two wallets and go someplace, get out, count to ten. I took the elevator down, leaning on the back wall and muttering to myself, kicking my heels as the offices slid past, then the silent storage, the low-angled sunlight streaking across the lobby. The cage jerked to a stop in the basement and I got out. I raised the roller door and pink light poured into the loading dock. My car stood beneath a canvas cover. I pulled off the wrap and bundled it against a pillar.

I folded my jacket and laid it on the passenger seat, then fiddled to lower the window on the driver's side where the handle had broken. I stopped it on the street and got out to close the basement door and the car stalled again. I pumped the choke and re-started it and nursed it down a back street with my foot heavy on the gas pedal, the double skin of rust in the side panels shaking like angry applause. I turned right on the road that snaked away from the city and towards the eastern bays. The long stretch would give it time to warm up. I flicked the radio on and twirled the ossified plastic dial: 'Peg'. 'Tambourine Man'.

The 1971 De Tomaso Pantera is a low-slung wing of a car which is impressive to anyone who isn't a serious collector or a mechanic. I bought it from a damp farmyard garage for $4000 and it takes several miles to come alive, but it is big and powerful and the brown leather seats hold you like a giant hand. With the windows down it stays cool inside and there are a few roads in Auckland on which you can keep moving and moving, even if you eventually have to turn and come back. I coaxed the choke back in, and felt the V8 warming until accelerating made the body drop and hug the road. And then

I opened it up and watched the traffic fall away.

The faster you travel, the slower your surroundings seem to be and the calmer you become. I believe this is because, as you accelerate, you experience a minute fraction of the effect described in the theory of relativity, which states that when a body approaches the speed of light everything viewed from it appears to come to a halt. Hanging on to the corners, hugging the shoulder and stepping hard on the floor, the car and the road were all that counted. Tangiers was not real, this morning never happened.

The sun was still falling, basting the harbour waters. I drove until they were red and then took the corkscrew road up Achilles Point and down again, tracing my route back to the city, overtaking everything, running orange lights and thinking about nothing but the noise of the engine and the building façades and the quickness of their passing.

The Regent Hotel looked busy. Cars were queuing in the forecourt and the room windows were lit salmon-pink all the way to the eighth floor. The brasserie was a jumble of diners and tables and table service. I pulled up at the steps and turned off the engine to save it stalling again. The doorboy came trotting down the steps.

'Leave it running, sir,' he corrected me. 'We'll just take it round for you.'

'Sure.' I started pulling up the driver's window with my finger-tips.

'We'll lock it for you, sir.' He pulled the door away from me, holding it open. 'Please. Do you have any luggage with you?'

'I'm meeting someone.' I gestured to the handle. 'Do you mind? The handle's broken.'

'We have a twenty-four-hour breakdown service available – we could get that looked at, if you'd like.'

'Thank you, but it's no worry.' I sandwiched the glass between outstretched hands and raised it until it was closed. 'The clutch is also very short,' I warned.

'We'll be sure to take care.'

I stood at the bottom of the steps putting on my jacket. 'Well, you do have to be careful. You have to rev it a lot but let the clutch off a very small amount each time.'

'Look,' he said, tugging at his studded ear. 'Please, sir. Relax.' He smiled at me and wrenched the ignition. The car roared, lurched forward and stalled.

'See?' I said. The other doorboy laughed from the top of the steps.

'I've got it,' he said, bunching his lips, and stalled the machine again. Guests stopped to watch. The machine was jerking forward, its massive engine gulping. The retractable headlamps blinked open when the engine started and clapped shut each time it stopped. I was nervous that it would flood or the steering would lock, but there were more people gathering and I didn't feel like performing for a crowd. I left him to it, his face turning red, and passed through the big swing doors.

I descended again, this time on carpeted steps into the sunken, split-level lobby, my shoes noiseless on the dyed pile. The concierge nodded good evening, speaking sotto voce into one of his telephones. The reception desk spilled over with flowers. A wedding couple were checking in, the bride still wearing her long white gown. The chairs were draped with fat tracksuits and couples nursing airline bags. At the back of the lobby a baby grand stood like a black clam with a pianist crouched inside, carefully extracting the riff from a Bacharach song. A jazzectomy. Removed, the melody divided itself into ornaments and frills, dead pieces that rose to disappear high in the ceiling with the voices and the ringing telephones, lost in the tall white pediments.

I opened the bar's smoked-glass door and stepped into the applause of recessed lights. Natives and travellers slouched in the deep couches, faces yellowing in the side-lamps. Anonymous, gold-lensed spectacles peered through the shadows. Hands draped from armchairs and whispers carried smoke. The only loud noise came from a corner where some teenagers were laughing. I took a deep breath of cigarettes and leather and slowly released it, blinking. My tongue pressed against my teeth. I made shaky plans to eat later, or maybe order from the bar. Things seemed easier in this room. The difference you made to it was just enough, and not too much.

The barman, Tony, was shovelling ice, his hand rolling the stainless-steel shaker. He was short with a buzz-saw haircut and his arrowhead moustache implied a zippy little grin even before he smiled. I chose a counter stool. He winced as he opened a bottle of obscure liqueur. 'All gummed up,' he said, rinsing the top under a hot tap. 'How's it going?'

'Not bad.' He poured the blue liqueur and added cream.

'Looks good,' I said.

'Oh yeah.' He sniffed at the teenage corner, the girls' white arms sticking out from their gowns, the boys stiff in hired tuxedos. 'End of term. Some city high school. They should go get a milkshake.'

'You were young once.'

'I was never rich, but.' He capped the shaker and shrugged, flicking open his Zippo with his free hand. A businessman had taken out a cigarette. Tony lit it, smiled and made the lighter disappear back into his waistcoat pocket. 'Some people have it good,' he said. 'I got an old guy who orders his drinks through room service, one at a time. Five-thirty: one martini. Six-fifteen: one martini. Forty-five minutes later, another martini. I say, I'll send you a pitcher, but no – one martini every three-quarters of an hour. And he tips every time.'

'That's the good life.'

'He's one of the regulars. We have guests on the top floor who've been here for years. They never go out. I couldn't think of a worse way to live.'

'How long have you been here, Tony?'

'Coming up three years.'

'You should celebrate.'

'Bad policy. You don't want to remind your customers they've been coming to the same place that long.'

He tipped it out and planted two paper umbrellas in the froth. Then he had one of the waitresses take it away.

'Gin and bitters?' he asked.

'Thank you.'

I met Tony the first night I came here. It was the week they razed my old regular, the Meridian Room – took out all the '60s decor and filled it with tubular steel stools – and I was looking for somewhere new. He looked exactly as he looked now, like he'd just got up from sitting with the debutantes. He had a young face but he had worked bars since he was fifteen and his mind was a lot older. I will always remember meeting Tony on that first night at the Regent, but not, of course, because of Tony.

He made the gin somewhere between short and long, and carefully added the bitters.

'Heard about that guy they found?'

Suddenly I wanted to say that I hadn't, but he was treating it as commonplace news, enough to open a conversation, and I couldn't feign ignorance of something which had taken place so close to where I lived. 'I heard something,' I said.

'They found a body – an old man – all cut up in a rubbish bin.'

'I heard it was a recycling bin.'

'With the broken bottles still in it? Jeez. That's horrible.' He set my drink on a paper mat. 'So, yeah.' He rolled a lemon across the cutting board and chose a knife: 'They haven't identified him yet. There are cops all over town.'

Now I wanted to take another look at who was around us in the bar but I couldn't. I sipped my drink and listened to the reel feed out.

'A guy came in here this afternoon,' Tony said. 'Totally out-of-it guy.'

I bet.

'They were checking the guest lists, you know, seeing if anyone was missing. They asked me who drank here, I said everybody. They weren't like real cops. They were sort of weird. They didn't even have photographs of the body for you to look at. What's the story there? Who interviews potential witnesses without photos? Nobody. First thing you see anywhere, eight-by-ten glossies. It's an industry standard. Envelope, eight-by-tens, recognise anyone, ma'am? McCloud does it, Magnum does it, McGarrett: eight-by-tens. Fundamental.' He shook his head.

I folded my arms over the lump in my pocket. 'Doesn't sound like they know much.'

Tony scooped the lemon segments into a bowl. 'A dead man all cut up, you'd think there'd be plenty of clues.'

'Brass candlestick,' I said. 'Lead pipe, secret passage.'

'Haven't seen that one.'

'It's a game. Board game. Cluedo, by the Parker Brothers. They did Monopoly.'

'Monopoly.' Tony tipped his head so the word rolled back and forth inside it, but still it didn't ring any bells. Because he spent most of his hours behind the bar he had little time for entertainments other than television. He had a Sony Trinitron perched on the end of his bed at home and a Watchman 4cm colour LCD tucked behind the till which he eyed while wiping down the bar tops during slow patches in the afternoon. Home video rentals had only slightly broadened his vision – his working hours made it impossible for him to catch prime-time programmes, let alone visit a store. He lived off repeats and dead-zone budget series, generic rip-offs. His world was second-hand with ad breaks, retouched black and white, none of the colours ever quite true.

'There was a lead pipe in *McCloud* the other week,' he offered.

'Plumbing's all plastic now,' I said. 'I don't know where you'd find a lead pipe. You ever held one? Found one on a demolition site, I could barely lift it. Heavy and soft. Dense. Perfect weapon. In fact, you pick it up and that's the first thing you think of – what a deadly weapon it would be.'

'So it puts the idea into your head, huh? I've heard that argued in a courtroom.'

'You have?'

'*Ironside*,' Tony nodded. 'So that glass-bin guy, that make sense to you?'

'Not really.'

'Doesn't make sense to me. It's so public. Y'know? Gruesome.'

'Cops blamed it on the Mardi Gras.'

Tony sucked in his lower lip. 'Is that right?'

'At least they'd like to. I wouldn't mind.'

44

'You should cheer up a bit about the Mardi Gras, Mr Penrose. It's a chance for everyone to let their hair down.'

'What if I don't want to let my hair down?'

'S'true. Never picked you for that.' He uncapped two Heinekens and up-ended them into two separate glasses so they sank in their own disgorged beer. The glasses filled without spilling a drop.

'It's not as if I don't want to—'

'Of course.' He waved the thought away. 'I like a party. Not everyone does, though.'

'I keep to myself, I guess.'

'I can understand that.' He dropped the bottles behind the counter, trying not to smile. 'You're a hard worker, right? I respect that.'

'Give me a break.'

'Nah, I mean it.' He took the beers along to the other end of the bar.

I leaned over the counter. He threw his empties into two black plastic rubbish bags round the corner: beer bottles in one, mixers in the other. The alleyway dumpster offered environmentally conscious citizens three different holes for bottles to be recycled. Suburban white glass: white wine, gin, vodka, sauce, vinegar, pickles, onions. Blue-collar amber: beer, beer and beer. And sophisticated green into which the victim had been thrown: Beaujolais, claret, burgundy, port. The deep end. A genteel demise: red wine with red meat. I turned my hand slowly in the gleaming bar lights and wondered about the colour of the man's flesh at the time it was cut: was it red? Or paler, like veal, before the blood rushed in?

Tony strolled back.

'That guy,' I asked, 'how long would it take to die like that, do you think?'

He shrugged. 'Death of a thousand cuts.'

'Right. Why kill someone in such a particular way? I guess it comes down to one of two reasons. One: you want everyone to see what you have done. Two: you've forgotten people are looking, you don't care what people see. The act is staged for you alone. It's your indulgence.'

45

'To do something like that you'd have to believe that you'd never be caught. The indestructible man.'

'Haven't seen that one,' I said.

'It's not a TV show. What I mean is, you think you're indestructible. Like Steve Austin, or similar.'

'On TV the good guys have to be indestructible, to survive for the next episode.'

'Not so.' Tony set down my drink, his face thoughtful. 'They have their weaknesses. Someone like Rockford really works up a sweat. And TJ Hooker, or Columbo. There's always a minute in there when things are really tight, really sweaty, and in that moment we come closer to them as people. When they really face the abyss, you know? When man looks into the abyss. That's the truth of someone like Columbo: the camera grants us that intimate moment in which we examine their deficiencies, their shortcomings. We see ourselves in their dilemma, just for one moment. They're a reflection of us.

'The establishment can't solve a crime. It takes an individual. The lone investigator can manoeuvre – that's why they succeed. They're like you and me – independent thinkers. They see things differently. Columbo doesn't move like the rest of the force because that would be superfluous – the rest of the force are moving that way already. Columbo knows he needs to take risks, break the rhythm. And you know what else? The lone investigator knows the streets.'

The ice glinting in my glass, the trace of bitters thinning like a melted branch.

'I know the streets.'

'We both do. These are men who know the real world. They see past the trees, you know? That's their strength.'

I sipped. 'It's years since I saw *Columbo*,' I said.

'It's still a great show.'

'Promise?'

'Cross my heart.'

One of the waitresses came over with a tray and Tony excused himself. I sat and finished my drink and when that had gone I ordered another.

And that is how the night went on. The evening got older but the bar remained a gentleman and never asked her age. The shadows remained and the low lights burned. When guests left, new ones entered and took their places in the empty chairs. Tony topped up the sink with fresh ice and wiped the wet top dry. I rocked on my stool, leaned on one elbow, talked to people in passing without saying that much. When the gin lost its taste I asked for the bill.

'Aren't you gonna stick around for dessert?' Tony asked.

'Not tonight. I'm tired tonight.'

'Wilhemina was asking about you,' he said.

'She was?' I took out my wallet. Tad Ash's wallet. 'It'll be interesting to see how that case turns out,' I said.

'Without the lone investigator, the case will go nowhere.'

I looked again through his cards, his notes, his receipts. 'I think you're right, what you said about the police. They won't solve anything. They need someone with insight. Inside information.'

'They need clues,' Tony said. 'A good lead, information that's everything.' He nodded at the wallet. 'Problem, Mr Penrose?' He winked.

'I've just taken on a new client,' I said.

'No problem.' He took back the bill. 'I'll put it on your tab.'

I stood up a little shakily and said goodnight to Tony and some people I didn't know.

In the lobby the pianist was winding up the last song of the set. Finished, he straightened himself and combed back his grey hair, occupying himself with the middle distance in case someone should break into applause. I put him out of his misery, clapping as I passed. He smiled thinly.

The doorboy didn't smile at all when he saw me return. He winced when I spoke and refused to fetch my car.

'Sorry, sir, you're way over the limit.'

I formed my lips very carefully around the words. 'Fuck you,' I said. 'I'm fine.'

He tugged at his earring again, his subconscious begging me to shut up. 'If you want to drive, you should learn to control your drinking a little more,' he said.

'You stupid little shit.'

47

He held open the door and smiled. 'Have a nice fucking night.'
I waved him off and started walking.

The night had transformed the office windows into a mosaic of mirrors. Their surface echoed the harbour streets tenfold, the neons and pedestrian lights, the taxis leapfrogging for a place at the stand. Silhouettes moved slowly through the streets. A breeze tickled my eyes. A plastic bag inflated by the wind scuttled along the roadside and, lifted by a sudden gust, crossed on to the sidewalk and disappeared. It was waiting for me around the corner, bobbing in the darkness. Litter rolled like dice across the bitumen's white-painted lines. The bag was keeping pace with me, pausing when I slowed, blowing faster when I went to stop it. I finally got it at the traffic lights and screwed it up in my hands.

Then I stopped and looked around. Opposite were the church and the pie cart, cars waiting at the intersection. I was standing across the road from the Dilworth. A beaten-up Holden grew tired of waiting for the signal and ran the red light, the exhaust roaring. The pie-cart diners cheered.

A police car followed it. I saw it and stepped back. There would be cops watching Insurance Alley, especially at night. Looking for witnesses, maybe for the killer to return. The wallet was evidence of interest to the police but common sense had left me now. The stronger part of me did not want to give it back. The law was procedure and routine, and I already had enough rules to follow. I didn't want anyone to spoil the mystery, just as I didn't want anyone to point out that the beauty of the city's reflection owed everything to the science of refracted light and environmentally unsound urban development. Tonight I wanted the city to look beautiful and the dead man's wallet as mine to unravel.

Just along from the pie cart was a blonde woman standing in a long leather coat and smoking a cigarette. As I admired her, a taxi swung into the kerb and she got in. I saw her again as it passed, sitting on the back seat, her face turned away. I wondered where she would be going at this hour. Two a.m. I had seen it many times before yet tonight stood enchanted before the office windows

48

and the likeness they had captured, the crooked sequence of vehicles and faces like a photo-strip from a portrait booth. I counted out the rice-paper moons and their fragile, luminous rhythm. Something had lifted from me. From where I stood, I was anonymous and safe. From this corner, standing in the breeze, I could glimpse sense and purpose. The movement of people in the streets was as complex as the stars. Answers, like oblique trajectories, would appear only if I tracked them.

I sniffed the pie cart's aroma of onions and cheese and the spit of the short-order stove, and crossed the road to the Dilworth.

In my office I tangled my clothes as I undressed and had to shake them out. I ran my hands across the city map and marked Insurance Alley with a black-beaded tack. Then I poured a glass of water and switched off the lights.

The edges of the office window panes flickered with the neon of the church sign that burned below, EKALE OTOPO AIEU, EKALE OTOPO AIEU.

And now P. Tangiers would be out there, in the streets, looking for the wallet.

He wouldn't find it.

I stood in the place where dawn would fall, naked as a dead man, my skin cast blue by the unsleeping neon.

6

I was in the shower the next morning when I heard the phone. I got out and dried myself and checked the answering machine: it was Brands, calling to ask why I'd missed the meeting. I called back and told them I'd been sick and asked for the relevant documents to be put on a courier. Then I got dressed and took a taxi to the Regent where, it turned out, my car wasn't.

The doorboy had said he was going to park it in the hotel car park but after a half-hour of walking around I had to agree with the concierge that it wasn't there. I walked round the corner of the building, to the place where the doorboy was most likely to have left it had the engine flooded, and found a tow-away zone. The towing company on the sign was called North City. I walked back to the Regent repeating its number and knowing I had lost an easy game. The man who answered the phone laughed and said they had my car, then laughed again.

I took another taxi to North City Towing. It was in a gully at the top of town, wedged between two other yards. The entrance was blue-painted brick. The oily cement forecourt was ringed with chicken-wire gates. Sunlight fell through the barred skylights onto the unevenly parked cars. A man-sized door marked 'Reception' was set into the wire, its upper half open. Inside was a dog lying in one of the patches of sun. It was a little cross-bred terrier with a sawn-off nose and a squint, and when it saw me peering it kicked itself up to sit on its rump and panted, pink-jawed. I knocked hard on the door.

A man with tattooed shoulders came out of an adjoining garage, scuffing his feet. The dog's ears twitched. It stood up as he got closer, and then barked. He swore at it and tipped his chin at me, not looking me in the eyes.

'I've come for my car,' I said.

'Hundred and forty-five, mate.'

I wrote out a cheque with the registration.

'That cash?'

'It's made out to cash.'

'You got ID?'

'Here.' I fanned out my credit cards and driver's licence. He copied the details from the licence and one of the cards in green ballpoint, then wrote me a receipt, holding the pen in a fist between his first and middle finger as if he didn't have a thumb.

'Out the front mate – drive it round. Keys.' I dropped them in his oil-cracked hands. 'Sweet,' he said, poking the dog with the toe of his jandal. 'Charles, boy,' he told it. 'Hey, Charles.'

I waited in front of the garage, by the air hose. I heard the Tomaso before it came out of the door. The people working out front stopped to watch. The tattooed man drove it gently up to my feet and got out. 'Needs some work,' he said.

'I know.'

'Brakes are really fucked.' He smiled. One gold tooth and one tooth missing.

'I haven't had any trouble.'

'Nah, they're fucked.'

I got in the car and strained to release the handbrake. The engine popped and almost died, but I held it and pulled away. The tattooed man stood idly in my mirror, getting smaller.

I found Ash Antiques at the top end of Symonds Street between the Khyber Pass intersection and a bus stop where an old woman was sitting on the bench and talking to the person sitting next to her, even though there was no-one there. I patted the wallet in my pocket. I couldn't return it; I couldn't afford even admitting that it existed, now that I'd denied that to Tangiers. But I couldn't ignore its contents and where they were leading me. I had to solve the puzzle, finish the sentence. It was my investigation now, no excuses.

Across the store windows, in white poster letters as tall as a man, ran the legend LEASE SALE: CLOSING DOWN. A smaller sign conceded OPEN.

The door rang when I pushed it. Looking around in the hand-painted shade revealed nothing precious. I pushed my way past a white enamel dentist's chair and a trio of poker stands, a cast-iron bicycle, a mower with a cracked wooden handle. There was a wind-up gramophone with a paper-mâché trumpet and a box of fibre needles. Shelves and display cases were lined with stacks of 78s in brown paper sleeves, stereo viewers, bone-handled cutlery and yellowed ceramic dolls. From the ceiling's cracked plaster hung a half-dozen rusty scythes. Most of the back wall was covered by a huge velvet painting of a blonde woman and a unicorn standing on a vaulted chess board.

At the front of the shop was a small davenport tucked against the wall. On it, carefully arranged on a blotter, stood a cash register, the telephone and a dozen second-hand books. The till's printed docket recorded two sales a day apart, $50.60 and $14.04, both cash. The blotter was unmarked. The only proof of its use were business cards tucked into its gilt and leather corners. I found cards for Ash Antiques – the same as those in the wallet – and also for Veale & Associates, the number I'd called. Knowing them was troubling. Both were tainted by things I shouldn't have known. I put them back, looking for something fresh.

The other cards were all for experts in the second-hand: Worts Leadlight Merchants (stained, etched, stick-on); Castors from Goknar (New Zealand's biggest range: twin-wheel, ball & glides); T.A.M. Bookbinding (comb, casebound, legal). I pocketed one of the two cheesy billets (cartoon samurai) for the downtown Yamada bar (ramen, licensed, closed Monday) and then slipped a folded piece of card from the fourth corner. It was an order of service – for a funeral.

The funeral of Thaddeus Velim (Tad) Ash. I drew in a breath. I was here.

When I heard someone entering the back of the store I put back the card and turned quickly to one of the books on the desk. It fell open where it had been marked by its *Star Trek* trading card. Episode 23: 'Skin of Evil'.

'Particularly rare,' said the man from the back door. 'To be handled with tweezers.'

I shut the book carefully. 'I didn't realise.'

'No, the card.' The man waved a long finger as he approached. '*Star Trek: The Next Generation*. Depicting Tasha Yar in holographic form. Quite rare, at least according to younger clients. I use the cards as bookmarks but they handle them with white gloves. Literally.'

'Trading cards are a big market.' I spoke slowly, fighting the churn in my stomach.

'Do you collect?' He stopped an arm's length away.

I couldn't answer. I shook my head and stared, hypnotised. I knew his face, instantly, but I couldn't think from where. I knew every part of it – the high forehead; grey hair neatly trimmed; the long, thin nose; the clear eyes – not as a person, but a moment I had glanced, frozen clear and sharp. Still staring, I remembered the elements it lacked. It was clean of blood, uncut by broken glass. The last time I had seen this face was in Insurance Alley.

I was looking again at the dead man, from the glass bin.

Calmly, he watched as I brought up the only name known to me. 'Tad Ash,' I began. The shop owner blinked slowly and smiled.

'Was my other half,' he replied. 'My twin. I am the older by three minutes.' He extended a bony hand. 'Dede Ash.'

'Pleased to meet you.'

'But you feel as if you already have met me. That's not unusual' He dropped his hand to his side and straightened. 'Had you known Tad for long?'

'I didn't know him,' I said, and let the rest drop into clumsy silence.

Dede blinked with weary courtesy. 'I've answered so many questions in the last day,' he said. 'Which department are you with?'

'I'm not a cop.' I cleared my throat. 'But I saw your brother. I saw the scene and – there was also a P on the lid. On the bin, where Tad was found. He drew a P. And my name's Penrose. Do you see?'

Dede smiled. 'You do collect,' he said.

'I found it and I couldn't not ask.'

'It's all right, I understand.' He went to the front door and hung up a small BACK IN TEN MINUTES sign. 'This business was built on shakier impulses.'

He talked about the things in the store as we passed them, guiding me through the inventory: this was so much at a garage sale, this was handed down; this we found in the street; this we purchased by mail. Origin and provenance, sale and resale: it had all passed through many hands, the layering of affections describing the shape of each item more acutely for Dede Ash than a price or a name, which he recalled automatically. Instead of things, we were passing by owners, admirers, beneficiaries. These objects were their tracks and markings.

At the same time, I was holding back. He'd pulled a sharp trick: dead but still alive. He had the genetic drop on me, and I resented it. He spun a hanging bicycle wheel with his bony pink hand to demonstrate how the rubber had perished. I nodded, biting my lip.

When we came to the velvet painting he lifted the frame away from the wall. I stepped behind the painted sunset and into a bare, boarded space containing two office chairs and, between them, a small wooden box.

'We can sit here,' he said.

'You were behind here while I was looking around.'

He nodded, choosing the chair shaded by a unicorn. 'It's cooler, in summer.'

I sat down in the other chair and watched as he arranged himself with more care than he had other things in the store. He regarded the back of the painting where his fingerprints had left marks in the dust. Time had lent him more dignity than it had his wares – a well-cut suit, a venerable gaze. When he met my eyes I felt no need to look away.

'I should be wearing my gloves,' he said. 'This should be archivally stored. Every step should be taken to preserve it, protect it from acid and harmful environments. It's important to follow the correct procedure. What you're handling could be worth nothing or a great deal. You never know what you have. That's our trade, you see, or at least it used to be. Ash Antiques was once one of the most respected dealerships in the country.'

'What do you mean, "used to be"?'

'The business itself is not what it was. The goods we sell are getting older and rarer and worth more, but the competition is younger, faster. There are no cosy niches any longer, it's all one market. Everything is out in the open, prey to many dealers, with bigger clients, more determined people. Americans.' Ash sniffed. 'Extraordinary sums involved.

'My response was to move into a more conservative, low-risk market. I was thinking of our later years. Perhaps the elder always thinks ahead. I was always concerned to protect what you see here.' His fingers pressed against the back of the painting, stretching the velvet that separated us from the things crammed in the store, the blown-glass swans and movie cards, the plastic chairs. 'I compromised. Tad didn't like it. He accused me of shirking my business responsibilities – not pursuing sales aggressively enough. We disagreed fundamentally. He was good with new technology – naturally, I suppose, since he was closer to the generation which created it. He installed one of the first small business computers to help with his dealings. He compiled his ledgers on magnetic disks while I stayed up late processing the same figures by hand. Very little passed between us in recent years.' Dede's expression went tight for a moment, then softened again.

'Tad continued to work with rare books and antiques. Representing an overseas collector at one auction, he executed a bid for this.' He tipped his head at the box that sat between us. 'It seemed like routine, but after Tad had taken possession of the lot he realised it was worth a great deal more than he had paid. He and the collector argued over the fee. When a messenger was sent to collect the item, Tad refused to part with it. He was making arrangements to onsell it through an agent – when he himself didn't own the property. A shameful state of affairs. For two weeks he was consumed by this deal-making process: he refused to take other calls or open his mail. I hardly saw him. And the next thing I knew was, this.' Dede looked around the small, shaded space.

'He was dead,' I said.

'Yes. The police attributed his erratic behaviour to his age, his – lifestyle.' Dede moistened his lips, clearing them of a bad taste.

'That was why he wanted the business to make more money, wasn't it? To pay for drugs.'

Dede nodded.

'Do you think he was killed because of the argument with this dealer?'

He shook his head. 'As I explained to the police, the sums involved were very small. We are speaking of a few hundred dollars: Tad was hoping to onsell the lot for perhaps a thousand. The police don't believe murder would come that cheaply, Mr Penrose. Neither do I.'

'But you still think his murder had something to do with the purchase.'

'I do. *Caveat emptor* – let the buyer beware.' He stared at the box. 'Do you know what this is?'

'Is it dangerous?'

'It's an amusement.'

He uncrossed his legs and crouched to turn the box around. 'Dates from 1860,' he explained, running his fingers along the polished grain. 'Typical piece, elaborate veneer, here . . . here, do you see?' I nodded. 'Brass lock, broken. Inside,' he said, opening the lid, 'it's of rough deal. But that's not the point – this is the point.'

Using both hands he took out a square black and cream device and stood it upright along one edge as he fitted it with a handle. Then he took from the box a series of slotted cardboard discs, each about the size of an old vinyl LP. The discs were blank on one side and illustrated on the other with a series of intricate, sequential drawings: a man on a horse, two boxers, a child with a hula hoop.

'It's a zoetrope,' I said. 'They're toys. They make pictures move.'

Dede nodded. 'Almost. This is a phenakistiscope. But it operates on the same principle as a zoetrope. One positions the discs in the machine, turns the handle and views them through this mirrored slot, here. The device is older than the box. Early nineteenth century. Such a rare device to find intact, let alone in working condition. We've sold zoetropes and mutoscope reels in the past – there's one at the museum – but I myself have never seen a phenakistiscope in such an excellent state.'

He selected one of the discs and slotted it carefully into the machine. I could see the drawings on it: detailed sequential portraits of a woman dressed in what looked like Victorian clothes.

'See how well the colour is preserved?' Ash said. 'Collotypes. They've yellowed slightly – the acids in the pasteboard eat it away – but they're in mint condition, especially considering their age.'

'And you just turn the handle?'

'To wind the clockwork, yes.'

He fiddled with a mechanism. There was a flutter as the disc began to spin, its movement stirring the aroma of stale air. I crouched and peeked through the slot. The blur of movement transformed the many narrow slots into one uninterrupted view of the drawings inside, which themselves became a single animated image: the woman dropped her handkerchief and bent over to pick it up.

Ash smiled. 'She lives.'

The woman dropped it and bent over, dropped it and bent over, infinitely fumbling and recovering. Each time she rescued the kerchief her skirts flew up to expose her nude buttocks. Duplicity in her few living moments.

'Imagine, Mr Penrose, sitting and being entertained by such a simple illusion. Titillated by it. Hypnotised.'

It was hypnotic. The primitive eye watched while the brain waited for a break in the rhythm. The pattern became frustrating, a goad that she might walk away or look back. I even thought I saw it, a discrete action, but it was only the first plateau in the slowing of the mechanism. The energy stored in the spring continued to release itself until the woman stopped. Fixed, she appeared scratched and grey. I looked closer and saw marks on the disc. I reached inside but Dede stopped me.

'Fingers,' he cautioned, digging into his trouser pockets and

57

producing white cotton gloves. I put them on and carefully picked under the edges of the disc, sliding it off the spindle. It bowed with its unsupported weight. The woman's comely form was as restrained in detail as it was in motion. Her body was squeezed and moulded into an hourglass by a boned corset, her arse was bustled and her feet were bound in tiny shoes. Her eyes and mouth were as narrow and dark as the slots cut in the cardboard.

In a tight circle at the centre was the trademark, 'London Stereoscopic Co' and its legend, 'Wheel of Life'. Radiating outwards from the company name was a fine, wiry pattern. The ink had faded, but the indentations in the glossy pasteboard were clear.

Someone had written painstakingly around the disc, beginning at the centre and spiralling outwards. Hundreds of words.

'What is this?' I asked, my voice softening.

'The beginning. It's dated . . .'

I tipped it in the light. At the centre hole, the fine handwriting began with a later date: *October 1875*. I looked up at Dede. His estimate of the device's age was a technical valuation. I could see it was old from the moment I saw the box. But reading this, written by someone alive at the time, holding a pen and thinking lifetimes ago, made it worth something. I was excited by it. I didn't want to put it back. I wanted to slip it under my arm and run for the door, like I'd done with the wallet. This would lead somewhere.

'Turn it over,' Dede instructed.

It was the same on the reverse, except that on the board's uncoated side the ink had stayed clear. I tried to turn it but the gloves made me clumsy.

'There are more,' Dede interrupted when he saw me starting to read. He pulled a collection of similar discs from the box and held them out. All were scored with spirals of the same thick, cursive handwriting. 'I examined the writing itself but didn't think to actually read it. One often finds things vandalised or marked by subsequent owners. I dismissed it as obsessive doodling. Tad, however, had realised that the writings on the discs all connected up with one another in sequence to form a diary. Sections of it are rather erotic . . .' His voice trailed away.

'This is what Tad wanted to sell,' I realised. 'Not the actual machine, but what was written on the discs.'

'Yes.'

'Who wrote it?'

'A boy, born over a hundred years ago. His name is Palmer.'

Everything shifted. I felt instantly relieved and disappointed. 'Palmer,' I repeated. 'With a P.'

Ash hesitated, bringing his hands together. 'It was so intimate, so intense. I experienced great misgivings, the way Tad and now I had been poring over it. It didn't seem right to pry into such a private thing. I couldn't believe that its owner had parted with it knowingly. As if we were plundering a grave. No respect for the dead, Mr Penrose.' He looked up at me. 'I'm sure you understand my feelings of guilt, of shame.'

'It's necessary to break those rules, sometimes,' I said, wishing the words hadn't come out so fast.

'Necessary for whom?'

'You have to start somewhere. Everyone's working for themselves,' I said, clenching my fingers. 'You didn't get into this business to help your brother. You're selling these things to make money. What about the other possessions you've picked through? The clothes and shoes and children's toys? Do they send you on a guilt trip? Someone leaves a letter as a bookmark, you read it. Someone's speaking loudly on the phone, you listen. You can't say reading something – searching, looking . . . You can't say that's wrong.'

I stopped myself. He was watching me quietly. His expression was resigned, without anger. He was not accusing me of anything. I stood and he sat, breathing the same air trapped and warmed by the giant velvet canvas, filtered by the unicorn and the dusty shelves of bric-a-brac.

'You kept on reading it, didn't you?' I said. 'You hoped the knowledge would fix things. I understand that.' I put the gloves down by the machine. 'So what does this diary contain?' I asked.

'Well,' Dede said, shifting in his chair. 'It's rather hard to fathom.'

'Try me.'

And so, choosing his words with businesslike care, Dede began.

7

There is a handle beside where the disc goes. The disc is slotted, long thin cuts. There are different drawings but this one shows a man. The handle is turned and the disc turns round and round. The man is walking as if he is alive: left, right, left, right, left, right.

Mama prepares a white cheese. She places it on the cutting marble and removes its wrapper. Paper folded many times, unfolds like a flower. The oil from the cheese turns it transparent. We ate cheese like this, she says, when I was a little girl, when I was your age. The walls were plaster and smooth beneath my hands and the ground was dry. No school, Drew, no traffic, no gas lamps or telegrams. And the sun was hot.

My father shaves with a long razor. He strops each edge eleven times. He spreads lather across his face. You will do this someday, Drew, when you are older. Every day you will trim the hairs. What if I grow a beard? Shh now, you mustn't cough. He begins to cut. He starts at his left ear and finishes at his throat.

'Palmer begins the diary with a description of his mother – he gives her birthplace as Romania – but never mentions her name. In fact he never mentions it at any stage of the memoir. Reverence, perhaps. Or anger. He associates her with great frustration and injustice.

'Her story begins in her nineteenth year when, in order to reach London, she journeyed unaccompanied across Europe. She travelled at the height of the tourist season, making her way through the holiday crowds. It was part of her plan to lean on the wealth of the travelling classes, earning money from them wherever possible in order pay for her journey.'

'What did they pay her for?'

'Many things. Anything, in fact. From a dining companion to

more fundamental favours. She had sex with many men. And some women.'

'The boy wrote all this down? That his mother was a whore?'

'The diary is extensively annotated,' Dede said. 'Palmer's first impressions of what was happening were childish and uninformed: the insight is in the notes. He reappraises the main incidents from an adult perspective and checks them against other sources. There are many revisions. He is painstaking. Unflinching.

'He writes that she needed money, and was forced by others to perform acts which earned it.' Ash flipped nimbly through the discs as he spoke, tipping his head at familiar words. 'Palmer blames the travellers. His earliest entries record how much he hates them. He seethes at the white-jacketed husbands who tipped her for ten minutes in a hotel corridor, the socialite wives who examined her richly oiled skin, the bold young men who accosted her in dark corners. The looser morals of people who carried their whole lives in a bag, trundling between towns with nothing but hotel bills to remind them of the normal life they had left behind.

'After covering great distances on foot and surviving on practically no food at all, the girl arrived in London in a state of exhaustion. She took ill and was admitted to a central hospital.

'It fell to a Dr Baldwin, as a house surgeon, to examine the patient. He found her lying in her cot shivering with a fever. Her long black hair was damp with sweat. Sickness invested her dark skin with a luminescent pallor. Her hands were small and clasping, like a child's, and her breathing was faint. His eyes marked every detail. Her jewellery, the smell of her arms and thighs, her ragged white clothes as they were cut away, her richly callused feet, her grazes, her bruises, the strand of spittle on her lips: it evidenced her suffering and her distant origins, and it overwhelmed him.

'He doted on her, interrupting his scheduled rounds to monitor her treatment. He returned to visit her in the night. When her sweat soaked the bedding he changed it himself. He combed her hair. Her skin, hot with toxins, glowed in the gaslight. He sat at her bedside into the early hours of the morning, tenderly holding her hand.

'On the fourth night the fever broke, and her condition began to improve. Baldwin, conversely, had taken on some of her pallor. He was ragged with exhaustion and what one can only describe as distress at his patient's imminent recovery. He did not wish for her colour to return or her voice to grow strong again. Unafflicted by illness, she would leave him. He would lose his find – his precious object. And so, on the fifth night, he shared her bed.

'A doctor and his patient making love in the hospital ward. No violence or struggle, it is noted, took place. Nor hesitation, nor spoken words. Merely something else for the doctor to administer, something else for the patient to receive. And so she became frail once more. Baldwin drew a domestic scenario of sorts around them both, in which he could care for her and marvel at her tenderness uninterrupted. She was released from her sickbed nine months later, when she gave birth to a son: Palmer.

'Any murmurs of scandal were silenced when Baldwin entered into a private practice with another surgeon, Dr Mood. His aristocratic senior by two decades, Mood walked with a cane. He was respected by citizens and fellow practitioners, and had a reputation for even-temperedness. Gradually, his new partner was also accepted into polite society. Doctors Mood and Baldwin attracted the richest of the ill.

'Palmer declares a special fondness for his Uncle Mood. The first episode described in this diary is the occasion of Mood presenting Palmer's father with a phenakistiscope – this very same machine. His memory of that night is like an alighting bird: fluttering, then nervously still, straight-necked and elegant. Possibly he is thinking of his mother when he says it: he watches the machine from her lap, her arms encircling his waist. His father is waiting with a new disc in one hand, the room fills with the laughter. The people in the discs go on for ever, and Palmer watches them until he gets bored.'

Ash contemplated the brittle card.

'The family's life became as comfortable as the drawing room in which this little scene was played out. A warm household. Money, servants, a busy social life. Baldwin and Mood became companions about town, although Baldwin was the more reserved socially. In public he maintained a straight-backed pose.'

'What happened to the woman?' I asked.

'She was a wife, now, and a mother. She stood close to six foot. Her jaw was square, her angular mouth full. She retained her accent and her dark skin. She did not put her long black hair up – she wore it out, so it spilled from beneath her hat. Her long legs permitted her a man's stride. In an age of fashionably wan women, she could lift her own luggage, shout across the street. Now she was healthy once more, she began to view her marriage as a relationship into which she had been coerced. In the light of day she could never accept his authority. She sat contemptuously through social gatherings. People found her haughty and frightening. Literally, she seethed. Chomped at the bit.

'Her husband was unconcerned by her outsider status. It maintained her attraction as something rare and apart, something to be treasured. Milk-skinned wives steered clear. Men, however, did not.

'She met them on walks, in parlours, behind bars, in back streets. She frequented the East End, the bars and taverns. She strolled unchallenged into brothels to hire rooms and equipment. She knew many men, and the knowledge fuelled her contempt. No matter how tawdry or makeshift the coupling, it freed her, for precious moments. It gave her a voice.

'She began to fight with the young doctor, challenging him. Her arguments swelled under the pretext of household matters and then burst into violence. She would strike Baldwin and taunt him to retaliate. Baldwin did not understand. Clumsily, he defended himself with a tally of all he had done for her – cared for her, fallen in love with her, restored her health – and in doing so only made her more angry, because his care was the very thing she was fighting against. His tender affections were worse than redundant: they were a token of slavery.

'She began, in Palmer's words, to enjoy the company of guests. No longer did she walk the streets with men: she brought them home. She was careful to avoid being caught by her husband but also took pains to ensure that he knew what she was doing. She goaded him. It was revenge for everything he had visited upon her.

'From the top of the stairs, Palmer watched servants welcome a succession of strangers into the house and lead them to the drawing room where his mother was waiting. Following each liaison the boy would rush downstairs and remove any clues she had placed: a forgotten cufflink, a stained antimacassar. At first she was puzzled when, ushering her husband into the front room, there was no cry of disgust or alarm. When she realised the boy was foiling her plans he was locked in his room. So the following week, Baldwin discovered the things his wife had carefully left for him. She waited for her husband at the dinner table, her eyes gleaming, Palmer trembling at her side. Baldwin entered the room and greeted them both. The meal was served and the family ate in silence. The Doctor had chosen simply to ignore it.

'Palmer drew strength from his father's indifference. Now he stole a spare bedroom key and released himself each time his mother locked his door. As he became accustomed to the routine of her liaisons, he no longer sought to hide from her gaze. Soon the boy's stare was the admonishment, his mother the one who avoided eye contact. Daily he watched between the bannisters the same scene playing itself out: a knock, the servants' greeting, his mother's smile. Her insurgency was reduced to parlour entertainment. She merely mimicked infidelity, mechanically, with fading conviction.

'In public Baldwin maintained a professional air but in private he was attacked by grief and humiliation. He muttered that the stuff coursing through this woman's veins had thickened rather too much. He could not sleep. He lost weight. He gargled to hide his growing cough. And try as he might, his temper shortened. He was sharp with patients, less open to conversation, sometimes outright rude. His books emptied.

'He became a non-practising physician. At this stage of history there was a growing industry in death: a new fashion for dissection. Baldwin's books filled with silent patients. He became a dealer in the dead, and took on something of their air. He turned to drink. Mood made gentle enquiries but was fobbed off. He could see that his friend's fortunes had once more taken a turn for the worse.

*   *   *

Cakes are straw-yellow on the outside, inside like sour cream. Icing is pink and transparent as skin. Sweetmeats are small and hard. Old marzipan breaks into dust.

The room is dark and silent and through the keyhole I can see nothing.

Mama takes me into town. She is not speaking. She buys me aniseed if I will wait on the steps. Be a good boy, Drew. She kisses me on the cheek.

Mama comes back smiling and kisses me. She licks the aniseed juice. Drew, you are a dirty boy. A lovely boy. We walk home along the pavement home. She runs her glove over the black steel railings as a hansom clops by. Listen to the horse, Drew. Listen to its hard metal shoes.

Sometimes Papa calls out from the surgery: Drew, come in here for a moment, I would like you to meet a gentleman. Don't be afraid now. Here is Mr So-and-So.

Papa is drinking from a bottle. A white man is lying in the white sheets. The smell of the gas burner. He is blue-chinned. Why has he died before attending to his morning toilet, Papa?

Aha, Drew, my father laughed: after death, a man's beard will continue to grow for at least a day.

Will you shave him, Papa?

He bangs the bottle. That is a wretch's job, shaving the dead: that is the province of a poor man indeed. We are not concerned with appearances here, we are not concerned with being proper. God has finished with these men, their souls have left them. They are Bodies, now, and we do not care about their toilet. We are concerned with what is inside.

And what is inside, Papa?

Ah. Steel yourself, boy. And watch.

'Palmer was left to wander in the back-room of his father's surgery, alone amongst the medical texts and stoppered glass jars. He soon found his way around the extensive records of disease and deformation which they contained. It was here, during the late evenings and the hours in which his mother entertained, that Palmer took his first lessons in death. The idea of bodily decay was introduced into his mind. He saw foetuses in their early stages, plucked from the corpses' wombs. He saw a sailor's arm preserved for its tattoos. A two-headed calf bobbing in formaldehyde. And in the hand-coloured plates of the books he learned of diseases of the mouth, damage to the spine and bones. The placement of organs and the consequences of their failure. And the cadavers which passed through the the building, flayed for anatomists' sketchings and private analysis – a grotesque parade. A march of death.

'Palmer became aware of mortality. He began to understand that he was part of a finite world. He realised, with grim insight, that his mother and father would die. He realised he would grow old. Everything would decay and stutter and cease. Looking around him, at his mother, at his father's trade, there was nothing to reassure him. He measured his breathing and the beating of his heart and wondered when they would stop. He wanted to know what would happen to him when he died. He wanted to know where he would go.

'One person understood what was happening. Mood had been watching Baldwin and especially his son, and was certain things were getting worse. He decided to visit Baldwin's wife.

'When Mrs Baldwin rose from her chair to greet him, her eyes flashed with angry inspiration. Mood was a true opportunity. Baldwin's best friend, his professional partner, his confidant, his saviour. Slowly a smile spread across her face. Palmer watched Mood enter the drawing room, and the door close.

'Afterwards, as he dressed, she hid his cane and, when he had left, laid it carefully across the chaise.

'Baldwin found it that evening. Palmer watched between the bannisters as his father re-donned his still-warm coat and hat and stepped briskly out of the house, the cane in his hand. Baldwin took a cab across the city to Mood's place of residence, asked the servant there to bring his friend to the door and, when he appeared, used the cane to bludgeon him to death. He cudgelled the man's brains. A news article from the time records that the older doctor's blood ran down the front steps and froze in pools on the kerbside.

'Professionally, it was Baldwin's end. He was struck off before the court hearing. The judge and jury found him to be in a state of mental derangement, and committed to Murthlem Hospital, six miles out of London.

'In Murthlem, Baldwin was left alone his cell. The doctors and attendants – or should I say magicians and jailers? – set about relieving the pressure of blood on his brain by affecting his circulation. They administered evacuants and purgatives. Sodium bromide, chalybeates, embrocations to the head. He was strapped to the bedstead and douched with cold water. The only conversation between doctors and their strait-jacketed patient was conducted as if between parent and child. If Baldwin was unstable when he was admitted, he was well-mad by the time his wife and child were permitted to visit.

'The train journey to Murthlem was a source of anxiety for Palmer. Although he slept blissfully in his mother's lap for most of the distance, he was always woken by the noise of the train as it entered the last tunnel. He would cry out in the dark, rocking carriage, flailing. He came to fear the noise of it and eventually the tunnel itself.

'Nor did Palmer cope well with the visit. His father was in a state of extreme disarray. Unshaven and shouting. After a formal exchange of greetings the boy would be shepherded outside by one of the nurses and left to play. His mother was determined to make contact with the man who loved her. Young Palmer had no concept of what this contact was: the best he could imagine was a slight variation on his own stilted conversation. The idea of spying on his parents occurred to him as an innocent prank. He went back to his father's cell, climbed up on a chair pushed against the door and peered through the Judas hole, and instead saw his parents engaged in acts of unspeakable misery.

'His father was tied to the iron bedstead with sheets knotted round his legs and arms. He describes their lovemaking as a wretched sight, a thing of degradation: their wretched copulating in a building filled with howls and pus-stained sheets. Palmer screamed and ran. His mother called a superintendent. The boy was pursued.

'Palmer ran out of the Murthlem grounds, heading towards the train station. The attendant followed. At the platform Palmer jumped down and ran along the rails. The superintendent followed. Palmer ran into the mouth of the station tunnel, unhesitating. The superintendent followed him inside. Palmer ran, and stumbled, and got up and ran again. The superintendent was closing in the darkness. By the time the man caught him they were deep inside the tunnel, hundreds of yards, and completely out of breath. The superintendent shook Palmer and Palmer screamed. The man slapped him until he quietened down and they crouched there, panting. And it was then, over the noise of their breathing and their heartbeats that Palmer first heard something. He said to the man, do you hear it? And the man said, what? I heard something, Palmer said. What do you mean? said the superintendent: what did you hear? And Palmer said: a whistle.

'A train was coming.

'There was a desperate moment as the two tried to get their bearings. The whistle reverberated the entire length of the tunnel, disguising its source and the machine's direction. The superintendent dropped the boy and sprinted back to the light end of the tunnel. The boy followed, running as fast as he could. But it was too late: they had been running the wrong way. The machine entered the stone-walled tube with the compressed thunder of steam and metal, an enormous noise, an orchestra of pistons and grates and flame. The tunnel was only big enough to permit the engine's passage: there was no room to move on either side. There was no escape. A man of bleak reasoning, the superintendent simply stood paralysed as the monster closed on him. He was killed instantly. In the half-second it took the beast to close the few steps of distance between them, Palmer was filled with a reasoning of his own – a logic born of the most incredible fear. The train was on him. Death was certain. But he jumped.'

I squinted and asked him what he meant, but Ash only repeated himself with greater force, impatient that I hadn't clicked.

'He jumped, Mr Penrose. The boy simply jumped. He cheated death. His words exactly.' Ash stabbed his finger round the last phenakistiscope disc as he read it off.

'"Suddenly," Palmer says, "in that second, I released myself. I released myself from all mortal restraints, from fear, from responsibility. I released myself from my parents, from my father, from my mother's fury, from the dissecting table, from the bodies, from the organ jars, from the three score and ten, from the train and its tonnes of unyielding mass and metal. In that moment, I jumped. I had no room to do it. I had no chance. Logic said I could not. Science said I could not. God said I could not. But I did. I jumped. I moved quickly. I saw death coming and I jumped from him.

'"With one bound I was free."'

Would everything go dark or light – bloody or pale? Would he hear solitude's quiet or the blare of everything he'd known passing by? I could not comprehend an experience which could not be explained, let alone believed. But something in the idea of it held me tight, as surely as Dede held the disc in his trembling, blue-veined hand.

His face was bright. 'What do you think of that?' he demanded. 'Explain that, Mr Penrose!'

'Extraordinary.' I stared at the empty white gloves. 'An incredible piece of escapism.'

'A tremendous escape!'

'No; escapism. A fantasy.' I couldn't look at him as I spoke. 'Listen to me, Mr Ash. I feel terrible saying it out loud, but your brother is dead. I saw his body. He didn't jump. He died. Death caught up with him. I promise you it did, whatever precedent you imagine lies here.'

The words fell to the floor. I fidgeted, tried spinning the phenakistiscope, but its motor was spent. When I looked up his eyes were streaming. I wanted to convince him that the time he had spent reading me the diary was not wasted. I wanted to tell him not to worry, that his brother did live on – in his face, let alone in his heart. But I couldn't say anything. I just looked down, pretending it was all I had ever been able to do.

I don't know what I'd expected from the P initial, or what I'd wanted to hear. I'd known, instantly, that it couldn't be anything to do with me, but at the same time had hoped that it was. I'd been drawn in the most fundamental way to pursue it, but now that I had its meaning I didn't know what it meant. I had been denied the simple reward of recognition: everything was strange, and there were no links, no progress to report, nothing of practical value: only grief, and loss, and misunderstanding.

70

We sat, Dede Ash and I, and shared the last minutes of the morning. The velvet filtered out light and cast us in Tad's shadow. We compared, silently, our thoughts of him: Dede's lifetime, my moment of passing by.

After a long while I got up to leave, brandishing an excuse as old and as sorry as the items on the shelves.

8

Outside, two bodies were stacked on the bus-stop bench: two kids, whose heads were wrapped in their jackets. One was watching me through solvent-eyes, the other was sleeping, snoring through his sticky mouth. They were too stoned to pose a threat, too comfortable to warrant assistance. I turned and looked back at Ash Antiques as I walked down the road. Dede was still standing there behind the glass.

In my car I started the engine and rested my foot on the pedal. Then I dug through the glove compartment for the road map and a working ballpoint. Quickly, using the cleanest page (43: rural land and the Waitemata harbour), I wrote down the names and dates that appeared in Palmer's diary, everything concrete I could recall. Then I tore the page out, smoothed it across the wheel and carefully drew a top-plan view of Ash Antiques that showed the position of the door, the back entrance, Dede's desk, where we had sat. Beneath that I made a second sketch of the shop façade as it appeared from the street, detailing its lead-lined windows and lockable grilles. Then I sat listening to the running engine and thought out which of the places I had seen were most likely to facilitate forced entry, and marked each one with a little X.

Alongside that I added a list of the names I remembered from the business cards. I took out Tad's wallet and looked at the card for Veale & Associates. Editorial Consultants and Literary Agents. Tad was trying to sell the diary. Veale was the person I should try next.

The only other thing I could remember was the date and time of Tad Ash's memorial service: tomorrow, 11 a.m. So I wrote that down too. Then I folded the page, put it in my breast pocket, and pulled out.

I couldn't see Dede through the shop window as I passed, but I knew he was there. The kids at the bus stop were huddled as if a storm was coming, or maybe had already been.

I called Veale. It was clear he didn't recognise my voice from my first phone call but he did sound as if he had been waiting for me and that everything I said was nothing more than what he'd expected to hear.

His address was five minutes' drive from the city in a suburb that looked a lot less expensive than it was. Children were playing in a small corner park, any noise they were making drowned out by the traffic. The streets were lined with mismatched state houses and dry, rough-edged hedges. Veale worked – and lived, I realised as I approached – in a small dead-end street not much wider than my car. I drove up on to the footpath, parking on an incline. The opening door scraped the road so I had to half-close it and squeeze out. Veale's house was behind a red picket fence, a buzz-cut lawn, a porch and a fly screen. Rapping on the screen did not produce a satisfying knock. A huge set of purple enamel wind-chimes hung from the other end of the porch, gleaming and still.

A woman pushed open the fly screen. 'Hello,' she said. She was wearing sweat pants and a brightly printed T-shirt and held a scaling knife.

'I'm looking for Mr Veale,' I said.

'Oh yes,' she said, and had begun to say something else when a man came running down the stairs behind her. He was squat, in an equally bright yellow T-shirt and shorts. He stepped round the woman and pushed open the fly screen further, grinning as if he'd known me for years.

'Mr Penrose!' he smiled. 'You're very prompt.' The woman smiled at me again and left us, walking back down the hall. 'Isn't this weather great?' Veale said. 'It really is wonderful at this time of year.'

He leaned out on to the porch, wiping his domed forehead with a ruddy, crinkled hand. His appearance was a strange mix of styles, each of which had been a fashion sometime in the past. His hair was a ragged tonsure, a hippy shag trimmed to disguise a thinning patch.

His dyed eyebrows were especially thick, as if he'd been careful to grow them to twice their normal size. The flesh of his arms sagged and his body looked soft. He wore several rings and his fingernails were filed long. His clothes were especially bright and clean save for the dots of hair dye on his shoulders. His expression was a wide grin, hearty then wavering, unsure of itself.

He took me into the front room. The walls were salmon-pink, the cane furniture slightly bowed. There was a small set of office shelves lined with paperback novels, the spines of which had faded in the sun. 'Mind the fax, won't you,' he warned, pointing to a beige machine on a cane stool in the centre of the room. 'It's rather inconveniently placed.'

I picked the one chair in the shade. The cushion had been reversed to hide the wear. When I sat down it sank low on the floor: I was left almost hiding behind my knees. Veale looked around the room as if he'd forgotten something.

'As I mentioned on the phone . . .'

'Yes. On the phone.'

'I'm interested in the diary.'

'Yes.' He nodded impatiently as if he knew what I was talking about, but only silence followed.

I cleared my throat: 'I was in negotiations with a third party, Tad Ash. He showed me part of a document – a diary – which I was interested in.'

'Yes. Yes.' Veale had his fingers in his mouth, the exact character of his countenance masked by his eyebrows. 'I must offer you coffee,' he said suddenly. 'I always enjoy coffee at this time of day – it's quite the best hour. I have a machine. Cappuccino?'

'Thank you.'

He left the room. I pulled myself out of the chair and started looking around. He had a small desk behind the door and a large Imperial electric typewriter, and papers stacked in a cardboard file that opened like an accordion. I flicked through the papers. They described errant pupils and swishing canes, most of it reading as antique. The photographs were more explicit but again old. In vinyl sleeves were postcards with a narrative theme: 'A Windy Day'. 'The

Bicycle Ride!' 'A Travers les Coulisses'. 'Et Maintenant 'Toussez!' A lot of Veale's business was extra-literary.

At the back was a sleeve filled mostly with copies that had been made using the fax; the images were highly contrasted and jagged-edged, like black needlework. They seemed to be all images of swimmers, photographs taken from advertisements and magazines, and all were men. They had been grouped according to costume – caps, goggles, trunks. Where health magazine nudes lacked those items, they had been drawn in. In some, in which the distant figure was nothing more than a watery outline, a list had been typed on the fax paper of what the swimmer might have been wearing. And, although they were clearly all of different people, every one had been named with a label identifying them as one and the same person: Veale, E. Their careful compilation marked them as the items he cared for the most.

When I heard the coffee hissing in the kitchen I slid the file back into place and returned to my chair. Veale came back into the room carrying a tray of biscuits and two tiny cups.

'Here we are. Are you a big coffee drinker?' he asked.

'I am.'

'I drink it a lot. The machine was an excellent investment.'

'I usually just buy it.'

'I used to, but since having the machine I've found it really does make the best coffee, and now I find myself hardly buying it at all.' He handed me a cup. 'It's true it makes small quantities, but if the coffee's really good one cup is all one needs. Would you care for a biscuit?'

'Do you make those as well?'

'No.' He laughed. 'They're purchased.'

The coffee was awful. I balanced it on my knee. 'I guess I should tell you what I'm after,' I began.

'Did you want sugar in that?' he asked, eyeing the cup.

'I'm fine, thank you.'

The phone rang. 'Excuse me – that will be mine,' he said, getting up and crossing quickly to the fax, but I could hear the woman answering the hallway extension. He stood watching the machine

75

for a moment, then went to the door and listened. She was talking animatedly, laughing. He turned back to the sofa. 'She's taking it,' he reassured me.

'It sounds like you're busy,' I said.

'Yes, I'm very busy at this time of year. There's quite a demand for the work I do . . .' His raised his fingers to his chin again, half hiding his face. 'It's an exciting business, an exciting time. There's so much new talent around now, one finds there's lots to do. Some of my clients are very high flyers indeed. I can't say who, of course—' and here he let his eyes meet mine for a conspiratorial second '—but rest assured . . .'

'So,' I said. 'The diary.'

'The document dates from the late nineteenth century. Highly detailed, very colourful. Unique.'

'And you're looking to sell?'

'The owner is seeking a prompt sale.'

'Why the hurry?'

He bristled. 'There's been a great deal of interest since Tad brought the item to me. One has many clients and interests to represent. There are a great many factors to consider in a sale of this kind and one finds, at the end of the day, that not all parties will emerge satisfied. It's the nature of the game, I'm afraid. It doesn't much matter to me if I'm the bad guy in all of this. One does what one can to see that everyone's happy. One does what one can. If there's blood on the wall or tears before bedtime, I don't much care.'

'How much?'

He rested back on the sofa. 'Bids are, in effect, closed; I would be pleased, however, to hear yours. Bidding opened at eighteen-five.'

'For a single diary?'

'For a holograph, intact and complete. Authenticated.'

'It still seems high.'

'The market for rare and exceptional works is highly competitive. One finds oneself catering to specialised tastes. I represent a select number of clients who deal only in autographs and personal diaries, letters, memoranda. Private moments, people's lives. Priceless slices

76

of the past, of other existences. Memories. There aren't a lot of them around.'

'There's a moral aspect, Mr Veale—'

'Morality is whatever set of rules gets you into the least amount of trouble – the high-tide mark of a society that fell back a long time ago. Morality is a ring round the bath.'

'And you're comfortable with that.'

He chortled. 'I'm not in this for the good of my health. It's all about money, in the end. It's important to feel good about that. As one moves through life one finds, ultimately, all things being equal, that life is mostly about money, so it's important to feel good about the financial side of things. Once the thing is passed on to you, there's little point in not making money out of it. I think you'll agree that's best. One always aims to make the best of one's situation.'

'So what else is in the diary?' I asked. 'Names, places, what?'

'I'm really not at liberty to say.'

'Is it possible to read it myself?'

'Well, I don't keep that sort of thing on the premises. One never knows who's looking.' He smiled, impishly, as if we both knew full well, but there was something he was leaving unsaid.

'But you do have a copy, right?' I asked.

Now he simply smiled.

'I'd like to see the diary,' I demanded.

He sat back, his cheeks reddening. 'I don't know if I can help you there,' he said.

'Have you actually read it?'

'I'm familiar with its contents.'

'Have you got it?'

Grinning.

'Cash.'

'It's not that simple.' He unfolded his legs. 'Other parties have expressed an interest, and, much as one would like to facilitate a sale, what you're asking ... I simply can't give that information to you. If there's no offer made I'll be forced to conclude that the interest isn't there.'

I stood up. 'I only know some of what's going on here, but I think you know even less. I think you're bullshitting me. I hope you are. I hope you don't have the diary because the only other person who had it is dead.'

He glared at me, ruddy-faced.

'I'll see you out,' he muttered.

Veale watched me from behind the fly screen, the garden wilting in the heat.

I gunned the engine.

The owner is seeking a prompt sale. His erratic behaviour, his . . . lifestyle. Needle marks up to here. Tad had been after fast cash.

Veale was sad and old and not even old.

I rolled down the window and the air poured in cool and fresh. It was good to be moving again.

What was it about a diary that would get a man killed?

Memories.

Her wet, soft grin, wide with appetite.

I let the car take me where I wanted to go.

9

The city was gridlocked with Friday night, the air snarled with car horns and boosted bass and rumbling engines. Early-evening crowds blocked doorways and side streets. Corner bars no bigger than a bedroom were packed with drinkers and people trying to get a drink. Diners queuing for open-late brasseries were mugged by buskers and sidewalk performers warming up for Mardi Gras. It was cluttered and confusing and not much fun. The intersections flashed, playing hazard to the pinball drivers.

There was a different doorboy on at the Regent.

'Nice car,' he said. 'Is it old or one of the new ones?'

'Old.' I tipped him ten dollars, and made him promise to park it right. He grinned and took the note. And then the big glass doors were swinging shut behind me, blocking out everything.

A band was playing around the piano, strumming songs so familiar they didn't have names any more. A man straddling a fat double bass planted notes here and there which meant something as rhythm and very little as melody. The singer, a skinny black woman in a blue satin gown, was resting her voice, chin in one hand. On the other side of the wall, the bar was stacked and busy. If Tony was on, he had his head down. I chose a soft chair near the piano instead.

I rested back in the deep leather upholstery and rubbed my eyes until the lobby was filled with red, throbbing people. A group of tourists were sitting on the other side of the room, crowded into a single sofa. They were choosing from a line-up of desserts displayed on a sweets trolley. When one of them nominated a slice, the attendant waitress would serve it on to a wide, white plate and dress it with cream and icing sugar. When she bent over to serve it her black hair fell in her eyes and she tilted her head to one side, drawing away the bangs with her little finger. She kept tilting her head as she listened with a practised smile to the last man's order. He could have been relating intimate news. She smiled at him again, and wrote something in the long black folder lying on the table. Then she took up the trolley and steered it towards me.

Her navy jacket hung with standard looseness but hinted at her long body beneath. Her shirt collar was stiff and her lipstick was red. She wore a man's business tie with white dots. The dark uniform made her skin look pale. She had a long face and green eyes and there were hollows beneath them. I wondered where she hadn't been sleeping.

She gave me the same smile she gave everyone else.

'Good evening, sir. I'm Wilhemina,' she said. 'Could I interest you in some dessert?'

I leaned forward over the trolley. 'What have you got there?'

She counted off the tray's offerings on her slender fingers. 'Fruit desserts, we have Chestnut Mont Blanc and Gooseberry Huff. Creams include a French Flummery and the Everlasting Syllabub.'

'Everlasting.'

'Frozen desserts,' she continued unbroken, 'are Mango Parfait and Black Forest Bombe. Cheesecake: Italian cheesecake.'

'That looks nice.'

'It's very nice,' she acknowledged quickly. 'And if you'd like something hot, our chef does pancakes, fritters, and Spanish honey pudding.' Finished, she stepped back again from the trolley. But not too far: her fingers rested on the handle. Her eyes were steady, their colour now somewhere between green and blue.

'There's another cream there,' I said.

'That, sir, is Bavarian Perfect Love.'

'Is that on tonight?'

For a very brief moment she glanced upwards, and I followed her gaze. The marbled ceiling tiles looked immaculate but I knew they were soiled, darkened by clumsy overtures that stuck like dust on a drinking glass. I wished I hadn't said it. I found myself gesturing towards something else. I was beginning to realise how tired I'd become, how vulnerable. I'd been encouraged by the deep upholstery into believing myself to be among friends, safe to utter intimate remarks. The pianist embarked on another aimless number. I ticked off the discount paint-by-numbers abstracts on the walls, the geeky door-boys with their bad haircuts and ill-fitting uniforms. Why guard your remarks in an environment which indulged such artlessness? It was a trick, and we were all falling for it. And then Wilhemina looked down from the ceiling and reviewed me sitting there with an expression both lenient and benign.

'If you'd like the Bavarian Perfect Love,' she said, 'that would be good.'

She took a dessert plate from the stack on the bottom tray. The clicking porcelain sounded like chimes in the breeze.

The Bavarian Perfect Love tasted good, although I had nothing to compare it to. I could only think of milky drinks and late nights as a child, reading with a torch way after bedtime. I held the cream in my mouth, let it run round my teeth. Torchlight on a letterpress page, ragged-edged. The torch was shaped like an astronaut. In blue plastic scuffed by nails and two-cent pieces. Candy shaped like cigarettes. The skin of a mandarin. All the things I had hoarded in the mind's afternoon, my pockets so full I could hardly sit down.

I ate slowly, chewing up the time it took Wilhemina to excuse herself, lift the concierge's key and make her way downstairs. When I had finished I put down the plate, wiped my mouth with the napkin and walked behind the piano, turning right instead of left towards the bar. The staff access door was closed but the lock was wedged open by a folded docket. I slipped inside. The overlapping service lamps cast arched shadows along the corridor.

She was waiting at its end, outside the laundry door, swinging the pass key in her hands.

Inside the air was close. The only light was an insect grille that turned everything blue. I followed her through a maze of shelving stacked with linen, pushing open the swinging partitions between rooms piled with hotel sheets and pillow cases and tablecloths and countless monogrammed napkins. The last room was nothing but three walls of towels, starched white, reaching up to the ceiling. The flapping saloon doors slowed to a stop. Her eyes were wide. I could see her neck move when she swallowed.

The rattling air-conditioning was parching my mouth. Her teeth cut a white line along her lower lip. Experimentally, I took her face in my hands. Her eyes closed and her head rolled. I searched her face. She smiled, dozy, vouching that she'd been here all along – thinking about nothing but you, baby, my flesh smooth and alive and clean. All the hours I am away from you, Wilhemina, what passes your lips? All the things, I knew, she would never tell.

And then I put what her lips had done to one side and kissed them for now, told them they were missed. I dwelled on them, doodling on the curve of her neck. I bit her until she stopped smiling and then kissed her again. I licked her parted teeth and gums, tasting of almonds. I brushed her cheek and the clench of her jaw and listened to the sea.

I lifted the jacket from her shoulders. I undid her tie, fumbling to solve the knot back-to-front. She raised her shirt halves like butterfly wings and pressed her stomach against me. I pushed her back into the towels, hooked my fingers into her skirt so it fell.

Black hair in the blue light.

We shook apart sentences into single words. Baby. Higher. No. That. Yes. *Yes* was her instruction and my barter. I pushed into her, murmured pet names. Her eyes were open now and their gaze felt like applause. We were the only people in the room and she was listening, she was here, with me, she was here. All of her. She was awake.

I bent back her head. We were moving higher up the towels. I reached to steady myself and pulled down bunches of them. I kicked them away. She clasped me, lifting herself up. We stumbled. She shouted and slapped the wall and I held on to her as tight as I could, whining, not letting her move an inch. And then her face turned wet. I licked it. She twisted to one side, one arm out, legs apart, fallen from a great height and broken, a swastika doll.

We slipped down in the cascade of towels. She was laughing and I was laughing and then we forgot what was funny.

We lay on the floor. I pulled her up, on top of me. Her body was richly warm. I wiped her face. I rocked her, back and forth. She giggled.

'Wilhemina,' I said it like it was a promise.

She uncurled. I turned my neck.

'You were here last night,' she said. 'Tony said.'

'Yes.'

'Why didn't you stay? I would have liked to have seen you.'

'I was tired. I had some things to do.'

'He said you didn't feel like dessert.'

'I had to return something.'

'At night?' She looked disbelieving. 'What?'

I shrugged. 'It's a long story.'

She screwed up her face. 'Is this a work thing?'

'No. I haven't been in to work for two days.'

'Why not?'

'I felt like a break. I'm tired.'

'You don't want to talk about it.' She sat a little further away. 'And you don't want to see me. That's okay.'

She got up slowly and looked around for her clothes.

'So where have you been lately?' I said. 'What have you been doing?'

She took a long time to button her blouse. 'Things,' she said, finally. She shook out her skirt.

'I'm only asking.'

'Yes.' She stepped into her skirt and zipped it.

'It's a question.'

'I know.' She smoothed the fabric. 'I've got another job.'

'What doing?'

'Making a lot of money,' she said. 'I'm saving to go away, to Europe. I want to travel.'

'For how long?'

'As long as I can. I want to get away. I'm not doing anything with my life.'

'What are you going to do there that you can't do here?'

'You're not listening.' She looked away. 'Where's my tie?'

'Here.' It had fallen on to the floor.

'You should get dressed,' she warned. 'I'm back on soon.'

I sat up in the towels. 'It's comfortable.'

'I could get you a room for the night. If you're still so tired.'

'What are you going to do?'

'I've got another half-shift, then I'm going home.'

'Why don't we both get a room?'

She began knotting the tie. 'I won't do that, Ellie.' She drew the knot closed and found the tie was short. 'Damn.'

'Here. Let me.' I reached out.

She crouched in front of me. Doing up her tie was more difficult than taking it off. She stared straight at me while I made the attempt. It didn't work. I started again.

'How's your place?' she wondered.

'I painted the windows over.'

'Why do a thing like that?'

'Only in the bedroom. So I could get some sleep. But I still can't sleep.'

I shook the second knot loose. Something disappeared with a pop into the electrified mesh and turned her gaze the colour of roofing lead.

'I used to keep you awake,' she recalled.

'It wasn't just you.'

'Thanks.'

'You know what I mean. I think about things.'

'What sort of things?'

'I don't fucking know.' The third knot was failing and I was losing my temper. I whipped it off her. I pulled it round my own neck and tied it and loosened it and slipped the noose over my head, holding it out to her, but her gaze had settled on something far away.

'What is it?'

'I guess I haven't been thinking about you,' she confessed. 'I used to. I used to wonder if you'd come in when I was working late. I daydreamed about being paged on my coffee break.'

Mr Penrose to see Ms Litner. I imagined the look from the lobby manager, the polite, knowing acknowledgement.

'They'd do that, Ellie, if you just came to say hello.' Then she caught the look on my face. 'But you'd never do that, would you? It took me a long time to work that out. You want me to be there when you want, but not when you don't.'

'What am I supposed to say?'

'You're not supposed to say anything. I'm telling you something. How I feel.' She took the noose and slipped it on.

I watched her tighten it and said, 'That looks better.'

'Does it?' She folded down her collar. I nodded, straightening the knot so it was just right. Her breath was warm and perfumed. My fingertips touched her soft neck.

'I have to get back, Ellie,' she said.

I searched for my clothes. I found everything except reassurance in the details which usually put me at my ease. My socks were dirty and the waistband of my trousers stuck to my skin, and my skin itched. I kept my back to her. I dressed while considering at the same time that I didn't want to be dressed. What I wanted was running water to soften my skin and remove the dusty smell of the store. I probably would have taken a room if she hadn't offered me one first. The idea of being that close but not actually having her made me miserable.

When I turned round she was bent over, carefully combing her hair. The towels were twisted and scattered, marked with footprints and sweat. 'We've made a real mess,' I said.

'Yeah, well.' She stood up and threw back her head. 'Someone else can clean it up.'

I walked out of the laundry. She was having some difficulty with the lock but I didn't wait. I walked back through the long corridors. When I reached the staff door I stopped and listened, but there were no footsteps. I ran my fingers through my hair. I opened the door and stepped into the lobby and the deadlock clicked shut.

The lobby was busy with couples and parties, people meeting and continuing their evening. The pianist was playing without referring to the score, his bald head bobbing. He looked thin and pale, drained by the music. The veins on his hands were thick. The singer stood straight, eyes closed, dribbling scat. The bassist slapped around his double bass with the same bored, impatient energy. A different waitress was tending the sweets trolley, running through the specials for a fidgeting customer waiting to order what he always had.

One of the doorboys went to collect my car. I waited with my hands in my pockets while his sidekick entertained with automatic chatter. Have a good night? Looking forward to Mardi Gras? You liked the music? How was dessert?

10

I woke up in the empty bed. My mouth was dry. First light was streaking through the windows in the next room, building spires of pens, cathedrals of stacked books. I got up to watch the sun rise the rest of the way. The clouds were distant and mauve and beautiful. Above, the sky was empty. The air had a cool tinge that promised a hot day. I set the jug to boil and took down a black tin of tea leaves from the cupboard. My side itched where I'd been bitten by mosquitoes. They bred in the old guttering and flew inside to feed. I stood the teapot on the desk and sat down, scratching.

Brands had called some time yesterday. I turned up the answer-phone and drank my tea listening to some assistant leave a message asking if I'd received the courier envelope, and if so would I call the office immediately. I could see the corner of the envelope peeking under the front door. They had got back to me more quickly than I would have liked or expected. Time was money, but I was beginning to lose interest now more compelling matters had come to hand. I got up and brought the envelope inside. I opened one of the desk drawers, dropped the unopened envelope inside and shut it. Then I picked up the wallet and regarded it, blankly. It had become more familiar – it was my possession now – but its strangeness remained undiminished. I dragged my nails across my ribs.

Tad Ash was to be buried at eleven. I knew I had to go. If I arrived late I would not be spotted as a stranger. I could slip in the back and not have to speak to anyone. I decided to attend as a sign of respect for Dede, even if my introduction to the death had not been respectable.

I took my time in the shower. Afterwards I opened the window and let in the sunlight and rinsed the razor blade in silence, as if solemnity would lend something appropriate to the action. My head ached and my mouth tasted of Wilhemina. When I finished I splashed my face with cold water and dabbed it with a fresh towel.

The steam scrolled out the louvre windows. I combed my hair in the cabinet mirror, condensation hiding my face. I opened the cabinet and chose a cologne. In the bedroom I decided on a single-breasted suit, charcoal grey. White shirt, black socks, low-heeled boots with square toes. Black silk tie, which I thought about, then hung on the closet and practised doing up back-to-front. I got better at it.

I straightened my cuffs while I waited for the lift. The address of the funeral home put it at the harbour industrial area, the railway yards at the bottom of town. It's a good place to drive when you feel like taking the car for a spin, but today I wanted to walk, even in the heat. I wanted to be alone with my thoughts. I wanted to think about Tad Ash, and nothing else.

Downstairs the foyer was dark and empty. The slate was butcher-cold. Secondhand Magazines was open, its racks of newsprint shaded green and grey. The store was run by Louise, a spectacled woman in her late forties. She spoke practically no English, and had named the store herself. When you entered a tinny door bell announced you and Louise would glance up and then look down again, smiling into the cup she was holding in her lap with both hands. She always used the same one – glass, with a fitted brown plastic lid. To drink from it she prised the lid open a few millimetres, took a sip, then quickly shut it again to protect whatever was inside. At night that seemed most likely to be soup, instant sachets dissolved in boiling water from the jug she kept in a curtained annexe at the rear of the store. Once, snooping out the back for crime titles, I'd lifted the curtain and seen a small table with the jug and, laid out next to it on the red and white checked vinyl, two pale apples and a bowl of puckered mandarins. I guessed that she also used the jug to make tea, although I didn't have her pegged as a drinker of instant coffee. I'd thought a lot about asking her directly but could never bring myself to do it.

Louise rarely answered questions or looked people in the eye. She closed the shop one day out of three, with the door displaying a

BACK SOON sign scrawled in a childish hand, but I was a regular customer on the days it was open. I liked Louise and I think she liked me. She gave me a discount on photocopying, as well as keeping an eye out for the two titles which promised to come together, week by week, to form the ultimate reference library on their respective subjects, *20th Century Freeway: A History of American Motoring* and *Dream Cars*. Both wait half-complete in my office in their handsome imitation-leather binders. Louise also regularly held back for me copies of *National Geographic* as well as the occasional *New Scientist*, and she was instrumental in tracking down the missing sections of my *Britannica*. Often I would unfold my regular subscriptions and discover inside a page or clipping she felt would be of interest. I thought of returning the gesture but couldn't think what with. Last Christmas I bought her a Crown Lynn cup and saucer which she accepted with delight and has never used. It's probably still out back, waiting shyly behind the curtain.

Louise was hunched over a *Reader's Digest*, one hand steadying her cup's brown plastic lid. I tapped on the window as I passed. She looked up and smiled and waved urgently and bent down and pulled out a small stack of magazines – all in one scuttle, like an insect reacting to the light. I smiled and nodded and called, 'Later!' and she smiled and nodded and put the magazines back under the counter. Then she folded herself back up behind her journal, lowering her face. My footsteps echoed on the way out.

Outside, the morning sun was already dividing the streets into slivers of white and black. People squinted and looked down, weaving through the triangles of glare. Corner awnings cast shadows into the asphalt, offering a stepped respite from the heat. I took off my jacket and slung it over my shoulder and paced myself, trying not to work up a sweat. When the *Walk* buzzer sounded people didn't really want to cross to the other side, which lay brilliant and unprotected from the sun. They wanted to remain under the awning and catch their breath, safe in the semi-darkness.

As I went further on I counted less foot traffic and more trucks, signs for machine parts and timber. The air tasted of diesel.

The funeral parlour was brick-clad. A small group of mourners waited at the door. I kept on walking down the street to give them time to go inside. When my watch said five minutes past I put on my jacket and doubled back. At the door the funeral director greeted me with a smile and handed me the order of service. *Thaddeus Velim (Tad) Ash.* Printed in gold on ivory card, the words disappeared in the glare.

The reception area was small. The building had no opening windows. The parlour wallpaper was gold and white. The white ceiling was trimmed with ornate plaster moulding painted duck-egg blue. Candle-shaped lights flickered smokelessly. Ahead, from inside the chapel, I could hear the music of an electric organ. The hymn crept slowly along the carpet and pulled at my belly. I cleared my throat.

Inside the chapel, everyone was seated. I hovered. There were about thirty people and nearly all, with the exception of two small children and their parents, were Dede's age or older. I counted grey hairs and hearing aids, zippered nylon jackets. Old but easily donned shoes polished to an acceptable shine. Determinedly bright floral dresses. Business shirts that hadn't been worn to work in a long time, thin at the collar. Nylon raincoats worn over cardigans, regardless of the heat. Crocheted wool in washed-out colours. Their dress was a mish-mash of decorum and habit, bracketed by the effort it took to don. I straightened my tie, shrinking back into the foyer. I could watch from there, maybe even listen from outside: I didn't have to be here in this airless, muffled gathering. I took a step back, but my arm was steadied by a wrinkled hand.

'We're just about to begin,' he whispered. 'I saved you a seat.'

I turned and saw Tad Ash standing there: Dede, the perfect echo of his twin.

'I knew you would come.' Dede nodded at the gathering, his eyes twinkling. 'Do you think you can spot the killer?'

'Ha-ha.' I cleared my throat. 'Very good.'

His other hand joined the first on my arm. 'I'm wrong to joke, of course. I'm very glad you're here. For whatever reason.'

'I'm not sure what the reason is.'

90

'But you did come. You left so quickly yesterday,' he said. 'I didn't have a chance to thank you.'

'I was happy to listen.'

'I was very upset. Very emotional.'

'Please.' I motioned him to stop. 'You've suffered a great loss.'

'What I said to you . . .' He wavered.

'Yes?'

'It was all very important to Tad. Very important.'

I nodded.

'It's been so difficult.' He looked at the front of the room. 'One can't argue, now.'

On a raised dais, constructed of just enough glass and chrome to imply the role of altar, stood Tad's coffin. It looked large and difficult to carry, but there was nothing sombre to it, only polish and chrome.

'The reason why you came' – Dede's grip tightened – 'is within yourself.' He released me, and put his hands behind his back.

'I'm here to give my condolences to you, Mr Ash.'

'Thank you, Mr Penrose. Are you a church-goer?'

'Not really.'

Dede nodded. 'Tad was one of the first city dealers to lobby for Sunday trading.' The organ music was picking up. He pointed me to a space at the front. 'And now we should take our places. Here.' He pressed the order of service into my hand again. 'Would you mind?'

'Of course.'

I followed him down the narrow aisle, past thick glasses, loud questions about the hymns – and uncertain expressions, a lip chewed or a handkerchief raised to the eye, that could be either grief or a twitch of age. My seat was in the front row, to the right of the organist and his tiny Hammond.

Dede waited to see that I was seated before moving away, stopping to exchange whispers with people here and there. Gradually the people around me lowered their voices and straightened themselves, and for the first time I found myself staring at the coffin.

A week before, Tad Ash had been answering the telephone and pressing keys on a till and straightening books and dusting shelves and talking to his brother. Stumbling into the alley. Feeling the cuts, feeling his blood drain. He had been running for refuge and found it here, in a box. Everyone stared at it, weighing their memories of the body it held, but none of them had seen the body as I had, and nobody else had his wallet. Which meant that in a strange way I knew two things about him these intimate friends would never know. I felt charged. I wouldn't go so far as to say chosen, but I'd definitely been handed the job.

The minister entered from the back of the room, walked up the aisle and opened his tiny Bible on the altar. He announced the hymn and the mourners stood, some of them shakily, as the organist pressed out the first bars. The old men sang in high-pitched voices, the women softly droned. I couldn't find the key and my voice cracked. I had to mime the last verse and was relieved to sit down.

It was as we were sitting that I realised someone had entered late at the back of the room. I caught it in the organist's face: his eyes followed someone who came in, paused, then took a place directly behind me. The person was beyond even peripheral vision but something in the atmosphere, the movement of still air by microscopic degrees, made me want to look. But by then the minister had begun to speak and I couldn't risk interrupting, not with Dede sitting so close. I was surrounded by fragile mourners – I couldn't just sit up and jerk round like an impatient child. All I could do was sniff the air and run my hands along the moulded plastic edge of the seat, straining for signals. People coughed, sniffed. There were few tears. Dede sat patiently as he was informed at length in sympathetic tones that his brother was dead. The woman next to me flinched. Dede maintained the same half-smile he'd presented to me. It was bad news, but he already knew. He looked weary and alone.

I tried to hold that thought but as we stood for the last prayer all that was in my head was to turn and look at the last entrant, the person at the back. When the prayer was over, I told myself. And then the minister announced it would be followed by a minute's silence and I wanted to shout: another minute? Another? In which the person at the back would slip away, masked by the noise of people seating themselves again. 'A minute,' the minister said, countering my thoughts, 'for each of us to make our own peace in our own, private way.' And then it came to me.

I took a step forward. I knelt before the coffin.

No-one moved. No-one looked surprised. The minister looked on me with understanding, maybe a little respect. The chapel was silent, without a creak or a shuffle. Pretending to close my eyes I watched the sweep of my watch's minute hand for a full thirty seconds before carefully straightening my head and staring at the surface of the casket, inches before my face. It took a moment to adjust to the focus and decode the sinuous, wobbling forms, but it was enough: in the reflection of the casket's varnish, I could see the entire room. And there, behind me, right at the back, stood the last person to enter. Tall, dressed in black: black coat, black sunglasses, blonde hair. *I can see you*, I whispered. *I know you're there.*

Abruptly, the silence ended. People were clearing their throats, fumbling for their coats and bags. I stood up and turned round – just in time to see the long black coat disappearing out the door. I was still standing as the minister recited closing words and the narrow space between me and the door filled with old people. I couldn't push through them. I joined the mourners as they shuffled out. There was no sign of the stranger by the time I made it on to the street, only Detective Tangiers and his faithful extra checking the people shuffling past.

'How's it going?' Tangiers said. 'You know someone here?'

Dede was several people away, being helped into a car.

'No,' I said. 'I thought I should come. Having seen the body. I felt I had respects to pay.'

'Fair enough. I saw you at the front.'

'I got here early.'

'Right,' he nodded, checking over his shoulder. I had come of my own volition but was already waiting for his next question, or for permission to leave. He was restlessly looking an old woman up and down, eyes moving fast. And then he turned back to me, with the same alert, super-bright stare I'd seen when he turned up at the apartment. He'd found nothing and needed something and if I didn't move quick, I'd be it.

'Who's Veale?' I asked.

'Veale?'

'Dede Ash just mentioned him. You know Ash? He's the dead man's brother. The resemblance is amazing, actually. I didn't realise—'

'He said something about Veale?'

'Yeah, yeah. I went up to offer my condolences, you know, and he just mentioned that someone named Veale wasn't here today.'

'Ash dealt with a party named Veale.' Tangiers snapped at the extra without looking around: 'We've got his number, right?'

'I guess that must be him,' I said as innocently as I could. 'Do you think there's some reason that he's not here today?'

'Maybe, maybe. Very good, Mr Penrose. That's good work. If you were one of my boys it'd be my shout.'

The hearse pulled away, followed by slow, pristine vehicles, grey heads crowding the back seats.

'Damn.' Tangiers glared at the procession. 'That's the next of kin.' He turned to the extra. 'We're out of here.' The other man nodded and crossed to their car. Tangiers gave me a quick smile. 'You want a lift?'

'I think I'll walk.'

'Round here?' He was amused. 'You have business around here?'

'No.' I sniffed the rust in the air. 'That's what's nice about it.'

I watched his car drive away. Soon I was the only person standing outside the parlour, the yellow lamps burning in the sunlight.

I crossed the road and started walking towards the harbour. At its end, the street narrowed and became less busy. I turned and followed the railway yards along the waterfront.

The best of the harbourside roads were in the process of being marked down for redevelopment. I didn't look forward to that. I would miss the public works buildings and freight sheds and the railways, the lines that had fed the city as it began to grow. Now, from the road, the tracks looked rusty and varicose. I climbed over the siding fence and pushed through the toi toi bushes and knee-deep grass to the bottom of the cutting and stepped out on to the railway tracks. The rocks and fill rolled underfoot, kicking up small clouds of red oxide dust.

Yellow dandelions poked between the rails. I walked along the sleepers, pacing my steps evenly, head down, combing the ground. Bundled fence wire, a single steel bolt, dirty washers.

The station platform was pebbled with broken glass. Its fence was graffiti'd and its wooden seats had been smashed down to their steel wall brackets. On the far side of the building, sheltered from the seaward side, stood a forty-gallon drum cut into a brazier, carefully positioned on bricks and charred wooden supports. Its blackened metal was still warm.

I walked into the ticket office. The windows were boarded and the boards pasted over with band posters and closure notices. Even here there were posters for Mardi Gras: the big parade, come to the parade! The floor was covered in newspapers and smelled of shit. Every weekend itinerants converted the place into a makeshift doss house and every Monday morning the authorities nailed it closed.

Far off in the distance, I heard something. A whistle: a train was coming.

I stepped outside to look. It was a big diesel headed in on the eastern line, one short passenger cab and a long line of empty trucks. It grew larger, its lamp flaring in the low afternoon sun. The whistle sounded again. Closer now, it began to block out the light. The wheels scraped the metal rails like flint and the sound of the engine began to double back on itself. For a dark second it passed, clattering and shaking, whistling like a punctured bird. Passengers flashed past. It stank of oil. The rushing air lifted the newspapers and blew dust into my face. I put my hand to my eyes and then the trucks were clattering past and it was shrinking, faithful to the tapering tracks. The second of noise and fear had passed.

She would be gone one day, but I couldn't cope with the thought. I wonder, in fact, if people ever do manage to fill the holes scooped out by age and disease, watching as friends are slowly picked off like prizes at a shy, one by one, knocked down and given away. This morning it seemed better to remain alone, or at least limit yourself to people in passing. And I wondered if that was why Palmer hated tourists: because their comings and goings trained them for parting. When death did come they'd have the words for farewell. It was simply a longer version of the sojourns from which loved ones and relatives always returned some time.

The phenakistiscope diary was nothing more than a madman's scrawl, a cardboard fiction. But I was also sure that some element of it was linked to Tad Ash's death as directly as the train lines running back into the city. Everything connected somewhere. I counted the seconds of the engine's Doppler fade, its shape turning grey and indistinct. Tad Ash died there in the train yard that day, not in the alleyway two nights before. I waved goodbye to the rattling freight.

I started walking back to the city, hands in my pockets. They did some searching of their own and came out with something. It was the card for the Yamada bar, and I was hungry, so that seemed as good a place as any to proceed.

11

The Yamada was a ramen bar at the bottom of town, one of a chain that had started up in the city a few years ago. Its sister establishments were expensive steak house and sushi affairs, but when I finally found the Yamada it was tucked between a tourist café and a run-down booking office in a back street behind the wharves. The entire premises amounted to little more than a corridor with bar-stool seating along an imitation woodgrain counter. There were about twelve people inside, which made it almost full. There was an empty place at the back, and in the place next to it was Dede Ash.

A chef and his assistant were working behind the counter, chopping vegetables on a stainless steel bench. I squeezed along past them and the patrons hunched over their meals. Dede was still in his funeral suit, sitting straight-backed to read the menu.

It all adds up, really. All you have to do is follow the cards. It's true that I hesitated, wondering if I should, if I had the right, but beyond that was the sensation that this had all been laid out for me. He was here and I was here and that was it: he and I had to speak.

I walked up to him and extended my hand. 'I didn't get to say goodbye,' I said, but he didn't look up. He kept on reading, his Adam's apple sliding up and down the front of his dry, white neck. I cleared my throat. He closed the menu and turned to me and stared. He had come here after the funeral seeking a private moment, and here I was bursting in. 'I wanted to thank you for the service,' I lied. 'That's all.'

He continued to stare. I didn't know what to say. Behind the counter the taps, shrouded in aluminium foil, ran in a constant trickle, replacing the steam lost from the always-boiling pot. The older chef ladled its contents into two wide bowls, shaking noodles dry and tipping them into the soup. Then he called over the boy who carried the bowls outside the counter and round to some people at the back of the room. I had to step back so I didn't bump him. 'You'd best take a place,' Ash said, returning to his menu.

It was good to sit down. I shuffled off my coat and tucked it under my feet. The boy stepped back behind the counter and handed me a photocopied menu, the English translation marked in ballpoint.

The lights were yellow with grease. The diners held cigarettes but there was no smell of smoke. Fans above the counter sucked it away, along with the cooking smells. A muted TV played endless music videos but the music came from a thin transistor radio: hits of the '60s and '70s. It saved me from talking. I sat listening to the tunes and the other diners making conversation on our behalf. The older chef sliced meat with a sharp-looking knife. The tray-ovens sizzled as the boy oiled them down. He packed the trays with finger-sized meats and seared their pastry skins brown.

Ash ordered shoi ramen and tea, I asked for shoi and a Sapporo and we handed back our menus.

'How did the rest of the day go?' I asked.

'I'm rather numb to it, now.'

'You came here by yourself.'

'I wanted to get away. I'm tired of talking.'

'I know that feeling.'

'Do you?'

The assistant chef plonked down the beer. I picked it up. The metal was cold. The tab unwound in a widening spiral, unlidding the can and transforming it into a glass. I sipped the foam. 'Dry,' I said, not meaning much by it. Ash nodded.

'They like it dry.'

I sipped. 'You ever been to Japan?'

'No.'

'Friend of mine worked there. I've never been.' I smacked my lips and sipped again. 'I'd like to. There are a lot of places I'd like to go. I should travel more. One day, I guess.'

'I never felt I could go anywhere without Tad.'

'Because you were twins?'

He nodded. 'We preferred to remain near each other. At school we were kept apart – very difficult. Our anxiety couldn't have been apparent to others: we never dressed alike, we had vastly different personalities. But we did most things at the same time. Cut our teeth, learned to walk, caught the mumps. Didn't even like sleeping in separate rooms.'

'Go out with the same girls?'

'One of the myths, regrettably.'

'Ah.'

'Many of us are twins in the womb, however. When the cells first begin to divide, there is often duplication. The duplicate can survive until very late in the term. Many more people than you would realise once possessed a twin – at least one other person in this bar. Maybe you had one yourself, Mr Penrose, a little shadow, a doppelgänger. Hence your taking an interest.' He tipped his head, letting the suggestion fall. 'Tad and I are merely one of the minority of pairs who survived. But of course, that's over now.'

'You're still here.'

'Yes, and waiting to die.'

I looked at him.

'Twins die within hours of each other. You must know that.'

'But this is different,' I objected.

'How? Tad is dead. Now I am waiting.'

'Tad's death wasn't planned,' I argued. 'It was accidental. He was murdered.'

'Nevertheless, he is gone, now.' Ash stared into his tea. 'I am left overdue.' He lifted the cup and sipped. 'Do you like green tea?'

'I do.'

'Clears the head.'

The chef worked swiftly. Helen Reddy sang. I slipped the chopsticks from their hygenic paper sleeve and rubbed them against each other to clear them of splinters. The noodles arrived. We ate in silence. I alternated the soup with beer and flushed with the contrast. Ash ate carefully. I slopped mine somewhat. Dining, we slipped more into the ambience of the room, became part of the bustle. When my bowl was half empty I pushed it away and ordered another beer.

'That was good,' I said.

'I come here often,' Dede said. 'Today it tastes different.'

'Does it?'

'Salty.' He sucked in his lower lip. I untwisted the second can's spiral. 'I enjoyed seeing everyone at the service,' he said. 'I appreciated the company.'

'But you're here alone.'

'I was waiting for you.' He smiled. 'I know – I couldn't predict that you would come here, so soon, but I did know you'd return. I saw it today, when you knelt before Tad's coffin. You're looking for something.'

'I went and saw Veale.'

He shrugged. 'I can't imagine you were impressed.'

'He seemed pretty flaky to me. He doesn't even have a copy of the thing he's supposed to be selling. I don't think he set up any deal for Tad. I don't think he has a buyer for anything, much less the diary. But he was looking for someone to publish it, and maybe his talking about it made someone jumpy. Do you have any idea who that could be?'

Dede's voice was sing-song. 'Who knows?'

I smiled. 'Right. Well, the police might have missed it but I think I know. I think it's someone who wants to keep the diary's contents a secret.' I stared at him. 'I'm with you, Dede, insofar as I think the diary is the connection here.'

'And so the autograph finds another devotee.' He sighed. 'It's sad my brother isn't here, Mr Penrose. I'm sure that in you he would have found the perfect buyer.'

He reached down beside his stool and brought out a bulging red legal folder. Pieces of broken sealing wax dusted the string which held it shut. Dede's eyes were moist. 'Please read it. Tad would have liked you to.'

'What's so special about it, Dede?' I said.

He shook his head. 'It was the same with Tad. I recall him saying that the first part didn't convince him, but as he read on ...' He held the folder out to me. 'I'm sure you'll soon see.'

His hands shook as I took it. The shock of seeing Tad dead, being lowered into the ground: Dede was on thin ice. I made space for the papers on the counter: he watched, as I unknotted the string.

'I've been carrying it with me,' he said. 'I hesitated to give it to you on our first meeting. But I can see the late nights, Mr Penrose.' He touched the hollows beneath his gleaming eyes. 'I know how that feels.'

Inside the folder were pages, their edges soft and worn.

'Where did these come from?' I asked.

'The base of the phenakistiscope. They were taped into a recessed area of the wood.'

The pages were covered in words in two different hands. The first, reading left to right along the marked lines of the pages, was lettered in large, awkward characters, often misspelt. The second script was much smaller, consisting of tightly linked, slanting characters which ran between the lines of the first script and sometimes vertically, in instances when the page had been turned on its side. The maze of script and superscript was laid so densely on some leaves that it turned them into thatch. Accompanying each page were further typed notes.

'Who typed these?'

'The typed pages are Tad's transcriptions.' Dede ran his finger down the page I was holding. 'The larger hand belongs to a man named Odom Fray. The diary was originally his, and he made his entries in black Indian ink. Palmer's is the smaller hand – it matches the writing on the phenakistiscope discs. He was writing in invisible ink – lemon juice, and sometimes urine. As the pages aged and dried the ink started to discolour and show, but at the time it would have been quite invisible.'

Dede picked out a specimen and drew me closer. 'See, here, how Fray's script breaks into Palmer's? His nib pressed into the page after Palmer had written this entry. And here' – Dede turned a few pages in – 'the reverse happens. Palmer's ink moistens Fray's writing, carrying it a few millimetres. This proves that Palmer and Fray were both making entries at the same time, often within hours of each other.

'Why were they sharing a diary?' I asked.

'It was Palmer's joke. Fray was very secretive about his diary. While he was asleep, Palmer would enter his own notes in invisible ink. Fray never knew what his apprentice was doing.'

'His apprentice?'

Dede picked something between his teeth. 'Odom Fray was an ex-circus performer working his way around the west coast of America. He was an escape artist. Palmer was his young apprentice.'

I held up my hand. 'Wait a moment. If this is the same Palmer, he must be over sixty.'

Dede nodded. 'Palmer explains it. It is the year 1929. His parents are dead, he is living in America, and he is exactly eighteen years old. Fifty-four years have passed. Palmer has aged by only eight.' Dede tapped the folder proudly. 'It's all here, Mr Penrose. Every detail. As clear as crystal.' He breathed deeply, drained by speaking. He sat back.

'I see,' I said. 'Well, I'll go through it. I'm sure the thing I'm looking for is here.'

'It's a great relief to me knowing you are on the case, so to speak.' He raised his cup. 'No-one else understands. It's quite beyond them.'

He drank the last of his tea and counted out his share of the bill in dollar coins. He wiped his mouth and hands with the single paper napkin that had lasted him for the whole meal and then stood and straightened his suit and walked out of the bar. The cook called after him as he stepped through the door, and then the boy: thank you very much, thank you very much.

I ordered another beer and began to read.

Flicking through the diary I found Palmer where Dede said he would be: the west coast of America in 1929. The balmy San Francisco summer was attracting seaside crowds: tourists and travellers looking to be entertained. The resort was host to dancing marathons and motor rallies, carousels and freak shows.

Escape artists were not the latest thing that year. In fact, they were yesterday's news, but as a live act they still drew a crowd. Ignored by newsreel and cinema, Odom Fray – Jack 'Fearless' Fray to his audience – earned his living by working theatres in winter and seaside resorts in summer. It was the beginning of that year's summer when he found a young boy named Palmer bunked down beneath the pier.

Fray described Palmer as a teenage boy, his gangly height exaggerated by malnutrition and his ragged, too-small clothes. He was an orphan without education or trade. His speech was 'strangely accented' and his conversation, although naive, was confident. The showman knew guilelessness to be a crowd-pleaser. He took Palmer in, employing him as an assistant and apprentice.

On arrival in a new town it was Palmer's task to hand out and paste up posters for Fray's performance, to sell tickets and spread the word. He appeared on stage with Fray as MC, his voice cracking nervously as he narrated each feat. When Fray was handcuffed and nailed into a strong-box, then lowered into the water at the end of the pier, it was Palmer's job to count aloud from a stopwatch, visibly fretting as the seconds ticked by. And when the box was raised, miraculously unbroken, with Fray sitting cross-legged on top, waving to the crowd, it was Palmer who went through the crowd with a hat, gratefully collecting coins.

It was also Palmer's role to assist Fray in the part of the performances the audience did not see: the manufacture of tiny files and flat, easily concealed tools; or the dissassembly, oiling and re-jigging of locks to ensure they could be easily picked. In the case of Fray's famous strong-box escape, it was Palmer who guarded the box for the twenty-four hours prior to the attempt, during which time he would de-nail the planks along its base and replace the nails with thin wire staples. On the day, after the box had been inspected by officials before the audience and Fray helped, handcuffed, inside, it was the apprentice who rushed forward to shake his master's hand emotionally for the last time – passing him in the process a lockpick and a flat pair of wire snips hidden in flesh-coloured wax. By the time the box had been sealed, tied to the crane and swung out above the waves, Fray had already picked his handcuffs and started to cut the staples. Hidden by the water he kicked out the planks, swam outside and closed them again, waiting for Palmer to worry the crowd before swimming to the surface.

At these performances Fray was praised as a hero with supernatural powers, a man who had cheated death. As Palmer learned more secrets of the trade, he found it harder to look on the older man with respect. When he gained access to Fray's diary and his private thoughts, he was even less pleased to find himself described as a weak and confused young man. He began to resent Odom Fray. Fray described him as increasingly petulant and chastised him for not keeping his mind on the job. Palmer retaliated by mocking the ageing escape artist and denouncing him as a coward.

Odom takes me out fishing. We row from the end of the pier into maybe thirty feet of water. We bait the two-cent lines with bread and drop them over the side. I have never been fishing before. He shows how to thread the line round a finger, to be alerted by the slightest tug. How to listen for a fish about to die: it is nibbling, ja? And with a turn of the wrist he jerks back the line to catch the hook in its mouth. This is hooking a fish, he says.

He has the cracked hands of a father. This is the razor. This is hooking a fish. One day I will have a son and learn him. Find a beautiful girl, feel my skin turn dry.

Ach, you are fucking miles away. You dreaming of a better life? Forget it.

This is making a catch. The charming of snakes, ja? I call the crowd on the pier forward. I say: Ladies and Gentlemen. Sehr verehrte Damen und Herren.

I show them the box, ja? I use both my arms to pick up one corner of the box, lift just one edge and the strain, it shows in my face. A heavy box. I show them the chains. Pass the chains round the audience. The women do not touch them, because of the grease and rust. The men hold the chains. Some men test the chains. They strain on them! To be impressive, no doubt. I show them the padlocks. I show them the handcuffs.

You come to me, just a boy. Rags you were in. And where had you been before, I could not tell you. Nobody can remember, your face it is so forgettable.

Long face? Perhaps. Short face? Perhaps. A man? A boy? Some days I see this boy in the light and think, you are my boss, ja? You have the face of a businessman. Someone who owns a shop. A businessman, yes. A dealer. Eyes taking things in, darting, all the time collecting what he can see. Collecting, collecting. Awake! So awake! Everything he knows. What can we tell him that he does not know?

And then in the afternoon, the shade, I see this boy and think, ach, a bum. My respect for you it rises and falls with the fucking sun.

Ah. I teach you but. Everything you know. What escaping have you done before you meet me? I ask around. I ask friends. I write to my friends and say this boy, this Mr Drew Palmer, you have heard of him? But no-one has heard. No-one remembers. Forgettable performer. No star. Just you wandering, wandering. Before you meet me you never escape from a thing in your life.

In San Francisco, in 1929, a crowd assembles at the end of the pier to witness Odom Fray's famous strong-box escape. The box has been inspected by a local clergyman and Fray, manacled hand and foot, has been helped inside. A cold wind is blowing, lifting spray over the edge of the boards. The audience shivers at the prospect of meeting the waves. As usual, the young assistant breaks through the crowd and gives his master the final handshake, pleading with him not to attempt this escape. The crowd murmurs nervously. Fray will continue with the feat. He holds his assistant's hand for a little longer than usual before releasing it. The assistant is stepping back when Fray reaches out for him again, this time clutching his hand, shaking it furiously. The assistant acknowledges this gratefully but breaks the embrace once more. The crowd is moved by this emotional display but Odom Fray, crouching back in the box, appears less assured. The lid hides his face. As the nails are driven in to the inch-thick wood, Palmer absent-mindedly plays with the tiny snips and lockpick that remain in his trouser pocket.

A band plays as the box is lifted high by the crane. It swings out over the edge of the pier, its square shadow dancing on the messy green. The waves slap its sides as it is lowered. It disappears from view.

Fifteen minutes later the box is raised, stringy with escaping brine.

Although the distance between it and the pier has not changed, its return journey seems slow. The band has stopped playing. The crowd makes no noise. Some of the women hold handkerchiefs to their faces. It lands with an ugly thump. The authorities smash its side with a piking iron. The heavy timber does not give way. Finally they wrench off the lid, rolling the box forward against its rope, and a slack, grey body slithers out.

Palmer makes his last diary entry in invisible ink, writing from his hotel room. The night is maybe ten minutes old, the sky red. He is sitting at his window drinking Coca-Cola and wishing for something stronger that would dilute his fear and pessimism and growing scorn. He considers himself orphaned twice: by his parents and by Fray. He scribbles furiously.

From his window he can see the pier and the crowd that has been waiting there since midday. Some of its members are visibly drunk and some are singing, but most are sober. Some are shouting angrily and some are chanting, but generally the mood is one of calm anticipation. It would be difficult for them to express in words just what they are waiting for because what they long for is a thing not from their civilised world. It is not to be purchased in a seaside emporium or ordered at one of the local restaurants, although the spit of meat on hot iron betokens something of what they desire. What they wait for, Palmer knows now, is death. Fray's failure has whetted the appetite of normal people and awakened them, suddenly, to the animal within. They want to see an escape act from which there is no escape, and they want to witness death – Palmer's death. As if they know, somehow, about the train and the missing years of his life. As if they know he is behind on the unspoken agreement to honour God's three score and ten, as if they are clamouring for him to catch up.

The Yamada's windows were dark. My plate was cold. The last scraps of noodle and fish paste had sunk to the bottom of the thin chicken soup, the fat beginning to coagulate into little magnifying glasses that bumped together on the surface. I reached over the counter and asked for the bill. The boy smiled and wiped his hands.

I slowly turned back the discoloured pages until the very first page lay facing up, then gathered up the stack and tapped their long edge on the table top until they lay straight. I closed the cardboard folder. The chef waited patiently while I finished tying the string round the folder before he passed over a mint and a toothpick resting on a folded bill. I took out a ten and a five and added them to the stack of Dede's coins. I put the mint in my mouth and stretched back in the chair as I waited for the change, my back cracking in a hundred places.

I had seen fakes – company accounts, bank ledgers. Clearly this was one. Sure, it told me some things, but nothing about Tad, nothing at all. Poor Dede. He had stepped out into a night that didn't hold much.

It was not until I peered over my knuckles at the bar and its chattering faces that I caught the dark shapes of her eyes. She had been watching me from the shadows of the far booth by the door, sitting straight in the uncomfortable chair. I didn't know how long she had been there because I hadn't seen her come in. It was the woman I'd seen outside the Dilworth on my way home, the woman waiting for a taxi in the small hours. She was wearing the same black leather coat, her blonde curls hanging over the lapels. She held her chin just high enough to keep her face in darkness. Her cigarette was balanced between long, red-painted fingernails, and her wrists were delicate and white. It was possible that she lived around here but, dressed as she was, it was more likely she worked the streets. Bumping into those women from time to time, I was often struck by how pretty they were, and how smart. They really had experience, even if it was of something less than good, and they were interesting because of it, although you could never tell them that, and certainly it never made a lively subject for conversation. Their eyes glazed over every time.

I found myself looking back at her. I couldn't read her shaded face, but when, abruptly, she rose I realised I'd been staring. She got up from her stool, pulled her coat tighter round her, and walked out of the bar leaving the door swinging, her beer glass still half-full, the smoke from her cigarette curling up to the ceiling in a twist of forgotten white ribbon.

12

The streets were quiet, the harbour flat. The multiplexes had closed. The fast cars were parked back at home in the suburbs, nursing speeding tickets and scraped bumpers. The clouds were heavy with rainy thoughts. I pulled the folder tight under my arm as the first drops fell and moistened my skin, speckling my shoulders.

As I approached the Dilworth, a bus drove past and stopped outside the church. Its doors hissed open and the passengers loudly disembarked. They stood in a confused huddle at the church door, clucking in a language I didn't catch. I ran past them and across the road, droplets trickling down the back of my collar. The bus pulled out, tyres rasping against the slippery road. The water was coming down in rippling sheets. It was the last part of winter draining away. Soon the season would tip toward summer and blue, cloudless skies. At the very edge of the horizon lay a thin, bright line, a ceiling beyond the city belonging to a better place and a better time.

I ran inside the foyer and into the waiting lift.

My office smelled stale. I opened a window and looked down on the street. The passengers had gone. The rain picked up speed until there were no gaps between the droplets, only solid water pounding the glass.

I stripped off in the bathroom and towelled myself down. I found some dry clothes and rinsed out the percolator and put fresh water on to boil. The coffee grounds were a vacuum-sealed brick. I poked a hole in the packet to let in the air and massaged it, feeling it loosen and crunch. The good thing about living alone is that you always get to do that.

There were three new messages on my answerphone, all from

Brands, in order of increasing frustration. I opened my drawer and took out the courier envelope they had sent. I flicked through it. I made some notes along the top of two of the documents using red pen. I wrote out some more notes – numbers to ring, the first line of attack – on yellow sticky Post-it labels and fixed them to the front of the page. The rest I could do in the morning. I put everything back in the envelope and returned it to the drawer.

The coffee was perking. I poured myself a cup, took it over to my desk and sat down. I sipped it. I looked at the folder, and then I gave in and put the cup to one side and went through the diary all over again.

Palmer killed Odom Fray because the old man's existence challenged the disconnected notions Palmer had used to shelter himself from reality. This document was a confession. But the only person threatened by its existence was Palmer, and Palmer was dead. Right? Right. Because he was born before 1875. End of story. Dead end.

I couldn't see a link between these pages and a motive for killing a man in an alleyway over fifty years later. Dede's excitement was unfounded.

I sighed, disappointed with myself. I had been hoping as much as Dede that something in the diary would make everything clear. I closed it and took the wallet out again. Now the connection could only be in here.

I flipped it open and shook it upside down and counted its contents where they fell. The stamps, the business cards. Coffee house receipts, latch key, the sci-fi trading card. I stopped at the postcard corner and the photograph of the black cat. I picked out the newspaper cutting and read through its list of second-hand sales. There were six or eight numbers there. Then I turned it over, wondering for the first time if Tad might have cut it out for what was on the other side. A black, ten-line advertisement from the personal columns: Madame Sunde, Fantasy Mistress. With a phone number.

Hundreds of people called that number. Dialling it would give nothing away. I could have picked up a newspaper and found it of my own accord. In fact, given the city's size and the statistical average of links between its inhabitants, it's unlikely I'd be unique among its users even in the sense that I knew Tad Ash. I had always been curious about these services and now seemed like a good time to do some research on them. Certainly, if the subject of Tad Ash came up I'd be a fool to avoid it – I might even go so far as to raise it myself, just to clear the air. Meantime I was just another caller. I sucked in air.

I tucked the receiver under my ear and dialled Madame Sunde's number and waited for the beep and the click and the hiss, the prerecorded message: 'The Madame is not in. You must leave a message. Wait for the little beep. Leave the message. Goodbye.'

I hung up and gave the machine time to rewind, then called again. Message. It was such a soft word. Missuge, m'susche. I could not see it as it was said. I hung up and called again. The softness and click of the palate. A man saying it would sound like a cartoon. But the woman's voice was soft, the tongue turning a sharp S into a thick, cushy shh.

I rang the number again and this time spoke after the beep. 'I'd like to book a call,' I said, and read out my phone number and credit card authorisation. 'Call me please, as soon as you can.'

I hung up and put everything back inside the wallet, matching even the thicknesses of cards to the indentations in the leather. I paused at the photograph of the cat. It was a nice cat. Male or female? I couldn't tell.

I went into the bedroom and peeled back the sheets on the bed. I clicked on the side-lamp and lay on my side with one leg tucked beneath the duvet, the bed linen cool on my skin. I threw the wallet up a little way and caught it, felt its weight.

I finished my coffee and stood it on the floor and lay against the pillow and held up the leather to the glare of the peagrain bulb. The light hurt my eyes, so I closed them. It was only for a second, but in that second I heard the rain falling on the black street outside and was dry in the sheets, dry and warm, and then I was asleep.

The bell woke me. I knocked over the coffee cup getting out of bed and it clattered on to the floor. I picked up the receiver but the ringing continued: it was someone at the door. I squinted through the red spots left by the lamp. Two o'clock. I found the intercom and pressed the button.

'It's me,' Wilhemina said. The speaker split her voice into two pitched rasps. 'Can I come up?'

'Yeah,' I said and pushed the button. There was the beep of the door unlocking and the intercom fell dead. I was running the sink tap to wash myself when it sounded again.

'The door won't open,' she shouted. 'It's locked.'

'Try it after I press the buzzer.'

'I know how to do it. It won't open.'

I pressed the button. 'Try it now. Try the fucking thing now.'

'I'm getting wet. Can—'

'Fuck,' I said, and punched the speaker. I found a pair of unwashed jeans and padded shirtless downstairs, the staircase grime sticking to my bare feet.

When I pulled open the front door she was leaning against the security grate. Her hair was flattened as if it had just been cut with scissors and a pudding bowl, her fringe lying flat across her forehead. Her make-up had all but washed away. The rain had taken up her uniform's slack, pulling it tight against her body. Her Nikes were black with water. She was carrying her working shoes in her left hand and in her right a big brown paper bag bearing the Regent logo and the luminous grease patch of expensive pastries. I held the door open for her but she didn't move. She stood in the rain and stared back at me with deep eyes.

'How's the weather?' I said, but she didn't laugh.

'I've been working the graveyard,' she said finally. 'I got off at three. I thought I'd come down and see you. I thought you'd be awake. I thought you'd be working, so I brought you breakfast. I carried it all the way under my jacket so it wouldn't get wet.'

'Thank you,' I said. 'You should have got a taxi.'

'It's not far, it's a warm rain. I felt like the walk. I wanted to see you.' She paused. 'I meant it when I said the door didn't open.'

'It happens sometimes.' I wiped my face. 'When it's wet, actually. I think the circuits short when it's wet.'

'Do they?' Her voice trailed off for a moment and then she picked it up again. 'I don't like it when you swear at me, Ellie. Even on the intercom.'

'I just got up. I was asleep.'

'I don't like you shouting.'

'I said, I'm sorry.' The word 'sorry' always came out as if I didn't mean it. I stood watching her standing in the rain, her shoes in one hand and the bag in the other. She was waiting for me to say something and I knew that when I did it would be the wrong thing. My chest was cold. 'You should come inside,' I said finally.

'Should I?'

'Of course you should. You should.' Her slow burn was dying now, dampened by the rain. 'Come inside. Come upstairs.' I reached out and touched her forehead, wiping it. Her gaze fell but she didn't step away.

We stood like that for a while, the back of my hand stroking her damp cheek. I traced the dark edge of her fringe, the swell of muscles at her clenched jaw. With my thumb I nudged each of the diamond studs glinting in her ears, one in the left, two in the right, hoping to find in them some sort of switch that would turn her around. I felt through the short baby-hairs that ran down the back of her neck, the businesslike finger's-width looseness between her skin and sodden collar and rested my fingers there and bought my thumb up to the point of her chin. Her lipstick was no more than a stain on her mouth, her top lip, red and bitten, resting on its small pink sister, unmoving, unafraid. I stepped onto the street and brought her face close to mine until she twisted away.

'I'm almost too tired to care any more,' she said, and pushed past me into the hallway. I took a breath and reminded myself to be sorry and let the door fall closed.

In the swaying elevator she stood with her straight back to me and said nothing as the floors ticked by. Wilhemina annoyed me in a way that nobody else did. She had good posture, whereas I slouched. She was bright-eyed after a full shift. She walked home in the rain while I ducked under awnings. She didn't feel the cold. I could work longer hours and I could concentrate harder but I never had her stamina – I always got colds and headaches and the flu. It irritated me having to catch up. Her gaze was set on the numbered lights. When they reached four she stepped back and waited for me to swing open the grille.

Inside my office she dropped her shoes by the door, handed me the brown paper bag and crouched to unlace her Nikes. She was shivering.

'You're freezing,' I said. 'You should get in the shower.' I put my arm around her shoulders and she didn't pull away and she didn't rise. She stayed hunched against me until I knew she wasn't angry any more.

I patted her on the shoulder and lifted her up and she put her cold hands on my cheeks and kissed me and her mouth tasted hot and sweet, her neck slippery inside the dank, scratchy uniform. We walked each other to the bathroom, arms linked like schoolchildren playing a clumsy game, and I kissed her again beneath the flickering light of the fluorescent tube, her wet head pressing against the tiles. My hand found the tap and turned on the shower and when I opened my eyes the room was scudded with steam.

I pulled her underneath the shower stream and she leaned back with her eyes closed, her hands scooping water into her face as I twisted each button through its swollen hole, the hot water renewing the darkness of her skirt. I pushed back her lapels and pinned her arms and she stuck her chest forward to kiss me again, drawing me deeper into her mouth, past her teeth, her tongue. And then her mouth was moving up, kissing my cheekbones, the burning sockets of my eyes, and I was fumbling at her blouse until finally I was tearing at it and she was roaring extraordinary things, popping the heavy fly of my jeans and digging inside with her free hand. The fine white cotton of her blouse seemed to shred of its own accord, the embroidered R dropping into the water. The skirt's material was tougher and now, twice wet, so tough I couldn't manage so she pushed down on my bare thigh, legs apart, and hiked the skirt up, wiping the soap from her face and smiling, her hair lank, and then she was whacking at the shower curtain, feeling for the bar until I lifted her up and she hung from it, the effort stretching her throat.

I found the front of her pants with my middle fingers and pulled them down until her pubis appeared and I could test it with the front of my teeth, pressing their flat dentition against her petite, forested nub. The water running down my face slaked away all but the sharpest taste, its mucus sting teasing the length of my tongue. The backs of her thighs were still cold. I plugged the tub and pulled her off the rail and on to her knees and stroked her soft cunt, holding her face against my face as she struggled with the last of her clothes. She wrenched the skirt off, God knows how. Girls know things which boys never will.

Unsheathed, she was long and beautiful. I soaped her stomach and her breasts, rubbed my fingers along the red lines left by her bra, the flesh something more than a mouthful, her hands dancing the length of my arms like white spiders. At that moment the reasons why I was angry fell away. She had walked through the wet streets to visit, she was blameless and she was good and she was beautiful, ripe and lean and alive. We fell with a crash and lay beneath the cascade and my cock was inside her and she was twisting, loud and happy, the hot water falling in time with the rain. I coaxed words from her, a joke, a minor protest, and heard myself saying sorry, so sorry, so very sorry, and this time the word came out sounding as if I meant it, which I did, and I was – I very much was.

We lay in the tub until the water grew cold, then stood up and got dry without looking, talking or catching each other's gaze in the mirror. As we walked into the dimly lit bedroom she stopped and touched with her fingertips the single Polaroid pinned to the wall, its shadow fluted in the bathroom's light.

'You still have it up,' she smiled.

The painted squares of the window panes were an unreflecting blue checkerboard, muffling the traffic noises from below. I walked into the back of her and my arms fell about her waist.

'I only put it up because you were coming round.'

'You didn't know I was.'

'Yes I did. I know everything.'

'Like hell you do, Mr Penrose.'

115

'No swearing now.'

'Grown-up's privilege.'

She crawled into the dark side of the bed. I snapped off the lamp and stood it down on the floor. I rolled over to face her and pulled the sheets up high round us and she drew close and lay inside my arm. My fingertips drifted and I lost myself in soft woven valleys and pools, skin against weave. The shape of her jaw, her closed eyes. Her feet shifted in the linen. She was looking for purchase, some sort of proof that she might sleep over. And then her grip firmed just as mine started to slide, and unconsciousness became her guarantee.

13

When I woke up she was lying propped on one elbow. She had been watching me sleep. Her fringe was a black tangle. I raked my fingers through it and she smiled.

'What time is it?' I said.

'You have to be somewhere?' she said.

'No.' I pulled closer to her warmth. 'You want breakfast? You must be hungry.'

'Mm.' She wrinkled her nose. I kissed it and got out of bed.

The floor was cold. The office was flooded with weak, grey sun. I shuddered and put on fresh coffee and opened some juice. I tore open the brown paper bag and took out the pastries Wilhemina had nursed through six blocks and seven intersections. The croissant went under a slow heat. I sliced the Danishes lengthways and folded the empty bag before dropping it in the trash. I put the juice and pastries on a tray and took them back to the bedroom. She was lying on her back staring at the ceiling, one arm folded across her stomach, the other curled above her head. I switched on the side-lamp and her eyes went dark.

'Coffee's coming,' I said.

'Neat.' She sat up and rocked back on her hands. 'That looks great.'

'I had them delivered.'

'Yeah?' She dunked her croissant in the juice. 'What did that cost you?'

'I know this girl.'

She wiped away the pastry flakes with her little finger. The coffee came to the boil. She drank one and a half cups. I turned on the radio and we listened to the world news. She got up to go to the bathroom, padding across the office in the weak light. The coffee tasted exactly right. The weather man warned of storms in Jakarta. Wilhemina walked back slowly, reading the things lying on my desk and pinned to the walls. She leaned over the bench and looked out the window. She came back to the bedroom with her arms folded and dropped to her knees on the end of the bed. She fell forward on to her stomach and stretched out, arching her toes.

'What a horrible day,' she said. 'I'm exhausted.'

'What from?'

'The end of winter. I feel worn out.' Her head lolled. 'What about you?'

'I'm fine.'

'Are you happy?'

'Sure.'

Her hand found mine and held it beneath the sheets, clasped above her warm cunt. 'You never say you are.'

'Lots of things make me happy.' I searched the walls, fossicking through memories and letters and afternoons past. But they remained silent: there was no endorsement, no applause.

I stood the hot mug on the floorboards. I started pressing her tired muscles, squeezing out the late-shift toxins, and she groaned and reached out, her arms digging beneath the pillow. I worked on the hard little knots of flesh beneath her shoulder-blades and the base of her neck, pounding fingertips down the length of her spine until she emitted a fake squeal and pleaded with me not to press too hard. Prone, she felt smaller. I mapped out a massage proportionate to the pain in my own muscles. She tossed her head from side to side, sniffing. I traced her long white snowdrift sides, my fingers falling now and then to her breasts or distracted again by the crack of her buttocks, her cunt's fleshy tuck. She stretched out again and then stopped, turning her head, and brought out Dede Ash's wallet from beneath her pillow. Playfully, her head still on one side, she used one hand to unpick it.

'This isn't yours,' she declared finally, rolling over.

'No. It belongs to a dead man.'

'God!' She dropped it like a hot thing.

'It's clean,' I said.

'What do you mean?'

'I mean it wasn't on his body when he was found. He lost it long before he died.'

She regarded it with distaste. 'Where'd you get it?'

'I found it. Like I said, it's clean. No blood or anything.'

'What do you mean, you found it?'

'Just like you did then. And I looked through it.'

She looked at me but I wasn't saying any more. She picked up the wallet again and held it for a good two seconds as if it might bite her. When she saw it would not, she began going through the contents like a professional.

'You've done this before,' I said.

'I'm a waitress. I can tell a lot of things about a man from looking at his wallet.'

'What can you tell about this one?'

'He's a businessman.' She flicked through the cards. 'Antiques. Antiques and importing. Is he a collector?'

'Antiques dealer.'

'No credit cards. No phone cards, no swipe-ID. It's like a wallet that's ten years old.' She held her lower lip between her teeth. 'He's an old man.'

'Was.'

'But there's this,' she said, puzzling over the *Star Trek* card.

'He dealt in them – quite a trade. And used them as bookmarks.'

She turned it over. 'You tell Tony about these?'

'Yep. He didn't know there was a second series.'

She grinned. 'He's such a sweetie.'

'Is he? I hadn't noticed.'

'Well, he seems nice. The other girls say he is.'

I let it go. 'What else?'

She uncrinkled the square of newspaper and read the numbers. 'For Sale column. Junk sales. He's buying junk second-hand.'

'Wrong,' I said. 'Turn it over.'

She did. Her eyebrows went up. 'Madame Sunde, fantasy mistress. S&M a speciality.'

'He liked to talk.'

'So he didn't have anyone.' She took a heavy breath. 'It's sad. An old man's wallet. Everything in it's so lonely. The only people in here are business people and this porno number – that's everyone he knew. And this cat.' She looked at the photo. 'I wonder who looks after it.'

'You don't know the cat's his. It might be a picture he found. People find strange things.'

She shook her head. 'I see it some nights, it's gruesome. People wandering through the hotel sitting by themselves at the bar – the men sitting and looking, the women no-one wants to speak to. They just lurk around in the dark. One morning I was signing off and there was nobody there and the pianist was playing by himself. Did you realise what a fantastic musician he really is? He was playing Beethoven. The "Moonlight" Sonata. You know it? He played it beautifully. Properly beautiful, you know, proper piano playing. He's a real musician. I sat and listened to him. I asked how he could play to an empty room and he said even when it's full there's nobody listening.

'And this,' she said, going back to the newspaper clipping, 'this is grisly.'

'Some people like talking about it.'

'I don't mean that. Okay, the phone thing, sure, I don't understand it, but that's cool. The thing is, that person there, that woman, that's someone he talked to, and now he's dead. She knows – knew – this guy. What would she say if she knew he was dead? Would she even care?'

'That's what I want to ask.'

'Ask?'

'Yes. I called her. I'm going to ask.'

Wilhemina's jaw dropped. 'Let me get this straight in my mind,' she said. 'You're calling a dead man's whore?'

'I'm paying her to speak to me. It's a business transaction.'

She looked at the clipping, then at me. 'Why?'

'She might know something I need to find out.'

'I'm sure.' Her voice was dry. 'What does she do to get your attention?'

'I don't know. But I think you're right about him being lonely. I think she maybe was his girlfriend, in a way.'

'Who is this person you're digging up, Ellie?' she demanded. 'What are you doing with his wallet? What is all this about?'

'I don't know. That's what I'm trying to determine.'

She shook her head. She was angry now and looking for the right words to use. She was about to speak when the phone rang in the next room and she stopped. I got up and walked into the office. I sat down on the chair and put my hand on the receiver.

Wilhemina put down her cup and pulled back the covers. She pushed her feet into her trainers and picked up my raincoat from the chair. 'I'm taking this,' she said, stepping into the office and pulling the coat over her warm, unadorned skin. 'It's the least you can do.' She shook her hair and combed it with her fingers. She retrieved the pieces of her uniform scattered around the room, rolled them into a ball and stuffed it under her arm. She turned on her heel and walked to the door. The handle rattled as it turned. She stepped out and banged the door shut.

The receiver felt heavy when I lifted it.

'You have fucked up, yes?' said the voice on the other end. 'All the wrong things you have done.'

I waited a moment, just in case Wilhemina came back, but she didn't. Her footsteps faded down the hall. I heard the lift rising.

'Everything you do,' the woman on the phone said, 'it is worthless.'

'Oh yes,' I said, settling back. 'Tell me about it.'

Madame Sunde spoke thickly, as if she had been keeping pace with my waking hours, walking alongside me to crouch in the same cold room. 'Tell me your name.'

'Penrose.'

'I am the Madame. You have called me. I know because of this that you have done the bad things.'

121

There was still some juice left. I slid the container closer and poured a second glass.

'I know you,' she said, her voice purring. 'I know where you live.'

The glass tasted cold. 'My apartment?'

'That's right, your apartment. I have been following you ever so closely. I enjoy to watch you. I watch you walking down the street. I follow you up the path to your house,' she said. Except I had an apartment, not a house. That wasn't right. 'And I watch you jerk off,' she went on. 'Whack yourself off like the dirty little boy. The child. Don't you?'

The flesh of the fruit caught between my teeth. 'Yes,' I said, picking at it with a fingernail.

'My.' She allowed a reflective pause. 'My, my.' I could hear her breath hit the receiver, followed by the soft hiss of cigarette smoke being inhaled. Like the blonde in the Yamada, her white, whiplash roll. 'You are the cool one. Not even in the mood, no? Not in the mood for Madame's words.'

'No. I was in the mood last night, but not today. You should have called then.'

'You have been with someone since then. You have released yourself inside them.'

I looked back at the bed, at the wallet. 'I guess that's it.'

'You have been fucking, mm?'

'Yes. But she left.'

'Mm.' Her laugh was deep and clacking, lead knucklebones rolled in a palm. 'You fuck her and she leaves but you make this telephone call because she is not enough. She does not touch you deeply. You require some-thing more,' she declared. Her halting accent inserted spaces into sentences as if to emphasise them, the words coming broken down the line. 'Some-thing extra.'

'Maybe.'

'Maybe! Ha! It's your money.' The pop of nicotine and tar and my words considered. 'Tell me of your little girl.'

'She's a waitress.'

'She wears a little uniform?'

122

'I tore it off. It was wet – from the rain.'

'You tear her little dress, her little stockings, little shoes. You like to tear off her little clothes as if she is the girl and you are raping her. You forrce her,' she purred. 'She wants to be made to fuck. She is the slave to you. She loves your cock. And what do you do then?'

'Touch her.'

'You what? Touch her? This is nothing.' She snapped, teeth bared. 'You fuck her, don't you? You fuck the little girl. Tell me you do!'

'Yes. I do.'

'You fuck her. You fuck the torn little waitress. You fuck her between her smooth white thighs. Fuck her. You fuck the ripped and torn cloth. You enter her evil dark part, the dark passage, and you leave your message there, your white stain . . .'

I cleared my throat.

There was a long silence.

'You are enjoying this?' Her voice went little higher, standing on tip-toe to search a high shelf.

'No.'

'But you can take it. This is what you want to prove.'

'I'd like to see you,' I said. 'Meet with you.'

'You do!' She cackled. 'You need to!'

'As soon as possible.'

'Of course, of course. Let us make an appointment.'

She gave me the details and we made a time. 'You be there,' she urged, 'or I call. And you will be in worse trouble than before.'

'Sure,' I said. 'I understand. I'll be there.' And she hung up.

It was still drizzling outside. The morning sun had gone back behind the clouds. My reflection stood, bare-chested in the window, and rinsed the fruit pulp from the empty glass.

I spent an hour on the Brands folio but my heart wasn't in it. I rang one of their people at home and said the option was looking good but I wanted to wait until next week before giving final advice. The guy sounded relieved to hear from me and was full of questions about why I was putting them off. I made stuff up. I lied. I wasn't really sure about the option. I promised to call before the banks closed.

I pulled the turntable out from the bookcase and tried to get it going. When I got the top off I found some cracked wiring I didn't understand. The corners were occupied by a small spider, and the shavings from the rubber drive wheel had scattered and stuck to all the other parts inside. The degree to which the dust had accrued graded the workings as innermost. Green capacitors shone like cut jewels. It looked like something had burned out. It wasn't a repair I could make myself: I'd have to pay someone to fix it. I pulled out the phone book and rang round some places that ranged from unhelpful to overly expensive. I reassembled the turntable and left the screws in a little pile by the r.p.m. switch.

I went back to my desk. There were pens lying around. I picked them up and stood them in the empty Sapporo can and straightened my note papers. There was a small map lying open: I folded it and tucked it into a long manila envelope. I straightened the dictionary, the telephone directory, the Pacific *Who's Who of Business*, the copies of *New Scientist* with their specially marked pages (morphic resonance, a revised Hubble constant), pushing them back to the wall. Then I looked over the clippings tacked to the plasterboard and sighed and started taking them down. I stored them in another legal envelope, dating it on the flap. The pins I dropped in a clear plastic box.

I spent a while sorting other papers into the filing cabinets. Their drawers were swollen with notes: looking through them I realised I would have to tidy the other files as well. I replaced old folders with new folders, overwrote old name tags with new names and shredded those I didn't want. After that I had to check the cross-referencing system, which meant switching on the computer and re-indexing the new files. As the software booted up I was reminded to back up all electronic documents and label the new back-up disks.

I picked up the clothes lying on the floor and hung them on their question-mark hangers. I straightened my shoes. Two pairs I took out and polished. Then I went for the bottles under the sink, the lemon-scented scourers and cleaning rags, and started on the handles and fittings. When I had finished the rags were black. I threw them in the sink where the bubbles hissed in the dirty water.

The lampshades were dappled with insects and the husks of dead moths. I unscrewed the bulbs and left the shades to soak in the bathroom sink. There was fly dirt on the door frame. I pushed the filing cabinets, then my desk, then the chairs into the centre of the room. I refilled the bucket and took out some sugar soap and started washing down the walls. Absorbed in the depuration of every vertical plane, I lost track of time. When I finally stopped to look back the apartment was scrubbed and my office revised. I ran cold water on my hands and shook them dry and walked into the bedroom.

The pattern of the sheets was unchanged since she had stepped from them. Flecks of pastry lay undisturbed on the pillow. The lamp was hot to touch. I switched it off. I picked up the pillow and held it to my stomach. I lay down on it and closed my eyes. The sheets still smelled of perfume and hair and sweat, the promises of everything we had said and done.

14

The night turned out warmer than I expected. As I dressed my fingers made clumsy knots of my laces and tie, and in the mirror I looked older than I felt. I spent a few minutes trying to get my hair to part straight but couldn't, finally pushing it back wet so it would dry when I was outside and too busy to notice which way it fell. My appearance, my tone of voice, my walk – things didn't feel right. All I could rely on was the knowledge of experience which told me they were average but not bad, damaged but not beyond repair.

Out on the street there was a new building site, the hoardings wet with Mardi Gras posters like a fresh layer of skin. I used it as a short cut, jumping the rain-filled gutters of cement and clay, squeezing between the steel mesh gates.

I knew the address Sunde had given me. In the early '70s it had been the Limelight Bar, a locked door fronted by a tuxedo. If he admitted you, you walked down leopard-print stairs to be greeted by slate walls, potted palms, dark brown cork. There was a DJ booth for party bookings and a small bandstand for jazz quartets. The kitchen served smorgasbord. In 1978 it passed to new owners who stripped it, closed the kitchen, installed beer lines, painted everything black and booked live bands. Its name was reduced to Lime after skinheads tore down half the polystyrene lettering. The bouncers were hired security guards in blue and beige uniforms and there was no coat-check, only a middle-aged woman and a till. It was repeatedly raided by police. In October 1982 the small DJ booth was re-activated on Friday nights and Lime became Fez. There were younger people on both sides of the bar and cocktails available. The till was manned by a nineteen-year-old English girl with bleached hair and a mohair jersey. Bands played Wednesdays, Thursdays and

Saturdays, and, although by late 1983 bookings were falling off, the police attended regularly.

Fez lingered and died in 1984 when it was taken over by the DJs and renamed the Temple. The DJ booth was enlarged and the live stage replaced by a partitioned dance floor. Behind the bar was a mural of Niagara Falls. They put a man back on the door. The girl at coat-check decided who was admitted. She wore a white towelling dressing gown, fluffy white high-heeled slippers and a white towel wrapped round her head. Instead of a purse she used an overnight bag. Temple lasted two years until a kitchen fire emptied it in late '86. It re-opened on New Year's 1987 as Chabalaba playing all Third World dance and reggae, which lasted about six months. Chabalaba became the Basement, then Tunnel and most recently a live venue called Shaft, but I hadn't heard of it after that. Even the police didn't bother going there any more.

Now at the club address stood a panelled door, treated in expensive red lacquer. As I approached, a tiny guest light flicked on. I pressed a plastic-ivory button set in brass beneath the tiny legend 'C.C.' I leaned close to the intercom to wait for tell-tale background noise, but when it came alive there was only static and the clear tone of a woman's voice. 'Good evening, sir,' she said. 'Membership number please.'

'I'm not a member. I've come to meet Madame Sunde,' I said. 'I've an appointment for one o'clock.'

'Your name, please sir.'

'Ellerslie Penrose.'

'One moment please, sir.'

I stood and window-shopped for a long minute before the speaker crackled again.

'Mr Ellerslie Penrose,' she said. 'Welcome to the Cot Club.' The bolt slipped back and the door swung open to reveal black marble steps.

As I stepped inside and continued down below street level, a new voice sounded in my ears: 'Please enjoy your time with us. Remember to inform us directly if you have any special needs.' The door clicked shut and plunged the corridor into the half-light of fluorescents concealed behind zig-zag, Art Deco skirting. 'We care for you, and how you feel. We would like you to be happy,' the voice went on. 'We know you work hard. We know you are a good man.'

I followed the handrail. The voice belonged to Madame Sunde but it sounded young: softer, calmer, more soothing. 'We know how much you give, how much you try,' it said. 'We are so proud of you. And we are so glad you are here with us.'

At the base of the steps the lights dimmed and something brushed against my face. I pushed aside heavy curtains and found myself standing in a small, round foyer with a low ceiling: a circle of green velvet. I stood and waited for my eyes to adjust to the light. I was acutely aware of having nothing to do with my hands. There were no signs of the usual club traffic: the carpet was clean. There was a faint sound of music, a synthetic dance throb. And, if I strained, people talking.

'You look so wonderful, so handsome,' the voice went on. 'Tell us everything you want. Feel free and glad. You are safe here, and you are adored. Please step inside. Please come home and curl up with us to sleep.'

Before me the curtains parted at the hand of a girl. She was short and pale and stood slightly knock-kneed. Her feet and legs were bare, although her toenails were painted bright pink. Her short hair was centre-parted and held up in pigtails tied with one pink and one blue ribbon. Her eyes were thickly painted with the ineptitude of a child trying on its mother's make-up. If she wore lipstick it was hidden behind the baby's dummy poking from her mouth. She wore a singlet and a white diaper held with oversized safety pins.

She stepped into the circle, letting the curtains fall behind her. Up close she smelled of rosewater and talcum. With one finger she tugged at her pacifier, stretching the yellow rubber between her teeth, and then released it with a pop, grinning. She was wearing lipstick – bright pink. I looked at her. Early twenties, at the least.

'Welcome to the Cot Club,' she said softly. 'Come inside and play.'

'I'm here to meet Madame Sunde.' And I was already late. 'Have you been told about that?'

'Oh yes.' She seemed pleased. 'Mummy wants you to play with us,' she said. 'She promises not to miss the appointment.' She stepped back, taking my hand. 'My name's Angela.'

'Hello,' I began, but Angela stopped me by putting a finger to my lips.

'Mummy says you're Mr Penrose, and you're very grown up,' she cooed. 'Come and play.'

'What sort of game?' I said.

'Ring a rosy.' She grabbed my arms and began turning me round, giggling. Then she stopped and turned me the other way. When she had finished I couldn't tell what direction I was facing.

She raised her finger to touch the end of my nose, punctuating each whispered syllable: 'Come-in-side.'

She pushed me back through the curtains and I was in the dark. Something fiddled at my wrist and my watch was gone, and then I was standing inside the Cot Club.

The club proper was a wood and marble panelled chamber that preserved the general layout of the premises as I remembered them. A staggered bar and DJ box, the walls divided into conversation booths, a small dance floor laid with white and black tiles. The music was loud, enormous for such a small space, but between the baffles of curtains and table booths, there was a great deal of conversation going on. The patrons were mostly male, attired in a style appropriate to the local business district. They were well-groomed and healthy-looking, and I could imagine them at tennis and the Tepid Baths. They wore two-piece suits or business shirts with braces, discreet ties and lace-up shoes. Everyone else – the waitresses, the hostesses – was dressed as an infant girl.

Bare feet and knee socks. Mature arses were squeezed into disposable diapers and rompers. Smooth breasts lay unsupported beneath brightly decorated T-shirts – some busts had even been taped down to render the wearer flat-chested and uncomfortable. Their faces were crudely painted and, when not in a speaking role, they held dummies in their mouths. Their jewellery was gaudy plastic stuff from toy-store bargain bins: pop-together necklaces, chunky charm bracelets, rings bearing animal faces and cartoon characters. Long hair was plaited and tied in ribbons and short hair cut in clumsy, careless chunks with any loose strands restrained with clips and jackie bands.

Angela walked me to the bar. 'Come and choose something nice to drink. You can have whatever you like.' She put a light skip in her stride. 'Anything in the whole wide world.'

A barmaid called Marianne, dressed in a school uniform, took our orders. As a guest I could choose from a list of beers, spirits and cocktails; the hostesses drank from soda-pop bottles and lidded non-tip cups. A few were being fed from baby bottles, their heads resting in laps. One sucked her thumb, another leaned, eyes closed, on a businessman's shoulder. The others chatted amicably in adult voices, breaking only to suck on a dummy while the patron replied or to chew thoughtfully on a finger. They were chirpy and soft-edged, carefully mixing observant banter with clumsy postures.

I turned to Angela, who was slurping on a soda. 'I want my watch back,' I said.

She grinned and wiggled. 'No.'

'I need it.'

'No you don't.'

'I want it back.'

'Then come and get it.' She sucked on her straw. 'I hid it.'

'Where?'

She took my hand and pressed it against her stomach. 'Come and find out.'

'Angela!' said a voice, and we both turned.

Madame Sunde stood tall, a velvet smoking jacket over a long dark evening gown that trailed behind her on the floor. Her throat was shrouded in a dark silk scarf. Her plaited hair was grey. Her eyebrows were pencilled, her lips dark. She breathed through her nose, lips slightly parted, taking in my scent, examining me with clear blue eyes. She leaned on a long walking cane, examined me leisurely.

'Mummy says I have to go now,' Angela said. She picked up her Fanta bottle and turned, but the cane stopped her. She regarded the shaft and its possible consequences before reaching down the front of her nappy and producing my watch. She pressed the movement to my wrist and tightened the strap round the pale trace of my veins. Then she left the counter without looking back and lost herself between the booths. I picked open the buckle and loosened the strap by a notch. The leather felt damp and warm.

Sunde smiled with a dead front tooth. 'Angela is a naughty girl.'

I took a mouthful of gin. 'Does that happen often?'

The cane tapped the floor. 'They enjoy their work. You enjoy it too, I think. But of course you say nothing. You are the cool one. Everything hidden away. My.' The chuckle, rich and deep. 'My my. On the telephone, I imagine what you are looking like but . . .' She shrugged. 'I never am right in what I imagine.' She extended her hand, offering me liver spots and varicose veins and four heavy silver rings, the largest filling the space between the first and second joints of her thumb. 'Madame Sunde.' She smacked her lips, working up saliva. 'Did you imagine me, or am I wrong for you also?'

Silently I measured her against the cheap newsprint advertisement. It wasn't enough. Her voice had been the only real precursor. Even her breathing seemed to gleam. Something phosphorous streaked beneath its rattle.

She guided me through the crowd, feeling her way with the cane. The stick was tillered by searching motions equally methodical and fast, pointing its way between tables like a leash tethering some invisible, impatient little animal. As Sunde passed, guests greeted her with a smile and her girls checked themselves – straightened up a little or, in certain cases, slouched more. The guests were barely acknowledged. The worse-behaved girls raised a faint smile.

We stopped at a booth in the far corner of the club. She laid her cane across the table and seated herself on the plum leather. She slid across the seat to just beyond the candle flame and, safe in the brief second which manners required before I also sat, violently coughed. For a moment her expression became uncertain and she sat back, eyes glazed. She wadded the phlegm in a paper napkin which she tucked into her left cuff and worked to control her breathing, taking deep breaths, siphoning oxygen into her lungs. Her jaw tightened and she smacked her lips, working up saliva. A few seconds later she was awake again, her head snapping to one side as she looked around for service, her fingers scratching the starch in the tablecloth.

For a short while we talked about nothing. She had a lot to say about the menu and begged me to choose only after carefully laying down the best order – a German white, one of the most expensive on the list, and this after it had been made clear that I would be paying. She insisted I was hungry, when I was not, and that we order hors d'oeuvre, again recommending the most expensive item.

Marianne took our orders. I watched her walk away: Sunde was amused. 'You are aroused by the waitress?' She smiled. 'She reminds you of your own waitress girl?' When Marianne returned Sunde lifted her pleated skirt to demonstrate her piercings: a gold ring threaded through her labia. I tried to enjoy the wine and remain ambivalent, and faltered at both. She released the young woman and with the same fingers scooped out her caviar. She squeezed the juice from lemon segments and scrubbed the slippery rinds into the backs of her hands. 'Vitamins!' she cackled. 'Softens the skin.' She waved a tanned claw under my nose. 'You are not eating?'

'I'm not hungry.'

'You'd like something else? We accommodate many likes here.' She spread her hands. 'Big happy family. We accommodate many people who don't know what they want. They try this, they try that: they are never satisfied! But that's okay,' she said, stumbling on the two syllables. 'They visit me to experiment.'

'With drugs?'

'With whatever is their pleasure,' she said. 'You are very intelligent. But you are hiding. Not telling me anything.'

'Aren't I?'

She rubbed her fingertips together. 'What do you want? What are your dark thoughts?'

'I'm not sure.'

'I think you are. I think you know. I think you are afraid to say. How long can you live, being so afraid?'

I poured another glass. It amused her, watching me get up my nerve. The drink had lost its sweetness. It felt as if it would clog my sentences and slow me down. I remembered walking through the wet streets with the diary under my arm, carefully choosing my steps, wanting to break into a run without spilling the loose leaves, my head filling with questions. Talking to her was slippery and simple. Like crossing a street in the rain.

'Can I remind you of another caller? His name was Tad. His pleasure was drugs. Did he get them from you?'

She hesitated. 'You were a friend of Tad's?'

'I came by something of his.' I reached in my pocket for the wallet and laid it on the table. She stared at it.

'It's where I found your number,' I explained. 'I didn't understand its significance at first. But then I made the connection.'

'How did you come by this thing from a dead man?'

'I found it. Near his body.'

She shook her head. 'This is a terrible thing you do.'

'I saw where he was killed.' The words hung in the air, an inch above the table. 'I saw his body.'

'Why?'

'I didn't know who he was. But I somehow became part' – I winced – 'of what happened.'

She shook her head again, slowly flexing her fingers. 'How could you take this? His wallet? How could you do this?'

'I didn't know it was his.'

I leaned over and took her hands: she pulled them away, squirming. 'Why would you take such a thing?'

'He wrote something before he died, in his own blood. He wrote the first letter of my name: P.' She stopped and looked at me, her mouth half open. 'And I thought – it's crazy now, I know – I thought that initial somehow . . .'

'The letter P?'

'Yes, it's crazy, a crazy thing.'

'Nobody tells me this.'

'The police thought . . . it was the last thing he did.'

She grabbed her cane and stood. 'Get out.'

I went for the wallet: she flicked it away from me. Her face was pinched with anger but she couldn't storm away: she was cobbled by the table. She shuffled sideways, crablike, out of the booth, hissing at me as she went.

'Get out. Are you still here?' She waved me away with the flapping billfold. 'Leave.'

There was a half-second between her reaching for the table's support and realising she had missed. She looked down, confused by the gap in synaptic call-and-response. She was sweating. She looked up at me again. The walking stick wavered, uncertain. She dropped it, her grip gone; its clatter was lost in the throbbing music. This was more than anger: her consciousness was fading, distinct and quick. Her eyes rolled back. Her lips trembled with wine and unspoken words. Her shoulders slid to one side. She was angry and drunk and afraid and old. Her cane-hand clawed the air.

She passed out.

15

I caught her before she hit the ground, and almost fell with her: she was heavier than I expected. Marianne dropped her tray and rushed over and took the other arm. Sunde leaned close against me, her head on my shoulder. She muttered, her lips making a wet, popping sound. Her plait had unwound so that the loose tresses touched her cheek, an unkind contrast to her wrinkled skin.

'She needs to lie down,' I said. 'Somewhere quiet. With a window.'

'Her office,' Marianne said.

'Where?'

Marianne tipped her head at the stairs behind us. 'Top floor.'

'Christ.'

Some of the patrons were turning to watch when they were interrupted by a boom on the PA. 'Don't be afraid, boys and girls,' bellowed a sweet girl's voice. I looked up and saw Angela standing the DJ booth clutching the microphone with a bright, dirty grin. 'Mummy's drunk a bit too much,' she said. 'Everything will be all right. Won't you please stay and play?' Fresh music washed over the room. The relaxed atmosphere gradually renewed itself as Angela chatted over the mike. 'Who'd like to play with *me*?' she said. 'Who'd like to play with my *cunt*?'

'We'll have to walk her,' Marianne whispered. 'Left foot first,' she said, smiling tightly beneath her employer's weight. I stuffed the wallet in my pocket with my free hand.

It helped that Sunde remained partly conscious as we walked her. With each step her eyelids flickered and her head fell forward, nodding acknowledgement. We edged her back towards the rear of the club and slowly manoeuvred her up the two flights of stairs.

The stairs stopped at a door. There was a pause and a click before it swung open into darkness.

There was a flutter as we entered, a rustling of soft paper. Something scuttled along the floor and hid. Marianne guided me as we carried Sunde a good eight steps inside before lowering her on to a chaise. When we had laid her down Marianne crouched and began loosening her mistress's clothes. I stepped back. Sunde sniffed as her collar was loosened, then coughed and began breathing more easily.

'She's getting more air, now,' Marianne said. 'That should help. Could you turn on the light?'

'Where's the switch?'

'It's on the table.'

'You mean, it's a desk lamp.'

'Yeah.' She giggled. 'It's a desk lamp.'

'Well, if it's on a desk, it's a desk lamp,' I said, feeling around. 'If you want me to turn on the light, the switch will be on the wall.'

'O-*kay*,' she said.

'That sort of thing can make a difference.' A drawing-pin fell to the floor. Stepping carefully, I found the side-table and a wobbly lamp with a fabric shade. I wrung its grooved neck until I found the toggle of the switch. I snapped on the light: there were a phone and an answering machine on the table, glasses and a cut-crystal decanter. 'The way people describe things,' I said, 'can—'

I stopped.

The something on the floor meowed. A wide-eyed kitten, no more than half as big as any of the five or six other cats in the room. They blinked, watching us. But their animal stare was offset by the other eyes in the room: the women in the photographs. Polaroid snapshots, magazine centre spreads, airbrushed portraits, movie stills, postcards, art reproductions. From the base skirting to the plaster relief that edged the ceiling, the walls were papered with girls. Lurid smiles and coquettish poses. Bare thighs, lips the colour of plums. Backs arched like odalisques, a chain-draped ankle coyly hinting at oriental pleasures. *Déjeuner sur l'herbe*, *Le Rêve*, Bonnard, Balthus. *The Bar at the Folies Bergère*. Some were faded, many years old; others were brand new.

'This is Mummy's private room,' Marianne faltered. 'You can't stay.'

'The Madame is unwell. Very sick indeed,' I told her. She looked worried. 'But don't panic. I'm going to stay with her for a little while.'

'I don't know—'

'Marianne, if I don't stay, I'm going to have to ring an ambulance, and they'll come and take her away to hospital. She's very old, Marianne, very frail. You know what happens to old people who go into hospital. Do you think they'll let her out again?'

Marianne bit her lip.

'The best thing for her at the moment is peace and quiet. You go downstairs, look after the club. We don't want her to worry. I'll stay with her. Just to make sure she's okay.'

Marianne nodded. I led her back on to the landing. Shutting the door, I saw she was pinned up next to Veronica Lake, nude, without her infant make-up. A dull wash of music and muffled laughter crept through the floorboards. Downstairs was carrying on as normal. When I turned back to Sunde she was watching me. Her eyes had opened with the lock's sharp click.

'The police are investigating this,' I emphasised. 'They know Tad was a junkie – they'll trace him to you.'

She laughed.

'I'm not kidding. And the cop in charge is not your nice-guy type. He's quite crazy.'

'Tangiers?' she said. 'He is not mad.'

'You know Tangiers?'

She smirked. 'I obtain for my guests whatever is their pleasure.'

'*Tangiers?*' I sat with my mouth open. This was too good. 'Tangiers is a junkie?'

'Like his boyfriend Sherlock Holmes.' She tapped the crook of her elbow. 'The needle.'

'Shit.'

'You don't know this?' She shrugged as if she was telling me the plainest truth in the world. 'Here is the last place he comes to look. He will not come to me. He will not put me in jail.'

137

'He'll pin it on someone. He's that kind of guy.'

'Look out,' she purred.

I suddenly felt alone in the room.

'Would you mind?' She indicated the decanter. 'I would like something.'

I sniffed the stopper: vodka. 'Isn't this a bit strong?'

'It's my custom.'

I poured her a shot and took it over. She sipped it, sniffed, and coughed, keeping a wobbly grip on the glass. She sat up a little. 'That is better,' she announced.

'You fainted. You shouldn't drink so much.'

'My girls will look after everything. They're good girls,' she said absently, and then her gaze lost some of its focus.

I looked at the walls. The kitten came over and stood by my leg. It straddled my shoe, rubbing back and forth. I reached down and picked it up with one hand and placed it, spread legged, on the table. It blinked and flicked its tail. 'Cute cat,' I said.

'Travis.'

'His name's Travis?'

'Yes. They are all awake at this hour.' She introduced them in a faint, dreamy tone. Sushi, a black and white cat; a fat ginger tom, Apples, perched in the corner next to its mother, Basket. Two Persians, Thufur (taller) and Moonpie (louder). Boy Cat, lank and stupid-looking. Travis, the smallest, swatting the lampshade tassels.

I looked at the walls. 'And what about these?'

'My other girls. You know them?'

'I know a few.'

'You get around.'

I touched *The Turkish Bath*. 'Ingres painted this when he was a very old man.'

'I think it is the loveliest of his paintings.'

'He used the same girls over and over. They never got old.'

'Are there photographs on your wall?'

The grainy darkness, the flash catching her smile.

'Most of my things are filed. For my work. I need things to be accessible, I need to get to them in a hurry.'

'So we are alike. We both collect. We are both lying to the police. We are both dying.'

She closed her eyes.

Something in the wine and the living of these last minutes taught me silence and told me not to question, not just yet. There was something fierce in her, an angry self-preservation.

'You think you have travelled a long way, and learned a great deal. But I have to sit up and breathe: this is harder work than you can imagine. Every single moment is expensive. To the world I owe dollars, gold, cheques: sure. But in here' – she tapped her chest – 'the real debt. Heartbeats.'

The cats paced, curling round the furniture.

'I will leave behind this place, and my girls, and these thoughts.'

She opened her eyes. 'I have had many men. I remember them all. You want to know the name of one? Palmer.'

Palmer. I looked at her. Like crossing a street in the rain: now we were on the other side.

'Palmer who wrote the diaries?' I said. 'You knew him?'

She nodded abruptly: yes, yes. 'He was a beautiful boy, then. A child.'

'When did you meet him?'

She sipped the vodka. 'Look how old I am. Since fifteen, I have been doing this job.'

I listened.

'I started before the war. I was fifteen,' she repeated. She shifted, searching for the right position in the chaise. 'And I was no Madame. I was Miranda. My name – Miranda Sunde. The name of a girl.

'My hair was lighter, then,' she remembered. 'Almost blonde. I danced – more gracefully, I think, than other girls my age. The uniform of the house was a long evening gown, white silk. Very elegant. I felt very beautiful. In the lounge every night there is a performance. Someone plays the piano while we dance and undress.

'I remember one night a boy comes in. Not a man: a boy. Very young: my age. And he picks me – which is strange. Usually young men pick someone older. Whatever. I lead him to my room and undress him. I touch and kiss him but nothing happens. At first, he could not love me. No response. I lie him back on my bed and wrap his leather coat round him. Together like that, we sleep.

'In the early morning I find myself listening to the noise of the house: the radio, music, shouting. Smoke and vomit. Far off there is singing and the clatter of chairs being moved, doors opening and closing, the creak of beds. And this boy is talking, talking. He is telling me the story of everything which he remembers. His mother and father, how they argued. His mother takes a lover; his father drinks, cuts up the corpses. He feels he is responsible for their deaths.

'I laugh at him. The war is beginning, and people are dying and more will die . . . and suddenly one boy raises his hand because of three people. How can he even find their memories, stacked with all the others like firewood?

'But he makes me realise what I have become. My God. From a sweet girl to this, a whore. Paid to fuck. I am ashamed. And I say to him: I will redeem him. He will escape with me.'

I rubbed my forehead. 'How?'

She shrugged. 'I fuck the right people: U-boat men, a captain. Soldiers and airmen, they are fine in the war but no use when it is over: the only way out is the sea, yes? When the sailors run, they take us. We slip underwater, past the boats and the searchlights. We go south, across the equator, to good weather: where the gold has been hidden, where there are supplies, contacts. With the money, we move again, and we keep moving. We travel for a long time. And the years pass, and he remains beautiful to me. We talk. We lie together. We are very worldly, Palmer and I. Quite the couple. I earn money here and there. He is very good with cards. He gambles and wins. We travel with excuses and fake names. We meet a lot of people.

'I am very beautiful at this time.' She winked. 'Believe it, if you can. As a teenager I am too thin, too tall, but suddenly I am getting this wonderful shape. I even start to look a little older than him. We laugh about it. We keep moving. Do you know a language, Mr Penrose?'

'No, I only speak English.'

'Ach. I learn a new language every month! Just by listening. I pick

140

up local words and accents just with my ears! Instinct. No practising. I just go into the room and my brain collects the conversation, works it out. Two days later I speak like a native.' She grinned. 'I lost the habit a long time ago.'

'What about Palmer?'

'He's a good traveller. But travel is not the problem.' She was looking at the floor but way, way past it, looking at something buried deep. 'I am getting older, and he is not. He tells me he hates it. I am becoming someone different, someone wiser: he is still just a boy.

'He begins to avoid people. He hates clocks, watches. Never asks the time. He spends his time in hotels with the curtains drawn so he does not see the day pass by. He does not like animals, does not even water the plants. He has people send up his food. I go out, he stays home. If I am out at a restaurant he telephones me to talk, and we talk, and then I go back to my meal. I call him during the day, after coffee. I speak to him more on the telephone than in the flesh. He listens to music. In the darkness, he is very pale. All he knows is what I tell him and, later, what he sees on television.

'One day I come into the room and he is different. Not just how he looks. He is thinner more than just the body. He is . . . hollow. He is not the sweet boy any more. He is angry. Angry at everyone. And I am afraid.'

'What happened?'

'I pack my things. I leave. I come here where nobody knows me, where there are no reminders.'

She held out her empty glass. I filled it for her again. Her grip was steady now.

I asked, 'Did you hear from Palmer again?'

'I don't know where he is. I never thought about him until now. When you talk about Tad.'

'I'm sorry I took his wallet,' I said. 'It was a mistake.'

'He warned you not to. He wrote the letter P in his own blood as a warning.'

'A warning about what?'

Her tone bobbed, cool – ice in a glass. 'About Palmer,' she said. 'About Palmer's diary.' I nodded. 'I've read some of it.'

'He is saying look out for Palmer.'

'Beware of anything to do with him.'

'No. Beware of Palmer. Look out for Palmer. He is coming to get you.'

I nodded. I turned to the side-table and opened the drawer.

'What are you looking for?' she demanded.

'Something to write on.' On the inside the wooden drawer was unfinished chipboard with cheap zinc screws. I found a pen and an address book and tore out a page. 'Palmer starts his diary in 1875, right?' I wrote the date in large numerals. 'Let's say he's ten when he does that. Okay? Well,' I said, writing the sum out in full, 'that makes him a hundred and twenty-six years old today.' I held the figures up for her. 'I don't think he's going to be causing you trouble.'

'He is coming for us, for telling his secret. First Tad and Dede, for buying the diary. And then me, for selling it. He will be coming for me.'

She closed her eyes again. I watched her. After a few minutes Apples crossed the floor, jumped up on the sofa and climbed on to her stomach, testing its rise and fall with his paws. As he curled in his mistress's warmth, Sushi began sniffing round her boots.

The cats watched blankly, bumping sometimes against my shins and sniffing my hands. Travis crossed the dresser top and stood near the edge and opened his mouth with a high-pitched miaow. I found myself reaching out to pat his head, the crown between his ears still too small to be stroked by anything more than three fingers. He liked it. He spread his legs, bracing himself for more, and I obliged him. The cats' purring came from high and low in the room, a soft puttering that filled the hollow spaces between the ticking of the clock.

Travis stretched and yawned. I gave him a pat and put him on the floor. Sunde was asleep and everyone downstairs had gone home and if you had asked me why I was still in that office I could not have produced a good reason. It's like sitting up watching TV even when you know there's nothing scheduled. You make coffee and you wipe down the kitchen bench and you walk round the room and still nothing comes on. And so 2 a.m. finds you still channel-flicking, hoping chance will turn something up. Sometimes it does and sometimes it doesn't.

I closed the notepad. Putting it back in the drawer, it bumped against something: a thin, flat package. I checked that Sunde was asleep before lifting it out. It was wrapped in a yellowed page covered in writing which, as I unfolded it, was instantly recognisable.

All civilians have been issued with darkness. They apply it at sundown and the effect is overwhelming. Only the trail of sounds overhead proves you are alive.

We spend the last hour before midnight sitting in the train station. Miranda stares at everyone. When the watch says after twelve we walk out the back of the platform and cross the city towards the wharves.

There are hooded lights at the fence but the wire gates are open. Now we can see our breath. Miranda walks into the light in her long army trench coat. The soldiers do not look up. We walk past them.

There is a cave with a steel ceiling. The lamps make shadows of 12 or 15 men. Some are carrying boxes, some are talking. Their voices are loud. The sound of their boots crossing woven metal gangways. A crane lowers a net round with supplies into an open hatch. The hatch is close, maybe 30 feet away. It is at the prow. The prow is a long, metal hull. The hull is shaped like a cigar, with a deck of boards tapered at stern and bow like a private's cloth cap, rimmed with sharp cable railing. From its middle rises a beautiful oval tower marked with tall white letters: U-977.

The food on board is mouldy. Don't pull it apart, Miranda says. Piece by piece it is a nightmare. Piece by piece we all are. Look at this ship. Look at me. Details. Forget them. We are fighting the big currents now. She takes a handful of the rice and black bugs and puts it in her mouth. She chews it and she swallows. It's food. Eat it.

It is the end of the war. They can make machines so fast but they cannot build enough good men to steer them. We do not deserve this boat. We have won our passage too easily, we do everything with ease. The men drink and boast they can dive in this boat 600 feet. Straight down. But we will not be jellied by the pressure. We have no spines to crush.

On the third day Miranda puts her hand between her legs and shows me the blood. Thank God, she says. It worked.

She hugs me and says: don't cry. It would have been the worst thing to happen now. It was the right thing to do. There will be time for it later, in South America. All the time in the world. I will give you a son.

Don't cry.

Inside was a photographic negative in an old metal and glass transparency frame, the edges chipped with age. I turned it so the light reflected off the blackened silver and the image read in positive.

When I saw what it was, I held my breath. I turned round, panicked that Sunde had seen me with it, but she was still snoring. I quickly re-wrapped it and slipped it into my jacket. I unlocked the door and went down the stairs.

The club was a dim museum of safety lights and chairs stacked on tables. The sound system hummed to itself. Washed glasses drained upside down on clean tea-towels. Someone had mopped the floor. Everything stank of cigarettes and beer. A little pile of lost items – plastic jewellery, a Dunhill lighter – stood on the end of the bar. I found the fire door and cracked it open.

I walked fast. I stopped again when I was a safe distance from the club and unwrapped the negative and raised it to the dawn light.

The photograph showed a woman reclining full-length on a bed, her toes curling in their stocking tips. She was nude, not naked: her most intimate areas were concealed by the contrapposto pose. The stocking tops were black bands round her thighs, cupping her silken behind and the long unwinding track of her spine. Her face was young but knowing. She eyed the camera with conspiratorial allure, a single eye dark with make-up. Her other eye was lost behind the blonde curls that ran down her shoulders, and the black leather officer's cap. In her smile was a tiny flaw faithfully captured by the grainy emulsion: a dead front tooth.

The moment I had laid eyes on the image I had recognised her – twice. She was Miranda Sunde when she had met Palmer, when she was a young whore. And she was the blonde in the Yamada, the woman catching the taxi outside the Dilworth. Tall, in a long black coat, she was the one who had arrived late to Tad Ash's funeral.

144

I held her up to the light and stared at her for a long time, the noisy city falling silent around me. She was real and in my hands, proof that Palmer and I were sharing the same world after all.

16

I walked back home past Insurance Alley. At the entrance I stopped, shifting my weight from one foot to the other. The glass-disposal bin wasn't there any more. I took a quick stroll down its length but found no blood or brains, no trace of what Tad Ash had suffered. Someone had cleared it away. Oxygen loss, falling blood pressure, heart rate erratic, soothing chemicals flooding the system and the illusion of space and light, a welcoming hand at the end of the tunnel and then blackness, the last neural flicker like a film reel that has run its length. And then nothing, not even the muffled clatter of folding seats. Lying unaware of your own body turning cold.

The certainty that it would happen to me seemed hollow, even unlikely. Maybe I wasn't yet old enough, and it wasn't that close. Or maybe Palmer and I shared more than an initial now. Standing in the alley, for that one brief moment, I could imagine the fear but not the resource. Nothing in me could envisage moving out of the way as he had done, crouching and staying warm. I stood straight against the graffiti'd cement and the sticky posters and stared, waiting for the sun to pick out something I hadn't seen. The feeling that it might do so lasted for a moment, and then the alleyway turned silent again.

The initial sense of illumination remained, however, and I walked back to my office counting thoughts. Listening to my heartbeat.

To the world I owe dollars, gold, cheques.

Outside the Dilworth the pie-cart chef was unscrewing gas bottles and hooking up the tractor. I bought his last carton of milk. I sipped it upstairs at the window, watching as the cart was towed away to whatever home it enjoyed in the daylight hours.

I spent a long morning pacing, talking to myself. I drew it out. I kept going back to the negative, staring at it again and again. The arched back, the cascade of curls. Her grey-chipped grin.

At the beginning of his life Palmer had been an innocent, a victim of circumstance, and although his escape was strange his motive was simple: he wanted to live. He fled to another country. Finding work in a life-and-death sideshow must have complicated things, forcing him to contemplate the significance of his actions. So he ran again but this time met her, the blonde girl, and he fell in love with her. He tried to lead a human life. When he realised he couldn't, they split. That break would have left a hole in him, opened up his worst side. He'd turned ugly, and not only to her: a doctor's son, an intinerant – he would know what to cut and where to run. Sunde . . . I shook my head: she was old in her club and young in the streets, I couldn't explain how.

The significance of the diary was becoming clear. I was learning the truth of its pages, the knowledge other players in this game had held all along. I had been sold the story piece by piece, drawn in like the good client I was, hooked. It was time to tug on the line.

I got Dede at the store. He answered the phone tonelessly. 'Well,' he said. 'Good afternoon.'

'Shit, is it that late? Listen, Dede: I've been thinking. Tell me what you think.'

I turned the image in the flat sunlight. 'I found a negative, a photograph. It looks very old. Could you date something like that?'

'It's not my area of expertise.'

'It's a photograph of a woman. A woman who knew Palmer: her name's Miranda Sunde. And she told me last night that she also knew Tad. They had a business relationship. Did you know about her, Dede?' Silence. But I stayed on the line.

'This photograph is Sunde at the time when she knew Palmer. It's really something, Dede. She's beautiful. She has long blonde hair. Nude, curved. You should see it.

'But the thing about it that's really special is that she looks exactly like another woman I've seen around town, a doppelgänger for the Miranda Palmer knew. And this woman, Dede, this twin seems to know something about all this. I've seen her again and again. The night I met you at the Yamada? She was sitting in the corner, watching us. I think she came to Tad's funeral and sat in the back row. She's following me, Dede. She knows more than I do.'

'How could that be?' he said.

'Pretty weird,' I said, cheerfully. 'But I'm certain it's all connected in some way. I tell you what, Dede: I thought you could take a look at this negative for me, maybe consult some of your expert friends. We could date it and, I dunno, maybe you'd have some ideas. Do you think you could do that? Because if you could, we'd be closer to finding what we're dealing with.'

The light caught the dark patches of emulsion and brought them to life in perfect negative detail. White turned into black, black became velveteen silver. 'Maybe Palmer's not the only one who doesn't die,' I laughed. 'Maybe we've got a troupe of zombies running around or something. We should call in the papers, radio, TV, all those guys. Unsolved Mysteries. Unexplained phenomena. We'd make a—'

'Mr Penrose.' Dede cut me off abruptly. 'I have an offer to make.'

Here it comes, I thought.

'You have an excellent perception of business, Mr Penrose. I'm sure it will allow you to measure how deep you are in this matter.' His voice was spitty and terse. 'You were at the scene of the crime. You have withheld information from the police. You have met me to inspect the diaries, and Mr Veale with a view to purchasing them.'

'Silly stuff,' I said. It was all circumstantial, his word against mine.

'Most importantly, you have met with Madame Sunde and gained information about the illicit dealings of a member of the police force, a certain Detective Tangiers. If he came to know this, it would be to his advantage to view these connections as not so silly. Your position makes you an ideal buyer for the diaries. Don't you agree?'

'Wow, Dede.' I shook my head. 'And here am I thinking your brother was the salesman. It's like he never went away.'

No answer. I let him hang. The sound of the traffic moving on the streets.

'You have to give me time,' I said. 'I'm trying to work things out. There are so many angles to this thing that it will take me a while. I know you're bored, but that's the price you pay for being one step ahead.

'I've been thinking about your twin, Dede. I know you went to a lot of trouble to explain how different you and Tad were, but I'd lay money that if one twin is chemical-dependent the other is likely to be also. Am I right?'

Silence. I knew it. The phone crackled with the dead static of his guilt – and the dead static of a third party on the line, listening. I kept digging:

'I bet nobody knew,' I said. 'I bet you scored drugs for each other. I bet you posed as one and the same person. Which, in effect, you were. Both relying on the same source: Madame Sunde. And she was a safe, cautious connection: she paid off Tangiers – straight exchange, no cash. That protected her from the cops, but not the dealers. I bet that, for every dollar she made, he slipped two in a vein for free. I bet he milked her dry. I bet she's in deep, Dede.

'You were the one who decided to sell the diaries, to pay off her debt and protect your own interests. Your lifestyle, Dede. You were the salesman. Tad had nothing to do with it. He didn't purchase the diaries from auction: Sunde entrusted them to you, and you decided to sell them. But Veale was too good at talking up a sale. The wrong person found out about the diaries: the man who wrote them, the boy, Palmer. And he tried to stop the sale by killing you – and got the wrong man. He killed Tad.

'What feels worse, Dede, Tad being dead or you being alive?'

Dede coughed. 'The Madame came to me for help. We of course responded as professionals and as gentlemen. We were confident of arranging an excellent deal to meet her needs. Several private collectors expressed interest. The money would have been more than enough . . . for all our needs. The Madame was uncertain. We took the greatest care, but this, we never could have anticipated.'

'Dede, please: one collector to another, my amateur to your professional. You've convinced me but fooled yourself – selling the diaries puts you in mortal danger. I believe that now.'

'We have a professional obligation to honour the sale. The proceeds will satisfy the Madame's requirements promptly and safely.'

'How many people has Veale told, Dede? How long before Palmer works out that your're still alive?'

'It's a matter of twenty-four hours at the most. By that time we will both be gone.'

'He loves Miranda, Dede. He won't let you take her.'

'Nor would he do anything to bring harm to her. She has protected me from many things. Now she will protect me from Palmer.'

'Once, maybe, when he was a human being. He's a century old, Dede. He's beyond humanity, now. He's over it.' I clutched the receiver: the man was being so damn stubborn. I wanted to smash it into the wall. 'Dede? Listen. I'm coming over, okay? I'm going to bring back the diaries, Tad's notes – everything. I'll help out. No Tangiers, or I'll call the whole thing off. Okay?'

There was a click as he hung up.

I listened. I could still hear breathing. A deep inhalation, the suck and curl of her cigarette. 'Madame?' I said. 'Miranda? Are you still there?'

Silence.

'You've been listening all along, I know.'

'You have stolen from me,' she said.

'Madame, please.'

'My photograph.' Her voice was as shaky as his was calm. To Dede this was simply a deal between clients. He was prompting her, quietly brokering the whole thing. 'We need money and you are playing this game, playing with us.'

'I know you're grieving. I didn't mean to make things worse. But when I saw the photograph . . . Dede will tell you: we're both collectors. I didn't steal the negative. I'm going to give it back. But I had to examine it more closely, I had to work this out.'

'I woke up,' she accused, 'and instantly I know what you have done.'

'Madame? I took the negative because I had to know. The same reason I took the wallet.' She was still listening. 'You know what it's like to be trusted, don't you? A photograph, a memory – it's all the same. It's all trust.' I was working the skin of my forehead with my fingers. 'Palmer gave you the phenakistiscope, the diaries, everything. When Tad was killed you believed Palmer did it. Well, I believe it too, Miranda, because I found the negative. It proves there's a link.'

'I will call Tangiers.' She sounded weaker.

'You want to blackmail me? You want the money to escape? Fine. But Palmer knows you betrayed him. Tad's death was a warning. Palmer probably wrote the P himself to make sure you got the message. He has more than a lifetime to find you. He'll track you down. Listen to me, Miranda: you have to appease him, give him what he wants. You have to give his diaries back.'

Silence.

'You feel guilty about what you did. I don't blame you. It's the same with Dede – he's kidding himself that if he hadn't tried to sell the diary, none of this would have happened. Thinking like that serves no purpose. All you're doing is arguing over guilt. Believe me, I know.

'Miranda? Listen to me. You had nothing to do with Tad's death. You left Palmer long time ago. It's all in the past. All he knew is the girl you were. You were good to him then. That's all that matters.'

I waited. The receiver hissed.

'I'm going to come over with the diaries,' I said. 'You tell Dede that. Talk him into it, Miranda. We know you can talk. Bring him round to what you and I both know. We'll fix everything. I promise.'

The phone went dead for the last time.

I stood over it for a short while in case it rang again. When it didn't, I grabbed my jacket and keys. I walked downstairs with the diaries in my arms.

Louise shut the store every day at five, but she opened up for me. She had turned off the photocopier and we had to wait for it to warm up. I asked for one copy of the diaries and put it on my account. Twentieth of the month, she smiled. You bet, I said.

I sat and waited as she methodically worked her way through the

151

pages; pressing the document on the glass, closing the lid, pushing the button. The machine wheezed, each copy sounding like its last. The warm duplicates peeled into a tray. Lift, spread, shut, press. Louise was meticulous. When the lid did not close properly the light leaked across her face, a hot white beam scanning her concentration.

People are good, by and large, and do not deserve to suffer. Dede had threatened me because he was afraid. I had some stocks on high return I could pull and hand over to him. It was enough to get them overseas; I could oversee the business being sold. Everyone would be safe then. It was going to work out fine.

I folded a sheet of paper round the negative and put it in my pocket. It would have been sensible to copy that also if I'd had the time, but in truth it was too fragile a thing to commit to reproduction. The image of Miranda's flesh was as slender as breath on a window pane. I would stow it as a memory alongside the other things I had never touched.

I left the copy in my office. I stashed the real diaries under the passenger seat before gunning the car and taking the long way to Ash's store, a wide circle round town and across the bridge that ran over the motorway. As I approached the valley the traffic thickened. I considered hanging a left at the intersection and cutting back but stayed with it instead. It was only when I was over the crest of the hill that I realised I'd made a bad move: the traffic was backed up all the way across the bridge. On the opposite hill cars were stepped up the road bumper to bumper. Nothing was moving. Crossing the valley and climbing all the way up the other side was going to take a long time.

I slipped the car into neutral, pulled up the handbrake and spent the eight or ten minutes it took to cover the next block trying to retune the radio. A year ago when the Tomaso's dedicated stereo blew, I'd had a digital tuner installed and still hadn't got the hang of it. The sound was so precise that it picked out every pop and crackle in the broadcast. Now instead of music it seemed all you could hear was the atmosphere up close. Still, it was more expensive, which made it a better tuner – I recall the salesman's argument as being somewhere along those lines. I found some '60s easy-listening and sat back to check the queue.

Logic dictated that there must have been a major accident nearby but I couldn't see one. There was no nose-to-tail on the motorway, which was clear and flowing fast. I sighed and stretched out in the seat.

From way up ahead came the sound of a siren. I wound down the window and listened. It turned a corner at the top of the hill and faded. I wound the window up again. The Tomaso's engine was heating up. I bounced both palms against the steering wheel and fiddled with the radio's graphic equaliser, shifting different parts of the music in and out of focus.

I didn't have to see inside the other cars to know that the other drivers were getting edgy. All the way up the hill, brake lights blinked in sympathy with tapping feet. When the traffic did move, engines roared and cars lurched forward, only to stop suddenly before the tyres had made even a full turn. The Tomaso edged towards the base of the hill. The cars in front of me had reached the incline and were riding the clutch all the way. The station was playing a song called 'Sundown'. I surprised myself by knowing all the words.

The noise of another siren came down the hill behind me. I adjusted the rear-view mirror and saw a fire car with flashing lights. It couldn't go any further down the lane and couldn't reverse through the backed-up traffic. The driver was swearing his head off and shouting and looking around for someone to blame.

The middle of the road was marked by a low cement barrier, and the fire car began making ugly, inexpert lunges at it. The wall was just high enough to scrape the front of the vehicle and just low enough to convince the driver that he could make it if only he could get enough of a run-up. Each time the car fell back into its lane, the lights shook and the engine roared and the brakes squealed. People were yelling and sounding their horns, afraid of being rammed each time he rolled back. Finally desperation pushed him over. The drive shaft scraped the cement and then the car bounced into the opposite lane, screeched and sounded its siren again.

It got about ten feet before a Mercedes coming the opposite way

153

sounded its horn, swerved and clipped him on the passenger door. Everything stood still and then came a soft crumpling noise and the hiss of a thousand pieces of shatter-glass spraying across the road. The Mercedes spun round and smacked twice into the steel rail, the only thing that saved it from going off the bridge on to the motorway below. The fire car didn't stop. It kept on moving up the right-hand lane, swaying as the driver struggled to regain control. I watched him travel up round the bend in the hill listening to the sound of brakes and horns and his siren fading until it was only as loud as the others.

Some drivers got out of their cars and crossed to help the Mercedes driver. The traffic queue moved again as if the spectacle of the accident had released some of its tension.

The temperature gauge was tipping into the red. I pulled up the handbrake and flicked through the radio channels. A station was playing 'By the time I get to Phoenix'. I knew the words to that, too, but I couldn't remember them at that moment. Something else was getting in the way. I wound down the window and sniffed. The air outside was hazy and smelled strongly of smoke. The cold air was trapping it in the valley. I was far enough ahead in the traffic to see up the hill, so I leaned out the window as far as I could. I looked at the tops of the buildings and the growing plume of smoke and tried to place the fire.

I drew my head back inside the car. I wound up the window, switched off the radio, turned off the engine. I got out, shut the door and started to run. I ignored the steepness, the exhaust fumes, the noise of horns back where I'd abandoned the Tomaso. I pushed past the traffic cops who tried to stop me at the logjam at the top of the intersection. All I cared about was getting to Ash Antiques and all I could think was that, no matter when I did get there, it would be too late.

By the time I reached Ash Antiques I was wet with sweat and the flames were reaching so high they were climbing the sidewalk awning like fast and brilliant vines, feeding on everything inside the building. Four fire tenders were in attendance, the dented fire car parked behind them. A fireman signalled me not to get close, but

I was already close. Miranda and Dede were inside and that was wrong, that was unacceptable, because they would die and they couldn't die because I had come to fix everything, to even things out. I pushed through the cool spray of the hoses and into the noise of drums and exploding glass and wooden beams falling black and torchlit into the earth.

I don't know how far I got in. I don't know, to be honest, if I even made it past the door. But I got far enough for everything before my eyes to disappear into a wall of white and yellow and for my mouth to open and draw in nothing – no heat, no smell, no air. I tried to shout Dede's name but no sound came. The poisonous smoke had stolen my voice. I reached out and touched only heat. My hands felt wet. I couldn't tell which way was up. It was like being caught in the surf and rolled upside down. I couldn't even tell if I was standing. I couldn't breathe. And then I was being punched and grabbed and I was light. The firemen's gloves were black giant hands on my shoulders. They lifted me up like a toy and dragged me outside.

I woke up in the ambulance with an oxygen mask on my face. My gums were blistered and I couldn't raise any spit. I could smell oil and plastic and wood turning to charcoal. I tried to sit up. The ambulance man pushed me back down.

'You've burned your hands,' he said. 'You ran into the fire.'

'Dede,' I croaked.

'You nearly died, yes. Lost your sense of direction. Lot of people do that when they see a fire, you'd be surprised.' He cleaved the air with his hand. 'Just run right in to it.' He wagged a finger. 'Now, don't try to speak. I've bandaged your hands. See?'

I tipped my head to watch the fire. It was huge. The Ash Antiques sign was falling. I tried to take a closer look but the ambulance man pressed me back down in the narrow bed again. He dabbed ointment on my face. He imparted toneless advice about caring for the burns and gave me a fresh set of bandages which he stuffed into my raincoat pockets so I wouldn't forget, carrying on talking about bathing the flesh and how it wouldn't be a problem and everything would fade away, cure itself, as long as I looked after it. 'You're very lucky,' he said. 'A fire like this, some people lose everything.'

155

'I have a photograph,' I said, meaning of the people in the fire, but I couldn't explain. I pointed helplessly to my pocket. Obligingly he reached into it and took out the negative. 'Look,' I said, making him hold it up. 'Her.'

Puzzled, he held it up to the light and then understanding swept across his face. 'She's something, all right. Pretty nice.' He put the negative back in my bandaged hands. 'You're a lucky guy.'

I shook my head, trying to explain, but he wasn't listening.

He patted me patiently on the shoulder. 'You lie there and get some rest, okay?'

I lay in the back of the ambulance. The negative was tiny in my white-wrapped paws. Miranda in her blonde curls, her soft silver skin.

The flames flared each time they found a new thing on which to feed. A television, blue glass bottles. An ear trumpet, an adding machine. The windows exploded with soft, gentle pops and the heat rose. New, old, precious, worthless: it all burned. The firemen talked about a downwind which would help quell it, and said that the surrounding buildings were stone, which would not catch, and they turned the hoses on full, right at the centre of the blaze. But for a long time none of this made any difference to the fire, which continued to rage in spite of everything.

17

The ambulance men gave me a lift to the east side of town and dropped me in a street close to the bay, the lamp-lit streets saw-toothed with weather-board villas. The tide had gone out and left gaps of scalloped mudflats between the pohutakuwa trees. The ambulance pulled round in a circle and waited. I waved thanks with my white hands and picked a letter box, following the clinker-brick wall to the house at the driveway's end. The ambulance rattled back up the street.

The house was quiet and dark. White railings led to the front door. The security lights flicked on as I came close. I knocked but there was no reply. I could hear a radio playing inside. I stepped away and waited for the lights to go off again.

I walked round the garden to the front of the section. The lawn was trimmed crooked, decorated with scrawny rose bushes and a set of white cast-iron garden furniture. The sea-side wall was a long ranch-slider window leading on to a wooden deck. As I stepped up on to it another automatic light came on. I used the heaviest key on my key ring to flick the slider's lock. I stepped inside the lounge and shut the glass door behind me and the light went off again, leaving me in darkness.

'Wilhemina?' I called. I couldn't remember her flatmate's name. I wiped my face with the back of my bandages. I called again. The radio played on, alone.

A faded *lei* was pinned to the door of her room. Inside was dusty and smelled of flowers. A bowl on the dresser overflowed with pot pourri. A tarot card – the castle – was wedged into the corner of the mirror. The bed was a mattress on the floor with a puffy white quilt. The music came from the clock radio. I spent a minute finding which tiny switch turned off the music and put it back, its red light burning the dirty carpet.

Her work number was pinned in the kitchen, on the cork board above the phone. I dialled with the tip of my middle finger and waited while the desk clerk put me on hold; my gaze drifted across shopping lists and messages that someone rang and Polaroid photographs of sunbathing and theme-costume parties, crepe paper and champagne flutes, gym memberships, the spare back-door key rubber-banded to an ankh.

'Yes?' Wilhemina answered. And I found myself again. She waited. None of the words in my head seemed the right way to begin.

'Ellerslie?' she said. 'Ellie? Is that you?' I could hear her breathing. Even the sound of her voice recalled her perfume. My stomach felt tight. The desk clerk was talking quickly to someone else. There was a bumping noise on the line as she turned her back to him. It was wrong to ring her during work hours. She was probably in the middle of an order. It was probably the last thing I should have done.

'Ellie?' she said.

'Something's happened—' I stopped.

'What? Tell me.'

I folded my arm across my stomach. I leaned on the fridge and pressed my face hard against the metal. Dark patterns were welling up behind each eyelid in time with my pulse.

'There's been a fire,' I blurted.

'God.' She sucked in her breath. 'Are you all right? Your place?'

'It wasn't my place, it was somewhere else. I knew the people. An old guy. The man with the wallet – his brother. It's . . .' I opened my eyes and psychedelic colours danced across the room. 'It's complicated. You haven't been following and I can't—' I had to stop. I had said all that I could.

She waited before speaking again. 'Where are you?'

'I'm . . . at your house.'

'What? Did Liza let you in? Who's there?'

'Just me.' I laughed. 'I mean, I hope it's just me. Hope I'm not interrupting.' Suddenly I went cold. 'Am I?'

158

She sighed. 'No. It's just a surprise, that's all.'

'I'm sorry. I can go. I'll lock up and go.'

'No. Don't. I don't mind you being there. I'll be finished at twelve. What are you doing now?'

'Just talking to you.'

'Get yourself something to eat, Ellie.' She had that needy quality in her voice, like a schoolgirl extracting a promise. 'Will you have a shower and get into bed? I'll be home soon.'

I took a breath. 'Okay.'

'I have to go now,' she said. 'I'll see you after twelve.'

'I'll leave the door open.'

'It's all right,' she reminded me. 'I've got a key.'

I said okay, and put down the phone. In the fridge were a half-bottle of white wine, three Stellas and a camembert. The chilled air felt good, but I couldn't eat.

I went back to her bedroom and undressed. I folded my clothes and put them on the floor, next to the tangle of gym gear. I went into the bathroom, turned on the shower and stepped into it, not feeling my burns until the water soaked through the bandages and touched the skin and the fire was on me again, spiking every nerve. I yelled and tore the wrappings with my teeth, falling out of the stream. I slammed into the medicine cabinet and it jumped open, spilling Panadol and cotton wool and nail polish remover and suntan oil like a hygienic *piñata*. I kicked the sink, scattering lipsticks and foundations. Everything was wet and loud. My hands were steaming, burning. I howled and demanded that it stop. I knelt and made claws of my fingers. The water drummed against the plastic curtain.

I remember being afraid of the cold of the school swimming pool and walking towards the deep end one step at a time, feeling the ice rise. Getting in that way, as the other kids jumped and splashed, made me feel like a coward. Because it was only water, after all. But it was the only way I could do it, getting to know the cold's every increment, pressing the meniscus until it broke and became liquid, magnifying the goose bumps on my chest like chicken flesh. Chicken.

Slowly, movement came back, found its tools and got to work. It took for ever to get myself up off the floor. The cotton wool was in a zip-locked plastic bag. I picked it out with my fingertips and dabbed my wounds.

I stepped back into the shower an inch at a time with my hands above my head, lowering them for a moment until the pain got too much, then raising them, then lowering them again, coaxing my nerves to adjust. I opened my mouth and coughed. A blister burst. Each time I turned, the water seemed to find some new bruise or cut. I picked up the soap using the backs of my fingers and dumbly pressed it into my body with my fists. The soft cake moulded itself to the ridge of my knuckles. Almond. Juniper. I soaped myself until I was lost in the steam. Everything hurt but it was good that the water stayed hot. My skin turned a grateful pink.

When I heard her key scrape in the door I felt tired for the first time in hours. 'Ellie?' she called. She dropped something in the kitchen and smiled, carefully, as she came into the bedroom. Her hair was pushed back in a black shock. She was still wearing my raincoat. 'Ellie? I thought you'd be asleep.'

I couldn't speak.

'Ellie. Jesus, your hands.' She took me by the wrists. 'God, Ellie. They're burned raw.'

'From the fire.'

'My God, they must hurt. What did you do?'

'I don't know. The wrong thing. Not enough.'

I pointed to the fresh bandages in my jacket. She dressed my palms again and wiped my face using her free hand, and then her cheek and then her tongue. She put her arms round my neck and kissed me. 'It's okay,' she said.

'I can't stop it.'

'Everything's okay.' She held my face. 'Get into bed,' she said. 'Wait for me.' She peeled off the raincoat and went back to the kitchen. 'I brought some doggy bags,' she called, the microwave beeping. 'We have risotto, sirloin and tempura.' I heard her rattling through the drawer for a corkscrew. She came back waving two glasses and a bottle. 'Burgundy. Nice, yeah?' She untucked her blouse and shook it and combed her fingers through her hair. She poured me a glass. I took it. It was hard clearing my throat.

She went back to the kitchen and returned with a single plate, three servings freshly prepared by the hotel chef, their sauces tidily pooled, the food shapely and steaming. She balanced the plate on the clock radio and climbed under the quilt. She took a mouthful of wine and kissed me so that it ran into my mouth. I let it roll between my cheeks. Her breath had nourished it. I tasted its fruit and her lipstick, slowly. She drank some herself, then passed a second mouthful to me. I looked at the plate. 'Thank you,' I said.

'I like to bring things home.' She smiled. 'If I don't have something waiting.'

'It all looks perfect.'

'You never know.' She fed me a forkful of rice. 'The things I've seen in kitchens. People tasting, letting the sauce run from their mouths into the pot. People testing pans with spit. Dropped meals. Sweaty hands. You think of the steam in a kitchen – it's like a sauna.' She pressed a napkin to my lips. 'Old meat cooked up to hide the blotches. Rotten vegetables. Dirty tables. Rat turds.' She watched me chew. 'Does that taste good?'

'Yes. Have some.'

'I ate at work. Steak?' She cut me two small cubes. 'I saw a chef cook a cardboard beer mat. Dipped it in three types of batter and sauce, fried it in oil, served it with salad and chips. The guy loved it. Sent his compliments.' She wiped my mouth again. 'How do you feel?'

'Last night,' I said, 'that woman I was speaking to on the phone when you left – she was one of the people in the fire. She was caught and she's dead.'

Wilhemina sat back. 'Ellie, that's awful.'

'I didn't really know her, but I did meet her. I asked her some questions.' I blinked. 'Her name was Sunde. She had a club in town, she was the hostess. I was returning that wallet. She knew the man who owned it. She lives – lived – up there with all her cats.'

Wilhemina's face creased. 'Pussy cats? Who'll look after them now?'

'I don't know. She has employees. Someone will see to it. Won't they?' Angela's routine was a picture in my mind, all thumb-sucking and baby curls. 'I can't think about the cats,' I said. 'I can't think about every detail. I'm trying to piece this thing together.'

'What thing?'

'Sunde knew a man, a long time ago. She sold his diary to a dealer called Ash, who was later found dead. She and Ash's brother felt the diary had something to do with it. They were both scared. I couldn't see a connection. But when they were killed in the fire I realised.' I looked up. 'I should have worked it out.'

'Worked what out?'

'The man who wrote the diary. I think he killed them.'

'Have you told anyone?'

'The police already know but . . .' I shrugged. 'He started writing the diary a long time ago. He's very old now. In fact he's so old there's no way he could be alive.'

'So why do you think he is?'

'It's the only link. He has to be.' I hesitated. 'And there's one thing, one crazy thing, I can't figure: Miranda Sunde, who was very old, and is now very dead: she's alive too. But she's young. I've seen her. I know it doesn't add up but it does. It's like the numbers are running backwards.'

She stroked my face as if she was trying to smooth away the worried expression on her own. 'It doesn't make any sense, Ellie, what you're telling me.'

'Nothing makes sense. You take chaos theory, right, and try to put it with quantum theory and that doesn't—'

She put her finger to my lips. 'You're really tired.' And then she leaned forward and put her arms round me. 'I can't remember the last time you had a holiday. You should rest. You're headed for something bad.' She squeezed my shoulders and the warmth spilled down my back. 'Can you feel that? Feel how tense you are. Your skin's dry. You're dehydrated. Are you sleeping? Do you have dreams?'

'Not usually. Not lately.'

'That's a sign you're not sleeping properly. You're exhausted and

162

messed up.' She reached behind her clock radio and bought out a bottle of pills. 'Take one of these.'

'What is it?' I asked, putting it in my mouth.

'Sleeping pill. You have to sleep, Ellie.' She passed me a mouthful of wine and I swallowed the pill and held on to her, kissing for a long time. She put the glass to my lips and filled my mouth and kissed me again.

'What about dessert?' I asked.

Her stare drifted out of focus. 'Dessert comes last,' she said, attempting a smile, but her expression quivered. I knocked over the plate, pulling her down. Our stares were very close, black and dark.

I remember, it was the last hour of the evening. Tony and I were spending it comparing notes on the best episodes of *Hawaii Five-O*; with 'Mind of a Killer', in which McGarrett analyses a murderer's oil painting before a rapt courtroom ('the ladder: his desire to escape'), coming in as the mutual favourite. In between making the drinks and wiping down the bar Tony had begun re-enacting key *Five-O* scenes. He would take a step back to give himself a little room and crouch, hands spinning an imaginary steering wheel, or shoot over the top of the till with a loaded finger, sputtering sound effects and dialogue. Tony's version was almost better than the TV but I watched with glazed eyes.

My attention was drawn by one of the waitresses. As Tony talked I had become aware of her moving in the background, clearing tables, showing people to their seats, passing phone messages. I began to anticipate the moments when she would settle a table's bill, standing at the counter to fill out a yellow slip or double-check with Tony (unnecessarily, I thought) for a room number. She stood closest when she was clearing glasses, bringing them up two at a time and not always empty.

Tony moved on to *The Streets of San Francisco* and various Quinn Martin productions and I turned to watch her each time she drew closer. It was not her proximity which was exciting but her ease. She was unhurried. Her presence was tranquillising, her manoeuvres unpronounced – at least, to anyone other than the well-scrutinised patrons paying for half-drunk cocktails and endless credit checks. That last hour. It was early morning, around one-thirty. The pianist was warming to 'My Funny Valentine'. Tony was holding forth on *Starsky and Hutch* (Hutch challenges Starsky to a 48-hour game of hide and seek: Starsky contracts botulism). And then I finally felt her touch. She leaned across to choose a swizzle stick and her shoulder pressed gently against mine.

She didn't look up at me even then. She maintained her professional detachment. She made herself preoccupied with the swizzle sticks, picking through them with long fingers, leaving her shoulder against mine, maybe moving her hip a little closer. I could read her name tag.

Wilhemina Litner.

I remember the press of her shoulder and her averted eyes, her gaze hidden by her long fringe. The reflection of the bar lights, the pop and trill of cell phone coming to life beneath the counter top and calling for its owner.

I remember her stepping into the shadow of the potted palms at the entrance to the bar, heels together, hands clasped, one eye on the foyer and the other on me. That made it easy for us both: I could follow her or stay where I was, and no-one watching would be any the wiser. What would happen next was simply another part of a complex and efficient evening shift: reservations and numbered tables, tonight's specials, separate cheques and now, waiting with an almost imperceptible raised eyebrow: staying at the hotel, sir?

We met on the top floor, the luxury suite at the end of the hall. She opened it and welcomed me into the world of very wealthy, very absent guests: scattered clothes, a blinking lap-top, open suitcases. You see, she explained, unlocking the mini-bar and screwing the caps off two dolls'-house gins, you might get caught messing up an unoccupied room, but if it's already occupied, who's to know?

I remember the gin's taste. I remember hanging the DO NOT DISTURB sign on the outside of the door. NE PAS DÉRANGER, which always seemed to say: Don't Go Crazy. But we did, many times afterwards. Again and again. The sudden strength of her grip and the answer of my own, my fists crushing her shoulders, my knee

164

shoving itself between her thighs, her sharp little fingernails, gin and lipstick, the rip as her jacket gave.

All of that from the first eight or nine seconds, I recall. A memory per moment. I carry them with me like a bunch of keys, whistling and swinging them round a finger. Each one I know by touch, and the door it opens.

When we started out, the sex was good. I could make her arch and shudder and come, and afterwards she would lie next to me in the rain and I would fall asleep talking about things that didn't have to make sense. Complexity had not crept into it. But spring had found me lying awake again. Making love didn't patch anything up, didn't make me care any more or her any less. It was an angry bloom, independent of the season. A prosperity born of people tired of working with each other. I knew it wouldn't continue like this. She knew it too, but neither of us was about to say it aloud. It was turning bad, which was all the more reason for hanging on to the things that weren't.

She pushed the plate away from the bed. I drew her closer using the backs of my hands, the same way I had picked up the soap.

The light beyond her shoulder outlined a profile that softened over time. Our shapes gradually altered and grew to fit, her long elbows against my shoulders, forearms crossed behind my head. I nuzzled her neck and her eyes. She stretched her legs thin and crooked, pushing her toes between mine. The weight of her body did not rest at any single point, but passed from knee to chest to one of her shoulders until I pressed her down and she guided me inside with lowering eyelids and the occasional whispered things. We made love slowly, each not taking their eyes from the other. I watched as her pupils widened and her eyes brimmed with tears and tasted her mouth at that moment because I could no longer bear to intrude. All I wanted at that moment was for her to be happy, and I could make her happy.

Afterwards the few sounds of the bay drifted in through the window. Stray, trailing vehicles, the whisper of rain shifting dirt on the window pane, digital clock red. She was warm, breathing softly through her nose. My fingers grasped the sheets, raised them carefully across us. She had a dream about something, giggling. I dreamed about Miranda and was glad Wilhemina was there. Each time I came to, she kissed me and stroked my forehead and told me to rest, to relax, to go back to sleep. And each time I did, her body weightless.

When I woke up in the morning she was gone.

18

I got up and dressed. I went into the kitchen and cleared aside the stack of paper and foil and rang my answering machine. There was a string of messages from Brands. They had no fucking patience and I wanted to yell at them. I punched the number and said just to go with the option now, fuck even waiting. The guy said OK and hung up; he didn't even say thanks.

I knew my car wouldn't still be parked on the bridge. I called a taxi. I got my raincoat out of her room and went and waited at the end of the drive.

At North City Towing, Charles was still snoring behind the counter. A skinny kid with half a beard took my name in silence and checked the clipboard and went to get the car, kicking the chicken-wire gate shut behind him. The dog huffed, wanting to make a break either towards or away from me, it couldn't decide. I shook my shoe at it, called it over. It ran back behind the chicken wire and flattened itself into a snarl.

'Hey, Charles!' the skinny kid warned from my driver's window. 'Charles, boy!' He squeezed my car towards me, steering it through an alleyway of confiscated grilles and bumpers to reach the front of the garage. Charles wagged his stumpy tail.

The Tomaso chugged to a stop and the skinny kid stepped out, swinging the pocket knife he'd used to start it. I pointed to the car and the vicious little v-shaped dent that now ran the length of all four side panels on the driver's side.

'Who did that?' I said.

'Fuck.' He put his hands in his pockets. 'Must've been when you left it.'

'I left it on the side of the road. It was safe there.'

'Yeah? Shit.' He shook his head. 'Some people are pretty stupid, aye.'

'It must have got scraped when it was towed.'

'Nah mate they're real careful aye.'

I leaned inside. The seats smelled of beer. The diaries were still under the seat but back a long way, shoved by a dirty heel. I tapped the odometer.

'Seventy-seven six-oh-one,' I said. 'When I left it last night it was about five-seventy-five. It wasn't at six-oh-one, it wasn't that high.' There were muddy marks around the foot pedals. 'Someone's been driving it.' I got out of the car. 'You take it for a spin?'

'No way, mate. Brought it straight here.'

'Fuck,' I said. I walked round it and found a broken tail light and another shorter scratch. 'It's been thrashed.'

'Nah, mate. That wouldn't have happened. Must've been like that, aye.'

I stood and looked at him. He looked at the car. Then he turned and looked at the dog bowing to lick itself behind the gate. 'Hey, Charles,' he called to it, ignoring me. 'Hey, boy.'

My shoulders began to feel heavy. Standing straight was an effort. I couldn't even get angry: there was nothing I could do. He stood making kissing noises at Charles and pretending I wasn't there, waiting for me to work it out and leave. Charles snorted and smacked his pink lips.

I counted out $145. He wrote me a receipt. I said thank you and got in the car and left.

Ash Antiques was a pure black skeleton, its fallen sign singed in a dumb pun. I parked opposite and crossed the road. Things felt quiet in the light of morning, quiet and tired. It was the even, uncaring light that picks out every detail and makes it precise, turns bright colours sour and blues the skin beneath your nails. The whole street had been laid out for inspection, bleached and unpeopled. Even the smells were still fresh in the damp air. Dew and charcoal, rubber and paint. Car exhaust thinned by the asphalt. The building had been surrounded with fresh yellow tape saying DANGEROUS and DO NOT PASS. Last night's tape had been melted by the heat. It lay twisted in a black gut-string on the sidewalk. A skinny guy in a Camel T-shirt and his hands in his pockets walked past, muttering into his goatee: See that? Man, look at that fucking mess.

I stepped across the melted tape, my shoes crunching. The pressure from the hoses had shunted charcoal into the gutter and streaked debris across the path. All that was left of the store was a network of black, spiky compartments like the squares in a Mondrian.

A big man was moving between them. He was wearing a stiff black coat that flared like samourai armour and swinging a crowbar that he whacked dully against anything still standing. As I watched he took a big stride across a gap where the floorboards had burned through, and landed gracefully on one boot, testing the wood remaining before releasing his full weight. When he was sure it was safe he braced himself and swung the crowbar above his head. It hooked in the ceiling rafters with a crunch. I remembered that ceiling the first time I stepped into the store. Bicycles hung from it, and a rocking horse. He gave the black plaster a tug and it came away, leaving a burned stud and a chunk of sky.

I stood with my hands in my pockets as he worked his way around the building. When he noticed me looking he gave a little wave with his crowbar. It looked a dainty weight in his hands, like a folding umbrella.

'Store's closed, mate,' he grinned.

I nodded. 'Did you see the fire?'

He whacked the crowbar against the charcoal of a vertical stud, but it held. 'Looks pretty bad.'

'Anyone hurt?'

'I heard there was.'

'That's no good,' I said.

He looked around and then swung the crowbar up again. It dug in and black flecks fell around him. He jerked the bar right with both hands until something made a cracking sound, but it held. Satisfied, he wrenched it free again, testing the floorboards as he moved along.

His eyes were small and dark and sharp, pinching each detail like a thumbnail testing soft wood. He paused closer to me than he needed to. The cracks in the skin of his hands were laced with black and there were teeth missing from the side of his jaw. The fold of his coat collar was worn to a polish. With one hand he lifted the jimmy and scraped its chisel-tip along one of the front window panes, flicking out the last shiny pegs of glass.

'It looks like a real mess,' I said.

'Ah, it's not so bad. It's standing.'

'Will they rebuild?'

He squinted, looking around. 'It's all part of the same building, along here.' He used the crowbar like a pointer. 'They all lean up against one another. The guys'll come in tomorrow and brace it.' He let the bar drop. 'Most of it's sound.'

'You're making it safe?'

'Wax Demolition.' He looked at me. 'Contract's sealed.'

I shook my head. 'I'm not a contractor. I used to buy things here. I can't really believe it's gone. I was just wondering how it happened.'

'Someone burning candles.' He shrugged. 'All this junk just went up.'

'It wasn't all junk,' I said.

'The alarm wasn't working.'

I thought about that. 'Why? Was it too old?'

He pulled down the side of his mouth. 'Vandalised. Kids poured honey inside it.'

'Honey?'

He grinned again, nodding. 'Best thing for wrecking an alarm. It glues everything together. You trip it and the current sets fire to the sugar, melts the wires.' He stepped into the next space of existing floor and began swinging at a rack of coat hooks screwed to the wall. 'Beauty of it is, the cops stop you carrying a jar of honey, what's wrong with that?' He was enjoying the joke. 'They probably got it from the twenty-four-hour down the road.'

'You know a lot about it.'

He shrugged. 'It's my job.' He swung the crowbar extra hard and it hit the beam with an emphatic crump. 'Street kids fuck up everything around here. Cars, windows. They fix the alarms so they can break in at night and sleep. They have to sleep somewhere. We see it all the time. They get somewhere and the cops don't do anything. What can they do? Nothing. Kids have to sleep somewhere. They're sniffing and they're stupid – something always catches.' He nodded at the skyline. 'I reckon we end up here once a month, doing the same thing every time: cleaning up the back-room, the basement, somewhere out back where nobody looks. Cleaning out blankets and spray cans, bottles of booze. Where they've been sleeping.'

'Did you find that here?' I asked.

'No. But that's where the fire started, out the back.' He turned and started kicking at a foundation pile.

'In the alley?'

'Yeah.' He stopped. 'Shit.'

'What is it?'

'Animal.' He poked the jimmy through the floor.

'What is it? Is it dead?'

'Cat. Stray, probably.' He was unmoving in his big, black coat. 'Well gone,' he said, and then he moved the boards back into place with his boot. 'Never mind.'

My hands itched. Wilhemina had wrapped the bandages so evenly that the patterns of their binding made symmetrical valleys and peaks, gathering behind the joint of each thumb and fanning outwards again from clean fixed squares of adhesive tape. I flexed them and winced. Metacarpus, the ambulance man had said – I remembered the term now, in the way you recall things long after they've ceased to matter. Something about the metacarpus, and the difficulty of repairing damage to it. My thumbnail wept clear, sour moisture. I wiped it away. Beneath the gauze the pink skin was preparing to grow anew, to reiterate the same cracks and lines and folds in the flesh.

'How long will this take you?' I asked.

'Till it's finished,' he said, swinging the jimmy up again. Light fell through the roof, and tiny ashes swirled.

I waved to him from the car. He tipped his head back a little but his shoulders kept working. Swing and bite, step and swing, knocking at the space where Dede Ash had first showed me the phenakisti-scope, first read me the diary. Where the cardboard woman had first dropped her handkerchief and picked it up, dropped it and picked it up. I pulled out from the kerb.

There was a slow wind blowing. The billboards and storefronts interrupted the sun. Driving along the crest of the hill I could see the hospital, a brick stack of curtains and white charts and visiting hours, monitored heartbeats. Beyond it the city stuck up all ochre and slate, its windows dead, the harbour beaten flat. There was traffic waiting at the intersection. Then somewhere in a box a switch tripped and the lights changed.

I parked outside the Cot Club and got out, smoothing my bandages. I pressed the intercom button and listened. Eventually the speaker coughed.

'We're closed,' Angela said.

'It's me. Ellerslie Penrose.'

'What do you want?'

'I was thinking about the—'

'Go away.'

'I need to talk to you.'

She thought about it before she swore and told me to go away again, her small voice shaking with someone else's authority.

I kept my finger on the button until the speaker came alive with a different voice.

'It's all right, Mr Penrose, we can hear you.' It was Marianne.

'I'd like to come down,' I said.

'I'm afraid we're not open.'

'I know. But you're all down there, and it would help if I could come down. For a few minutes.'

'Now is a bad time. Everyone's very upset.'

'I need to check something. One thing.'

'Everyone's very upset,' she said again, in case I hadn't under-stood. 'The lawyer's told us not to let anyone in.'

'I'll clear things with the lawyer.'

'He made us promise.'

172

'I'll look after you.'

'Why should I believe that?' she said.

'Why should I lie? Marianne, I've got work to do. Let me in. Please.'

After a silence, the bolt slid back.

The stairwell lights were turned off. I felt my way down the steps.

Marianne was standing inside the velvet curtains, her feet shoved into in plastic sandals. Behind the curtains there was music playing, muted easy-listening, and quiet chatter.

'We've been keeping the door closed,' she said. 'We thought there was going to be trouble.' She rubbed her arms. 'More trouble, I mean.'

'We care for you, and how you feel,' came a voice, and we both jumped. 'We would like you to be happy.'

'Jesus,' said Marianne, pushing the curtain aside and reaching behind it. 'It keeps switching on.'

'Turn that fucking thing off!' someone yelled. Marianne swore quietly. Angela appeared at the door pointing a tumbler of scotch. 'Turn it off, Marianne!' she shouted.

'We know you work hard,' the recording cooed. 'We know you are a good man.'

'Turn it off *now!*' Angela stumbled forward, sobbing.

Marianne lifted one of the curtains. Behind it was a tape machine: she ejected the cassette and held it up. 'It's off,' she said. 'See?' Angela stood disbelieving, clutching the glass of scotch with both hands, wiping her nose on one wrist.

'Here,' I said, snatching the cassette out of Marianne's hand. I held it up for Angela. 'See?' I poked my little finger between its plastic teeth and wrenched out the tape to a full arm's span, the spools squealing. I kept ripping at it until the tape lay in a grubby scribble. I dropped the casing and smashed it under my foot. 'See now?' Angela nodded. 'She's gone now and it's over. I saw the fire, Angela. I burned my hands in the fire.' I showed her the bandages. 'See my hands? See what I did?'

Angela squirmed, her face knotting in the darkness, her head burrowing into Marianne's neck. Marianne stood stiffly, waiting for me to finish. I let my hands fall. 'I don't mean to shout.'

'Everyone's very upset,' Marianne said. She kissed Angela on the forehead, turning her towards the room. 'Go sit down, honey,' she told her, squeezing her hand. Angela disappeared behind the lacquered door, her shoulders flinching.

When she had gone I told Marianne I wanted to look upstairs. She began to say no but I held up my bandages again. 'I was burned too,' I said. 'All I want to do is sit. To remember her. Out of respect.'

'If Angela sees, she'll go crazy. And, I mean, the others, I . . .' The pulse jumped in her throat.

'I won't say a thing. And then I'll leave.'

She sighed and nodded. I whispered thanks.

She opened the curtains. Sunde's girls were sitting round tables piled on to the dance floor. They had taken all the bar spirits out of their pourers and opened up a crate of house wine, and the floor was snowy with chips and white popcorn trodden into the carpet. Music rolled easy from the dance-floor speakers, the turntables unmoving. Someone's My First Sony, green and yellow like a freshly hatched bug, was jacked into the PA. The cassette was running a little slow but it didn't matter. Tammy Wynette slurred her vowels and someone lit another cigarette, crouching low over a candle burning in a squat red jar. Smoke rolled between nostril and mouth, a glass chinked, black-painted lashes fluttered and winked, listless in the windowless mauve.

Angela was between friends now, clutching her glass and watching me blearily. I didn't look at her. Marianne made a show of pointing me to the kitchen and, out of the others' sight, the back stairs.

I stepped into Sunde's study. The room was cheap in the light of a bare bulb. The pictures were dirty and the chaise was worn. The floor was thick with dust. I replaced the lampshade and the room grew rich again.

I sat down on the chaise and took out a pen. I unfolded a piece of paper and drew the floorplan, calculating the footprint of each piece of furniture in a clockwise direction from the door: the side-table, the first bookcase, the chaise, the second bookcase. And then I marked seven Xs: one in the far corner, two on the lower bookcase shelf, one on the side-table, one in the near corner, two by the chaise. I dated the drawing and made a note of the time, and then I began shading each piece of furniture proportionate to the weight of its base. The bookcases were heaviest, followed by the chaise, then the side-table. I wrote in the initial of the name of each piece of furniture, pressing hard to overwrite the cross-hatching. I indicated the direction of the floorboards. The breaks in the floorboards. The panels in the door. The combination lock. I returned to the Xs and made them bolder, then circled each one with a small, dark halo.

Marianne pushed the door open quietly so she wouldn't be heard downstairs.

'Mr Penrose—'

'What have you done? Where have they gone?'

'I'm sorry?'

'Where are they?' I said.

'I don't . . .'

I stood up and showed her the map. 'Basket, Apples, Sushi, Thufur, Moonpie, Boy Cat, Travis.'

'Oh. The cats!' She smiled, resting the drink on the side table. 'She took them.'

'Who?'

'The woman.'

I wanted to grip her soft neck and shake it. 'Which woman?'

'The woman, um.' Marianne shrugged. 'About my age. Tall. Blonde.'

'Fuck.'

'Pardon me? I don't—'

'Tell me quickly. Everything. What did she do? What did she say?'

'It was some time after the police called, after we closed the club.'

'What time?'

'I don't know. We don't have any clocks here.' She smiled helplessly.

'What time did you *think* it was?'

'I don't know!'

'Fuck it. Fuck! What did she *say?*'

'She said she'd come to look after the cats. She said she was a relative. We didn't know. She had two big cages for them. We didn't know. How would we know?' Marianne bit her lip. 'Jesus. What's happened?' She put her hand to her mouth.

'Would you recognise her again?'

'I was drunk.' She was forcing the words through her hand, her voice louder. 'It's *dark* in here. I don't *know*. Why's it so *important?*'

'Please tell me. Did she leave anything?'

A single big tear rolled down Marianne's cheek. 'I can't remember.'

'There must be something. Anything! Tell me, Marianne.'

'What's *wrong?*' she howled. 'What's happened?'

Outside there was the sound of running and then Angela burst through the door. 'What are you doing?' she shrieked. 'Get out! Get the fuck out!'

She slapped my face. She bellowed and beat at my chest. I could hear the other girls coming up the stairs. Marianne just stood to one side with her hands on her face. Then Angela caught me in the throat and I jerked back, coughing. I tried to hold her at a distance but she kicked me in the balls and it felt as if my legs had dropped away. I bunched over and clapped my hands on her shoulders and shoved her back as hard as I could. She skidded across the floor and hit the wall, bringing down a sheaf of portraits. Thumb tacks and bodies clattered across the boards. She was still screaming and picking herself up when the others burst in. They were reaching out and yelling. Someone new stopped me and someone else helped them and I was pushed down this time, smacked in the ribs and shins. I covered my face and rolled over on the ground and pushed to the door. I ripped the lamp out of the wall and whirled the cord round in the darkness. The lead connected like a whip. I felt for the door, ripping down photographs as I went. The women were bellowing, punching. I slipped on shed Polaroids and fold-out sections. I found the door and the stairs and the curtains, and finally the street.

19

The cafés were dark with afternoon crowds and the noise from the tables sounded painfully loud. Patches of my scalp burned where hair had been torn away. My hands were shaking.

In the car I cleaned myself up as best as I could, my elbow bumping the door as I turned the mirror to look at myself. Dusted off the bandages, combed back my hair with my fingertips. My cheek was bleeding and one wing of my coat lapel had been torn. My elbow caught the door again and hurt and I swore loudly. A dreadlocked guy watched me from the sidewalk. I couldn't sit there by myself in the car, but there wasn't anywhere else I had to be. Couldn't sit, couldn't go. Dreadlock's friends were looking now. I swore, sitting there and being wondered about by strangers.

I started the engine and floored the accelerator and raced the engine once, twice, three times. I dropped the clutch and pulled out fast, the engine railing. Fresh air flowed through the passenger compartment. The steering felt tight. I leaned back and hugged the kerb.

I turned tight into my street and hit the brakes. The lanes were blocked by police cars. A line of old men were marching backwards down the street. They turned as one and pointed their instruments in my direction, then stopped marching and played the next few bars of a tune. The band leader called a stop and they broke formation, shuffling back to their original position. One of the cops walked up to my car.

'Parade's starting here,' he said. 'You'll have to drive round the other way.'

'I live just down the road,' I said. 'I need to get home.'

He bent down to the window with one hand on the door and shook his head. 'Can't drive through here.'

'Could you make an exception? I'm going to that building.' I pointed behind him to the Dilworth but he didn't look round.

'You're bleeding,' he said. He looked at my hands. 'What happened there?'

'I slipped. Can I get through?'

'We can't let anyone through.' He leaned further into the window to look at my torn clothes, my trousers grey with dust. 'This your car?'

'Yes, it's my car.'

'Got your licence there?'

'Yeah.' I found it and handed it to him. He stood straight to read it, leaving me staring past his belt.

The brass band were lined up again. Some of them tested shaky notes. Marching girls stood around in clusters, chatting. A two-storey-high green frog was lolling on a truck flat, gradually sitting erect as it filled with gas. More parade floats were lined up all the way to the bus stop. Groups of people were moving past, jostling each other for space on the sidewalk. They were carrying chilly bins and six packs and folding picnic chairs. Some of them were singing along with ghetto blasters and everyone else was talking. There were hundreds of them, all passing within yards of my office. Their good cheer spelled out their easy lives. They had stepped out of decorated interiors and tiled bathrooms, arranging their expensive clothes to look casual. They had parked up on the hill by the university and along the waterfront and just rolled on in. And afterwards they would go home to trimmed paths and mineral water and music softened by a stereo remote.

I leaned out the window and looked up at the cop. He was reading my licence details into his hand radio. 'So can I get through?' I asked him.

He looked down. 'Had anything to drink today?'

'Nothing.'

His face didn't move. 'You should get that seen to.'

I wiped my cheek and it stung. When I took my hand away the bandages were spotted with an uneven line of blood. 'Well, if I could get home—'

His radio interrupted, rasping nonsense. He turned away, holding it close to his cheek. Then he turned back. 'That's fine,' he said, handing back my licence. 'If you just drive round the other way, sir, you'll be right.'

'But I need to go this way,' I said. 'To park.'

'Can't go through there. Parade's starting there.' He waved me on. 'Please drive round the other way.'

I made a U-turn and drove back up the hill. The sky was beginning, just perceptibly, to darken at the horizon's edge. Soon it would be pink, and then it would be dark. You could sense night clouds in the blue sky, thunder lurking just out of sight. Wind whipped the banners hanging from the streetlights, shook up the litter along the pavement. It was the time of afternoon when you felt anything could happen, even though the city had only one thing on its mind. The Mardi Gras crowds were gathering in pubs and on office-block balconies. Some people had put on their masks and amateur costumes. Television crews were setting up at strategic vantage points. Electrical leads snaked out from the cameras.

The trees around the Regent entrance were draped with ribbons and luminous strips. I stopped at the front doors.

The doorboy tugged at his earring as I got out. 'Can I help you, sir?' he asked.

'Just the car, thanks.' I put the diary under my arm, carefully holding the door open for him, but he didn't move.

'Are you all right, sir?'

'Oh.' I gave him a conspiratorial grin. 'Thanks, I'm fine. Bit of a fuss. Had to help someone.' I waved at the car. 'Keys are in there.'

'We're full tonight,' he said, evenly. 'Mardi Gras.'

'I can imagine. Town's pretty crowded.' As I said it the car door fell shut. He didn't make a move. 'The car,' I reminded him. He was staring at the dent along the driver's side.

'A lot of people brought their cars this evening,' he said.

'Right. Of course.' I pushed a $10 bill into his hand. 'Thank you.' My wallet snagged in the coat's torn lining.

The doorboy gave me a shallow smile and patted my bandaged

fingers shut on the note. 'I'm sorry, sir, but we're full. Why don't you go and enjoy the parade from somewhere else?'

'I've come here for a drink like I always do. What's the problem?' Holding the bill made my voice shake. 'Is there a problem?'

'No problem at all sir, except that we're very busy tonight.' He opened the car door and waited by it. 'Please.' His little laugh implied the self-evident. 'You're hardly in an acceptable condition to enter the premises. Management, sir.'

I looked around, chewing my lip. Police cars had pulled up across the street. Traffic officers and workmen wearing bright orange vests were laying out road cones and detour signs.

'Well, I can't turn back now,' I said, nodding at the cordon. 'The parade's coming along here later.'

'You still have time to get out, sir. Thank you.' He reached forward and touched my shoulder.

I held up the $10 between the straightened fingers of my right hand. 'You should take this anyway,' I said, and pushed it into the base of his jacket collar, just beneath the Adam's apple. He broke away and coughed. I was back up the steps and opening the hotel doors when he grabbed my arm again, more firmly this time.

'Sir,' he croaked, red-faced. A security man was taking big strides towards us across the lobby. He was about to take my other shoulder when Tony called out.

'Mr Penrose!' he smiled, quickly stepping between us. 'How's it going?'

'Kind of shaky,' I said.

'Hey, they're giving you a hand here,' he said, patting the big doorman on the back. 'You know Adrian, Mr Penrose?' He waved back the security man and turned. 'You can find a space for Mr Penrose's car, can't you, Mike?'

'Mike,' I said, grinning at the doorboy. 'See you here all the time but I never knew your name.'

'Hi.' Mike bit his lip. 'The car park's pretty full, Tony.'

'You can find him a space, can'tcha?' Tony took the bill from my hand and gave it back to Mike, talking steadily as he did so,

181

drawing me inside the hotel. 'Come inside, Mr Penrose. Thanks, Adrian. Thanks, Mike.'

'Thanks, boys,' I called. Mike was holding the crumpled bill before him like a dead carnation. Adrian watched us, round-shouldered.

'Just doing their job, Mr Penrose,' Tony said, leading me quickly across the carpet. 'You do look kind of a mess.'

'I had some trouble.'

He steered me away from the bar. We stopped behind the potted palms, out of sight of the rest of the floor. 'What happened to your hands?' he asked me.

'I fell. Grazed myself.'

'Is that what happened to your face?'

'No, that was somewhere else.'

'Your coat's torn. Your pants.' He looked me up and down. 'Are you okay, Mr Penrose?'

I couldn't tell him. I didn't know if I was okay.

'Tell you what,' Tony said. 'I'll get you a room, you can clean up – I can get your clothes cleaned.'

'You don't need to.'

'I think I should. I think you need a rest.'

My eyes narrowed. 'Have you been talking to any waitresses lately?' But he maintained the same bland expression. He led me round the back of the lobby. A mahogany magazine rack stood next to the elevator, newspapers draped over brass rods like laundry. Tony folded an evening edition into thirds and tucked it under my arm. He called the service elevator. When it arrived he held the doors open and took a room key from his pocket.

'Four-fourteen,' he said, pressing the big wooden pendant into my hand. 'I'll send someone up.'

After a moment, I said, 'Is she up there?'

'She's not on yet, Mr Penrose. But when she comes in, I'll tell her you're here. I promise.' He patted me in the small of the back, gently motioning me inside. He put his key in the elevator console, pressed for the fourth: 'Four-fourteen, okay?'

I leaned back against the rail. I nodded.

He removed the key, flipping it on its chain, and tucked it into his waistcoat. The doors shut and the elevator rose. I felt my stomach shift. That's how it would feel, living longer than you should: an Otis that never stopped, a snippet of zero-G. I turned the room key in my hand, ran my fingers over the smoothly routered numerals. The elevator lights hummed.

I unfolded the newspaper. On the front page was a photograph of Tangiers, a head shot, his face surrounded by network microphones. He was smiling at someone off-camera. Next to his photo was a peppery identikit portrait of a hollow-cheeked man with a goatee and tattoos. I looked at both pictures for a long time, and at the headline running across the top of the page. ALLEY MURDER ARREST, it said.

An Auckland man has been charged with the murder of Thaddeus Ash (71).

Simon Eedie (29), a Mt Wellington labourer, was arrested in a dawn raid on his home by armed police.

Police spokesman Dean Tangiers announced the arrest as the murder investigation was entering its sixth day.

Local residents have been shocked by the brutality of the killing, in which the murdered man's body was discovered naked in a glass-disposal bin in the central city.

Detective Tangiers said the man's death was 'drug-related'.

Police are not seeking anyone else in connection with the case.

And so on.

The fourth-floor corridor was empty. I walked alone along the carpet track. Room 414 stood at the high east corner of the building, past a bend in the corridor with a faceted bay window. In the room the patterns of light shimmered behind white floor-length drapes. I dropped the newspaper on the chair. I lifted the lid of the writing desk and put the diary pages inside. I took off my coat and put it on one of the monogrammed plastic hangers in the bedroom closet. I went through the mini-bar and got out two gin miniatures and a bottle of tonic. I made myself a drink and sat at the desk.

Something was missing, something wasn't right. The front page of the paper stared up at me. I didn't believe anything Tangiers was connected with, not one word. The man they had arrested was not the killer. He couldn't be. It was too perfect, too easy: Tangiers mopping up witnesses, settling scores. But I was too tired to work it out.

The porter arrived while I was making the second drink. He gave me a menu and a wine list and asked for all my clothes. I undressed in the bathroom and put on a monogrammed towelling robe. Carrying out my clothes in a dirty pile, spotted with blood and dust, I felt ashamed handing them to him. My coat and pants hung over his arm like rags. I hesitated to give him my shoes until he pointed out that the heels were down. I made him promise everything would be returned within two hours. He even balled up my socks and took them. He asked for my order but I couldn't decide. You choose, I said, passing back the menu. He closed the door as he waved away any offer of a tip. On the house, he said. Everything's taken care of.

The last rays of daylight disappeared, blurring the shag pile. When it got dark, I turned on the lamp.

The champagne arrived while I was in the shower. I came out and found it jutting from its bucket at the end of the trolley. Caviar next to a rack of trimmed toast. Beneath the lid, lamb cutlets, potatoes and asparagus with Béarnaise sauce. A small bowl of strawberries in kirsch. Coffee, cheese. I sat, wet in my robe, and ate, gripping the champagne bottle by the neck.

Afterwards I lay back on the bed. My clothes would be returned soon and then I would have to decide what to do. I knew I couldn't sit here all night. Time was passing, and it was important to keep track of it.

20

I woke up with my head pressing a damp pit into the pillow. Someone had taken away the trolley and laid the bedsheets across me. I hoped I knew who my attendant was. I thought I knew. They had left the curtains open and the room was filling with faraway sounds.

I sat up. My mouth was dry and my eyes itched. The night sky was ink-blue, peppered with satellites. It was a long time since sunset. Far off, I could hear fireworks.

I was still wearing the bathrobe. I straightened it as I crossed the floor and opened a bottle of soda water. I found my clothes hanging inside a plastic dry-cleaning bag behind the door. My shoes gleamed like new in the light of the lamp. The shine was spit-perfect and they had been resoled in leather. New laces were coiled inside the heels. I put them back on the floor and watched my reflection, sipping soda in the dark. It tasted better than the champagne. I wanted to do the whole thing over again: have another shower, eat a second meal, fall asleep and wake up, each tranquillity overlapping the next, another notch on the index of quietude.

There was a secondary drumming on the glass. I walked over to the window. A helicopter was circling the building, poking the street with a jittery blue spotlight. The street was swollen to bursting with the parade. A station wagon mounted with loudspeakers drove slowly down the middle of the lanes, blaring FM rock and telling people where to walk.

TV cameras lined the balconies opposite. A presenter was peering down at the crowds, wedged between the technicians and a furry microphone boom. Confetti fell from the roof tops, each piece curling in a perfect echo of the one preceding it, descending in a flurry of mathematics. Behind them floated a cloud of a hundred thousand foil squares the size of fingernails, flickering golden in the lights.

The bands were playing and the float characters were going through their routines, but from the window it looked as if things had jammed solid. Marching girls stepped on the spot. Crowds jostled round the floats and displays. The big green frog bobbed in the middle of the street, revellers tugging at its moornings. A mermaid was stretched out on a polystyrene rock, dragged along by dancing sailors.

I pressed my face against the window to try and see what was happening. Two hundred yards up the road a hanging banner had fallen across the intersection, blocking the parade and preventing it from moving further. A large area had been cordoned off to permit its removal but the flashing lights and the cherry pickers had done nothing to dampen the fun. I sipped the soda, my forehead cooled by the glass. The helicopter cast its fluttering spotlight. Anyone struck by the alien ray lifted their shirts and sprayed beer, silver balloons whipping back and forth.

It was the lack of movement within the beam which first caught my eye. She was in shadow at first, until the beam fell on her upturned face. She took a step backwards and then one to the right, training her vision on the hotel building. I was unable to swallow. As she stood, the helicopter moved again and her blonde hair fell into darkness. The soda bottle felt cold in my hands. And then again she moved into the light, exposing herself to the same silvered tremor that had fixed her in the photograph.

Miranda Sunde.

Staring up at me.

I counted the flights of stairs between us. She would run as soon as she saw me move from the window. She would be lost in the time it took me to find my shirt. I couldn't do anything except stand and look down on her, while she looked up at me.

She looked exactly as she had when I'd seen her before: a tall girl draped in a long leather coat. I was held simultaneously by the sight of her and by the impossibility of what I was seeing: an old woman killed in a fire now alive and standing a half-century younger across

186

the street, awake and untouched by the years between then and now, animated by the same black magic as her beloved. Passers-by didn't speak to her, refusing to confirm the anomaly. The crowd's current formed a polite cordon as it swirled round her on either side.

Just as her photograph showed as I'd seen her standing on the road outside the Dilworth; at Dede's funeral, the ramen bar. But now I couldn't look at her the same way. Each encounter had brought her closer until now, standing distant, she was much more than something from a dream. She checked over her shoulder, moved out of somebody's way. Her gestures betrayed her uncertainty. She wasn't enjoying being out in the open. And she kept looking up at my window, I was certain.

I waved. Slowly she lifted her hand and opened it towards me, then let it fall. Then she looked up at the helicopter's light as it moved away and left her in the darkness. But I had her now. I knew where she would be standing.

I banged the bottle down on the dresser and pulled off the robe. I pulled the dry-cleaning bag off the hook on the door and tore open the plastic and swore. My shirt wasn't there. It hadn't been returned. Then I saw the box on the dresser: it was inside, the collar and sleeves pinned, every button fastened. I frantically ripped the box and then the shirt apart. I shook out my pants and tore off the dry-cleaning tag and pushed my feet into the legs. I put on my socks and crouched to re-lace my shoes. My hands were shaking. It would have been easier if I'd turned on the main light to do it but I didn't have time to get up and turn it on and crouch down again because I was almost finished now, almost. I grabbed my coat and ran out the door.

The light in the corridor hurt my eyes. I squinted and ran its empty length, my feet pounding on the carpet. I took the stairs three at a time, and sprinted across the lobby, my freshly soled shoes dangerously unsure on the marble. Adrian saw me coming and opened the door and I rocketed down the steps so fast I lost track of them and fell forward. But this time I didn't go down. I put out my hands and met nothing but softness, the impervious clamour of thousands of people.

Making my way towards the street I could see only a small part of the crowd at a time. I fought the impulse to walk fast, to get to whatever was ahead. Anyone who wasn't drunk had succumbed to the crawling pace, and so the rabble moved at two distinct speeds: one sober and irritable, the other pissed and happy. I hid myself in the happy part, slipping on my raincoat as I walked. A policeman stood behind us at the far corner of the intersection. A fire-eater belched flame. The wind dropped and the two-storey frog rolled towards me with a giant smile. I took my hands out of my pockets.

I could see her, not far from where she had been standing. Her back was to me and she was moving away, towards the dancers and stilt-walkers. I broke into a run, breaking through the flames and kerosene smoke. An assistant in harem pants yelled at me as I ducked between the forest of stilts, running sideways through the aisle of amazed, flame-lit faces. The stilt-walkers loomed above my head, twirling their canes and plastic skulls. Someone shouted at me. The dancers shook tambourines and bells to blaring music, changing direction on every beat and blocking my path. She was getting away. I shoved the middle dancer aside, yelled sorry, kept running.

Now Sunde was moving through the military band, running straight down the aisle of trumpets and bugles, ducking the swinging trombones. I could see the flash where her coat-tails split, a diamond of arse and seamed stockings. Passing the bass drum, I caught the player's stick with my arm. A trombonist turned to check the off-note and I pushed him back and he howled, clutching his teeth. I couldn't wait. Ahead were the farm floats and Sunde was already running into them, pushing past the hay bales and ambling horses.

I changed to the sidewalk, jumping the puddles of urine and shit shovelled into the gutter. I could track Sunde as her coat appeared in flashes between the cowboy shirts. She was making her way towards the mermaid rock. At the moment she glanced back, head away from me, looking behind her, I was exactly parallel with her, an arm's length away. I could have reached out and touched her hair, her shoulder. Pinned her to the ground. She was mine, at last. I could bring her close and smell her breath. And I shouted. Miranda, I said. Miranda. Happy, most of all. Happy and triumphant because she was mine.

She ducked her name as if it was a bullet. And then she lifted the blue and green cellophane and disappeared beneath the waves. I was left yelling at the top of my lungs. 'Where'd she go?' I yelled over the music. 'Which side did she come out?' The Mélusine shrugged her glittering shoulders, her tail banging the papier mâché.

I pushed my way round it. On the other side of the float I straightened up and ran through the sailors and pirates, all the time straining to see Miranda. I circled the siren's rock again, looking back at the hayseeds, the stilt-walkers tall against the harbour lights. A St John Ambulance man was running towards the brass band. I spun round looking for Sunde. I couldn't have lost her now.

I found her behind a wall of sparklers and champagne party corks, her blonde hair bobbing as she spoke with someone I couldn't see. I crossed the space between us in two long steps and grabbed her shoulder and turned her round fast and she swore at me and grabbed my collar because it wasn't her, it was a boy in a wig and a ton of eyeliner. I dropped him and took a step back into a wall of silver and black leather, of fancy-dress Nazis and motorcycle cops, hooded slaves on chains. Someone shoved me and I slipped and cannoned back into the crowd, caught someone else, burst through to the other side and the narrow gap between buildings and people. Nobody seemed to mind. Nobody understood.

I started running along the sidewalk, stopping to stand on seats and rock gardens wherever they jutted from the buildings, trying to see her. The music swelled and changed, scraped my ears. I rubbed my face. I put my hands on my hips, stepped backwards. My feet felt heavy. I pressed my back against the wall. My neck hurt. There was blood all over my neck.

Running, her hair loose, within the stretch of my arm.

So close. And then gone, without turning to look.

I opened my mouth and shouted at the top of my lungs over and over again for Miranda to come back, and the moment I stopped her name disappeared beneath the screams and air horns and the machine-gun thudding of the helicopter above.

I took a step forward and then took a step back and turned to the left and then looked right and then looked ahead and then leaned back again. I walked up to the intersection and leaned on the traffic lights and tried to catch my breath.

The cherry pickers had finally hooked the fallen banner and were raising it into position. There was a cheer from the crowd and the parade, collecting itself like some giant boneless animal, began to move. An unsuspecting car crossed into the intersection before coming to a dead stop among the throng. The driver leaned out of the window and tried to wave people away until a woman in a swandri shirt and clown make-up leaned on the bonnet and, smiling, laced his windscreen with beer. The crowd cheered again. The parade was moving, filing past the lights. Cowbells and pirates, cardboard cutlasses flashing, the marching girls, the bands, children running between them trailing silver balloons and the dancing girls performing their endless striptease: dropping their clothes, picking them up, dropping their clothes, picking them up.

Carefully, I pulled open the left side of my collar and pushed a finger down inside it. A dry-cleaner's pin had stuck deep into my neck. Wincing, I slipped it out of the cloth and the flesh. It was covered in blood. I dropped it and turned away.

I crossed between the floats, anxious to avoid anyone I'd pushed past before, and started back towards the hotel. But the crowd's current had become especially strong. I stopped at a duty-free store and sheltered inside the door, pressing against a window of bonsai gardens hung with scent bottles and watches. My eyes followed the branches and their twisted training wires. I tried to concentrate on their tiny rocks, the cool of their perfect shade.

She hadn't wanted to speak to me. I didn't know why she had shown herself, only that she had. I knew if I saw her again she would still get away. She knew everything I was going to do.

Inside the store a TV wall was broadcasting the news pictures of Mardi Gras. Huge faces filled the multiple screens. The parade moved forward endlessly and uninterrupted. The confetti cannon kept on firing until it was raining paper the length of the city. The picture was busy with white details, a perfect signal thick with static.

21

I didn't go back to the Regent that night, not directly. I didn't sleep. I stood and watched the parade break up while numbness set into my limbs, everything turning over in my head. The crowds departed, trampling confetti. The cars pulled out, the streets emptied.

Around 5 a.m. I went back to the hotel to clear out my room. The dry-cleaning bag was still lying shredded on the floor. I drank a glass of water and opened the drawer.

The diaries were gone.

The only thing left was the cover sheet. Everything else – the phenakistiscope discs, the notes, the negative – had been taken. I looked in the other drawers, under the bed, between the sheets, under the mattress, the cupboard. I pulled open the drawers in the bathroom and peered under the sink. I looked behind the curtains and the window sills.

Gone.

In the foyer the night porter promised me nobody had cleaned the room. When he asked what had been stolen, I couldn't explain. Important papers. Personal material. He picked up the phone and started to dial for the police. No no, I said. It's a police matter, he said. I clapped my hand on the cradle. I said it was nothing of material value, and I was sure it would turn up. He hung up, dissatisfied.

I made him check the register but Wilhemina had gone home. He came away from the monitor shaking his head, his face firming with the expression I'd been trying to avoid all these months. You're the one, his eyes declared; it's you. He gave me a bill for the room and signed it off. I said thanks and dropped the key in the slot and waited red-faced out front until the doorboy walked back saying he couldn't find my car anywhere, sir, and was I sure that I'd left it?

The doorboy trailed behind while I spent an hour going round the car park. My Tomaso had been stolen.

He asked me for the registration but I couldn't remember. He asked what time I had parked it, if there were spare keys or an alarm, its exact model and make. I couldn't recall anything. I sat down in the middle of the asphalt.

A breeze caught the cover sheet and blew it under a van. Embarrassed at my suffering another loss, the doorboy got down on his hands and knees and hooked it with the tip of his shoe, tearing it on the ground as he dragged it out. He brought the page over and held it out to me. I sat and looked at him. The sun was coming up. His thin white wrists stuck out from his uniform sleeves and the breeze flapped the paper like a small, limp flag. He asked me if he should call a taxi. I said I'd walk.

Along the streets everything was shut tight, deeply hung over after the big party. The window of a camera store flickered with shapes and colours no camera could ever capture. My silhouette led with its right foot, complementing my own tendency to favour the left. Its shoulders were rounded and streamers were sticking to its shoes. A lonely outline, as outlines go. The cover sheet fluttered between my fingers.

A pair of yellow cleaning trucks were moving up the street, buffing the kerbs on either side. They rolled past playing music in a thin, sweet harmony, both drivers' radios tuned to the same station.

There was still so much trash to collect. From the square onwards, where the parade had ended, the road was ditzy with the pastel Morse of confetti. Leaflets and paper cups, streamers, gold-painted things. I stopped at the lights and scraped my soles clean.

In the square I watched a man in a patched coat guiding the pigeons in to land – a difficult job in the absence of runway lights. He had to run in order to cover the sixty or so square metres of paved ground, both arms extended like little wings of his own. His signals were the same as the ones policemen use to guide traffic: hard right-angle arm with raised hand for stop, deft index finger to nominate a group of two or more, a quickly beckoning right for advance. The birds swirled round his bare feet in a grey blanket, and when he clapped to arrest misdirection or crowding the flapping of wings was like the sound of wet firecrackers, a soft, arrhythmic popping that raised my fingers to my face, my skin, the pulse beneath.

A cat had caught one of the birds and killed it. I found the body in the dirt not far from where its fellows were gathering, the head ripped off, one wing broken. The grey feathers were slick and delicate with oil, tinged with the metallic pink of corned beef and sea shells. I picked it up by its bloody tail and dropped it in a litter bin. It must have been a sight for anyone watching at that hour: one man barefoot, barking instructions at the flurry; another nonchalantly disposing of a dead pigeon – but it worried me that the Bird Man might stumble on the corpse and consider it his mistake, some sort of crash landing. I didn't want him to blame himself.

I walked down into the car park underneath the square to wash my hands. The rest room smelled clean. Janitors had swabbed it with disinfectant and scattered deodorant crystals in the urinals like giant sweets. I put the cover sheet down in front of the stainless steel mirror. The bandages on my hands were soiled and torn. I had left them on for too long. I unwound the gauze, twirling it on to the floor like a dirty lasso. Exposed, my burned palms were pink, and sticky with ointment. I plugged the basin and splashed myself with warm water, examined my vandal-proof reflection.

My face was pale and there were tracks under my eyes, deep blue hollows. The front of my shirt was brown with dried blood. Gingerly, I undid the top button and peeled back the collar. The hole where the pin had entered my neck was looped with a rich, black corona. I dabbed the bruise with my wet fingertips but felt no better. The blood had soaked into my raincoat as well. The scratches on my cheek, twelve hours older, were closer to healing. My hair was greasy and dark in the strip-light that ran above the mirror. My forehead was lined. I massaged it but the creases returned. My eyes were wide with the same electricity, the irises bleached, the whites tinged with yellow.

I combed my hair back with my wet fingernails and dried my hands gently on the roller towel and straightened my coat. It was the best I could do. I walked out and up on to the street.

The buzzer sounded *Cross*. I turned up the hill, taking the long way round to the Apollo.

I pass the Queen Street shops so often people must be getting to know me. Like the old woman who stomps around with folded arms or the Chinese cripple who reprises his ballad in long, unsteady notes. It's a long time since he's played. Winter tests his arthritis, his swollen fingers clawed around the one-string bow.

Balloons were trapped beneath the awnings. The newspaper hoardings were full of headlines that didn't seem to matter. I walked, counted, compared them with sleepy eyes.

The Apollo was busy with the dawn crowd, a gang of kids with their feet on the furniture. Lee was banging the filter handle clean. I stood at the counter. His friends were shedding their outer layers of coats and sweaters and swandri jackets. Lightened, the girls flashed half-tops and pierced navels, and the boys were divided into two sizes, muscled and skinny. None of them looked fat. They talked under the music, compared tattoos, ornately re-laced their second-hand boots. A couple were kissing, tenderly negotiating silver spacer bars.

I ordered a long black, an orange juice and two soft-boiled eggs. And then I blurted, 'You should go surfing, Lee, take some time off.' He pushed back his glasses and blinked. It's just, I told him, that you deserve it, all this work you do, you should look after yourself, if you don't give yourself a break nobody else will. He held up his thumb and forefinger so I could call the soldiers' desired width. I made them about an inch. I said I'd been working late. He said that was cool. I thanked him and chose a table outside. My face felt hot.

The table wobbled when I sat down. I folded the cover sheet into a wedge and pushed it underneath the short leg. Then I sat back in the light of morning and the freshening breeze. The shadow of a seabird moved gently towards me across the street, floating slowly in an updraught. I stretched out the cramp in my legs.

A guy in a pinstripe suit was walking past talking on his cell phone. He finished the call short of the Apollo and snapped the

194

phone shut. He smiled. 'Hey, Ellerslie,' he said. 'You look like shit.'

'I'm fine,' I said. I couldn't remember his name.

'Can't blame you, after yesterday.'

'After the parade, huh?'

'After Brands. Deal took a dive midday after they bought it – closed at nearly half. Your boys lost a lot.' He mentioned some of the numbers as he talked. 'How are they taking it?' he wondered. 'They pissed with you?

'Easy come, easy go,' I said.

'I got a printout – want to see?'

'No, thanks,' I said. 'You keep it.'

'You win some, you lose some,' he said. He walked off.

Later – a short time, a long time – Lee brought out salt and pepper shakers, fresh paper napkins, an extra triangle of butter, ice water and jam, and set them down without looking.

I unfolded one of the napkins and wrote down the numbers he had given me. I did some sums. When I had finished I sat staring at the numbers. They were very bad.

I picked up the water. The glass left a ring of moisture on the table top. I wiped it clean, but you could still see where the glass had been standing. I sniffed the dish: apricot, and fresh. The Apollo has the best jam. Many people would forget that but I don't. It's a detail that's important.

I used one of the napkins to make a note to myself: *7.40 a.m. – Now Lee won't consider a holiday without also thinking of me.* The first catch of the day.

I folded it lengthways. Putting it in my raincoat pocket I found another tissue scrawled with a makeshift list: *the telephone cord worn and dirty beyond all reasonable explanation; why some old records sound good yet others sound terrible; the absence of worthwhile drama on television.* I turned the napkin over and used it to make a map of the lane and the tables outside the Apollo and the table I was sitting at and a rough list of the kids inside. I put it in my other pocket along with the card from the hotel dry-cleaners.

Soon it would be warm enough to take off my raincoat. Maybe

later, when the sun moved and brought the rest of the lane out of the shadows. The gull circled back. I could watch that gull for a long time. I'd be happy if I was up there, the breeze stopping my fall. I would be light and cool, warm where the sun touched my back. My face would be brushed with a soft, humming current like the last moments before sleep, a velvet weightlessness, gentle and safe. Real sleep. Like dying – falling asleep. Your body growing heavy until you are resting between existence and something different, teetering like a pen on the edge of a desk. Is there anything to hold on to, at that moment? Are you afraid? Is there anyone there? Can you roll over and touch them? Kiss the space between their shoulders?

The worst thing is, I've come too far to stop. Simple things are beyond me, now, my head so full there's no space for anything else. Folded notes and phone calls and pieces of paper, maps and photographs, other people's mail: the more I've collected, the darker it's become. Every year the canopy thickens and the things beneath it pale. The more I've found out, the more cause I have to worry. There is *so much* of everything, and I'm the only one keeping track of it. It's what I do. It's not my nature to leave people or things behind. What has happened before is important. I care about who used to be here. I'm not paid for doing it – I didn't even ask to be involved. I've had other jobs but never done them as well. Making sense of these memories is as close to a profession as I can claim.

Squinting into the sun I could feel the tears begin. They rolled down my face. I put my head down. My palms were awake to everything in my face, the oil and dirt, my wet cheeks. Unbandaged, the skin was too sensitive. I covered my face and bit my lip. My abdomen started to crunch, my muscles stammering. I struggled not to make any noise. I was aching for air but could only gasp. Crying was a relief, but not here, not on the street, not so early in the day – please. Not here.

Everything was going wrong. I was full to capacity. Other people could have put it behind them, but not me. It is a humiliating inability and I was lost because of it. The emptiness is painful. Not a bad pain, you understand. Not a terrible hurt, not unbearable, but a pain that's constantly present. It's like new shoes:

every step backwards or forwards, it hurts, it counts, you know about it.

My face was a red mess. I stupidly wiped it with one of the napkins and saw my map of the Apollo blot and run, and all I could think was: I'm going to have to draw that again. Or maybe not. Maybe I'll remember it. Maybe I could come back and do it later. Take a photograph. Eyewitness accounts.

I had blown the Brands deal. And now I was fucked. A moment's concentration, a split second, a lifetime. I'd fucked it up.

Breakfast tasted of nothing.

22

Entering the Dilworth I saw Louise waving at me from the back of the store. She was minding a small stack of my magazines. I thanked her and said I would pay for them and anything else owing. She rang up the total while I emptied out my pockets on the counter and looked through them for change. I asked for a receipt: she'd left the book out back and slipped through the curtain to get it. I smiled and waited, idly pressing flat the scraps of paper. The napkins, the hotel receipt, the dry-cleaning card.

Louise returned with the receipt book. Tax? she smiled. Tax, I said, nodded. Ahh, she grinned: lots of money. Yes, I said, lots of money. I was going to have to watch money now. As she wrote out the magazine titles one by one, I checked the hotel receipt. The porter's signature wasn't very clear. I thought about keeping it as a genuine bill and claiming on it as an expense. And the dry-cleaning, too. I checked the room account number on the back of the dry-cleaning card. It didn't match the number on the receipt. Instantly I felt stupid: Wilhemina had been in the hotel that night, but in a different room.

Louise finished writing the receipt and put the magazines in a bag. I took it upstairs.

My office smelled stale. I opened up the photocopy I'd made of the diary and set it on the desk. The pages were grey with toner, the black letters haloed with white. Now that they were all I had, the quality was not good. I called the hotel and asked to be put through to the holder of the account number on the dry-cleaning card. Sure enough, I recognised it: the number of the luxury suite on the top floor where she had taken me that first time. Between it and last night's bed stood four pale, cold floors, brass numbers and sheets turned back. Dial O for room service, *Notorious* on pay-per-view. I held the line, another guest waiting to check out.

The phone was picked up and a man said hello.

I masked the receiver and coughed. I carried the phone over to the window, bringing the street just that little bit closer.

'Hello?' he said again.

I sighed. 'Is she there?'

Now he took his turn to stop and think, figure things out. 'Not at present,' he said.

'The name's Penrose,' I said. 'I just wanted to thank her for the room. Is she working?'

He sniffed. 'When she is absent, it is not my concern.'

'How long has she been absent?'

'A good time.'

'When's she coming back?'

'The same hour as always.' He rolled the words.

'I need to speak to her.'

'You do. Penrose,' he said, intrigued. 'We share an initial.'

I turned and looked at the diary. The too-thick toner was dancing in the sun, the facsimile steadily decaying. His parents, his mentor, his wartime escape. Already fading. My shadow was long on the office floor, the receiver rigid in its giant hand.

'Please don't hang up,' I said.

'On the contrary, it's pleasant to hear a voice. Another friend of the Madame?'

'Yes, I am. A good friend.'

'She has many good friends,' he cackled, 'and supplies many entertainments.'

'It's important to be entertained.'

'Indeed it is. It certainly is, yes. I can tell, simply from your tone, that you understand what I'm saying. Everything's so gauche now, so bright and loud – one could not consider it proper. In my *life*' – he sucked in a breath – 'people's appetite for colour has *grown* so. It's ominous. People's hunger for pigmentation, for raw hue. Everything – mark me on this – costume, buildings, their toilet, their manner, everything is so much brighter now. The variety is frenetic.'

'You've seen a lot of things,' I said.

'Oh yes.' Bored. 'A multiplicity, but so narrow by the plotting. People have investigated everything: where's the mystery in that? I was born beneath a bigger sky. More was likely because less was known. Science knew its place. It surprises me, in fact, how much attention it attracts now. Why are you all so fascinated with numbers? Surely they are the world's lesser aspect. Bodies, minutes, species – I confess I've yet to come to terms with the tally. I'm told that I should, but there was never a place for me there. I've always been restless. It led me to cover thousands of miles. I investigated many places in the hope of purchase but found none. Despite the variety they were all the same. The monotony did not surprise.

'And of course, I have come to settle here. I sometimes have difficulty reconciling my existence with other things that have survived: in this city, reminders are thoughtfully culled. If it is old, it is torn down; if it has meaning, it is sold. Your city has no time for the past – it suits me very well.

'Strangely, it's only recently that I have considered the home I abandoned. I recall a map of the city on the study wall. The buildings were so thickly clustered they looked like skin, and the cracks in it were streets and lanes. That's what I always remembered. But then the other day I realised that I had been in error, and that it wasn't a map of a city, it was a dissection chart. It was a body I had been looking at, skin and flesh – not my home at all. I don't think it ever really felt like it. I was a restless child. My parents had my portrait taken but I was moving so I came out as nothing more than a blur. They are smiling. Their heads are clamped. It was taken before a painting of a field.

'I don't believe however, they were truly my parents. I was a traveller's child.' He shucked it off, laughing. 'I can't explain why this should have come to me now. These recent weeks I have been recalling all manner of events. I'm being revisited by my early life! I chronicled it, you know. I became a diarist at an early age. I would write on anything – the pages of books, cloth. I wanted to set it down accurately, and with good reason. When I was in America I worked in a sideshow for a time, with a man whom I tutored in all tricks of the trade. He noted it all in a book, but when I happened on it, I discovered he was relating the story as if he was the teacher and I the pupil. As you can imagine, I was bewildered and shocked by this ingratitude. I was forced to go through the notes personally and bring them about. Ironically I had not even completed the task when an accident befell him – he became a victim of his inexperience. A fool. But, still . . .' He rolled the thought in his cheek, swallowing the end of the sentence.

'I discovered Miranda in a similar state of folly,' he recalled. 'Sobbing in a brothel bedroom. A pale wretch of a girl, starving. She would have gone the same way as her predecessors had I not intervened. I found us passage from the place and we sat out the subsequent years in as cultivated surroundings as circumstances could afford. She was clumsy, unused to my citified ways, but gradually she improved. By the time we arrived here she was able to cope with many of the smaller details with minimum supervision. People paid us a great deal of attention, of course, something which I was more used to than she was. We had to conduct ourselves with discretion. She began to see the wisdom of leading a private life. Inevitably her suitors were disappointed.

'I don't write my diaries any longer,' he conceded, amused. 'I record them with an electronic device, a white box. I keep it by my bed. It listens for me to open my mouth, and the moment I do, it takes down everything I say. Clicks on, and the little spools turn. An awful lot of words. I never play it back. I have spent so much time becoming old, you understand, letting go of the things which youthful senses take for granted, that to have them recalled by machine, so loud and vivid, it's preposterous. An echo masquerading as reprise.'

He hesitated. 'If I wake up at night, you know, and I find myself alone in the dark and I am afraid for that moment, I speak out loud and the machine clicks on. Only a little click. But it's better than being alone.'

He cleared his throat. 'The device cost me a great deal of money. But I had a great deal. Without even trying, I had succeeded in collecting quite a bit over the years. There is no pattern to what increases in value: one decade it is combs, another it is carpets, another it is watches, buttons. Commonplace things to which you make no addition – all they are is older. At first I didn't understand, but . . .' I could hear his tongue running over his teeth. 'We crave the same fate, to become distinguished as we age. Do you see? We point to the worth of aged things and hope to inflate our own value.' This time the cackle was like spit. 'Ludicrous. And I could not of course recommend the parties whom I dealt with. The moment my back was turned they embarked on an endeavour which threatened me fundamentally. They dealt with an amateur, an imbecile who began to publicise my whereabouts, my past. They committed a terrible intrusion into my privacy, which is paramount. I am frail, and nothing I have ever done warranted treatment of that kind. It was boorish of them, and abhorrent. I confess, I became enraged.'

Tad's face, slashed and grey.

'It's no matter now,' he promised. 'The parties in question are no longer in business. We are all presented with the same opportunities, and I have made the most of mine. I can only express regret – my sincere regret – if others do not choose the proper path. There are many such vandals in the world and I have insured myself against them. I lead a solitary life. I avoid such people's attention.'

'You travel light.'

'I am accompanied by a great deal of luggage.' There was a smile in his voice. 'Therefore I employ a temporary staff. But it's difficult even to rely upon them. However sincere their initial service, they always come to judge me. I have judged myself in the light of many events – they have no idea of how little they count. So narrow in their perceptions. Things are so much larger than they imagine them to be, the marks they make of so little significance. They would pale if they could truly see.'

The line was silent in contemplation. I cleared my throat. 'When I first came across your initial I made the mistake of thinking it had something to do with mine,' I told him. 'Maybe I saw something of you in me, or felt like I knew you. But when I read your writings and met some of the people you've known, I realised that wasn't the case.'

202

'My writings?' he asked, puzzled.

'I have your diary.' I laid my hand on the sheaf of papers. 'I read it. It was given to me.'

'Impossible.'

'I know you moved to stop it going any further, but it did.' I picked through the pages. 1875, the long, dark tunnel, the train. 'I found a man in an alleyway,' I said. 'Tad. All slashed to pieces.' 1926: an old man, an escape artist who didn't escape. 'A few days later, Dede, his twin was caught in a fire. Locked in his own shop, couldn't get out. Burned alive.' The negative blonde girl, her grey front tooth. 'And a woman with him, she also died. An old woman. Madam Sunde. Miranda Sunde.' I scattered everything across the desk with my pink, burned hand. 'She's dead,' I told him. 'She died in the fire. And if I hadn't taken my time getting there I would have died with them.'

'I saw Miranda this very day, and she was as I have always known her,' he said. 'She comes to me each morning, after she has settled her business affairs. She unbuttons her coat. She sits at the foot of the bed. She remembers everything – the places we travelled together, people we knew. It's all fresh in her mind. Only in the afternoon does she leave. She puts on her coat and she kisses me goodbye.'

I rubbed my head, trying to follow his tangled thread. 'When does she come back?' I snapped.

'She arrives again the next morning. She undresses. Such a sight, such a sight. As lovely as she ever was. We talk for hours: there's so much to remember. When I travelled, she was my companion and we saw many sights together. There are almost endless details to recall – far too many for my atrophied brain! – but she remembers them all. She describes the fashions of the day, the hats and gloves she wore. We trace where we walked or stopped to admire a view, or the events we attended – the other guests present, what was being said in the room. Miranda delights in gossip and the machinations of social occasions and I took great pains to ensure she was the focus of both. She bloomed under my tutelage, a transformation which gave me much delight. I would still take time to encourage her, were I not confined.

So, in the afternoons she leaves me in order to attend to her business affairs. Sometimes I wish I could afford the time to go with her and supervise, but the experience of coping with her own affairs is a necessary one. I know she will return when she becomes bored.

'And sure enough she returns the next morning. Despite her time away she is still fresh and young – not in the least bit tired, which is excellent because in the hours that follow, we find so much to discuss. I knew her for a long, long time. We saw many sights together, met a great number of people. I can spend endless evenings simply discussing this with her. Before she sits down, she unbuttons her coat and hangs it on the chair. I am thrilled by it. And at the end of the evening she picks up her coat and puts it back on, and she leaves. She has many matters to attend to, both business and personal – it would be ungentlemanly to protest. No matter! She will return in the morning. She steps into the room. She unbuttons her coat and she drops it and we talk. We talk until all hours. And then she has to leave . . .'

I listened to his voice climb, to his story spin and yellow.

'I love her,' he broke in, suddenly, and the complacency in his voice was gone. 'I have always loved her. Always. She understands after travelling such great distances, sharing so many hours – she knows why she is here. None of you possesses her faith. All you have are sciences – you are alive simply as part of a table, a chain. You look for meaning in sequence, in the worthless things you inherit, and comfort yourself with statistics which purport to justify your role in the world. Don't you see? You are not alive because you *want* to be. You are alive because your science says you must be and if, tomorrow, someone invents a new formula or meaning that declares you unnecessary you will cease to exist.

'I want to be here,' he declared. 'I am here because I *wish* to be.'

'Then let me speak to you. Let me come up to your room.'

'You won't find what you're after,' he promised. 'No cape, no Nosferatu.'

'I want to meet the man behind all of this.'

'There's no man to meet,' he said.

I dropped the cackling receiver and ran. Out of my office, down the hall, down the stairs. Louise was putting out the day's rubbish. Very late, Mr Penrose, she said: late for your appointment.

The streets were brass, furnace-beaten, pitted by traffic and strolling, sunburned wanderers, dead windows, snaking gutters, car alarms boxing your ears. I ran, I ran, I ran. Four blocks and a corner and another block and a driveway, a Rolodex of flat storefronts flashing top-priority red-pen dead space leasing now. Everything in one street and how fast I could run it. Everything scattered and making no sense but making perfect sense if I could get to him, if he was there.

There was no breath in my body. He had taken it from me and I was going to get it back.

Jesus, I ran! I sprinted the fucking minute mile in hard shoes and a tie. I vaulted, jumped, landed silly and skidded and fell and rolled and got up and ran again. I shouted at people and cursed them. I punched faces, I shoved women out of the way, I ran. I calculated every mismatched inch of bitumen and paving, each crooked stone, wire basket, lamp post, band poster, storefront, angled sign. I pissed on the brief. I spat on the working week and waking hours of paper-trading dullards.

I ran like this when I was a kid. Bull rush. I was the fastest. Cutting a big arc wide in the field, shaving it close, closer than anyone. Remember? Big hand flashing at your collar, trying to get you down, brushing the fabric and that's when you pull away. Step on the gas, oh yes, big laugh through your body now, laughing through your milk teeth at the big guy grazing his knees on the summer clay. Fuck I was good. Remember? If you could have seen me.

Four blocks and a corner and another block.

A limo was pulling into the Regent's driveway. I ducked round it and up the steps to the amazed doorboy and the flash of the glass doors' parting. I ran across the lobby, everyone turning to watch. The concierge was already picking up the phone, staff stepping out briskly from behind the desk but before they could act they were behind me: I was taking the stairs two steps at a time, ignoring the pinging lift.

By the top floor I was so dizzy I was steadying myself with outstretched hands, knocking the framed lithographs off the walls. Stumbling on to the level I sent a planter crashing back down the stairwell, spraying dirt. I didn't look back. I ran trailing black footprints down the hallway, past the lift – someone was getting out and I slammed them, yelled get back, yelled. Pounding the walls. I screamed for him, I announced my entry, I demanded an audience. I began kicking the room doors. They flew open on people dressing and people watching TV and people kissing and people by themselves, young people and rich people and old people, with families and skin diseases and blue panties and sheets and jetlag and sticking-up hair. They were frightened and blank and shocked and annoyed and understanding, instantly, that this was very important, very special, and they all got out of my way. They didn't gather in a crowd, they didn't even stick out their heads. They stayed in their rooms as I eyeballed them and yelled and moved on. They knew what to do. They knew the drill. Where's Palmer? Stay in your room. Where's Palmer?

At the bay window.

At the end of the hall where it turned, where the hallway broke at a 45-degree angle, there was a bay window looking out over the city. And I saw him there and I reached out: a man, very tall. White ponytail. A long coat, checked trousers, his back to me. Looking out the bay window. Palmer, I yelled, and he didn't turn his head. He waited, for me, and I went to him, my whole weight, body tackle. Pin him hard, hold him down. Four steps, three steps, two steps. I jumped at him, I put out my arms and I jumped. And then on his shoulders I saw my own face reflected in the glass.

In the moment, the split-second moment before I went through the window, I turned my head and he turned his. Old face. Cracked skin. Bright blue eyes looking at me, cackling. He was laughing because he wasn't in front of me, as I had thought. He was waiting round the corner, and I was running full bolt at his reflection in the eighth-storey window.

Oldest trick in the book.

I hit the window and it exploded and fell outwards and I fell with it, my arms spread, my legs spread, my chest cold in the sudden wind. I twisted, trying to look back at Palmer but the rush of sunlight turned the hallway dark and everything in it invisible, framed with jagged edges. The edges became a hole, and then an uneven star dripping white, shining shards of glass. My feet floated above my head. The eighth floor shrank beneath me. I clawed the air, staring past my shoes, but he was gone. I'd had my chance at Palmer and missed. I tried to make the best of it, back-pedalling, waving my arms to slow myself down. The lower hotel floors were rushing past. Curtains, bird shit, streaks from the rain. Maybe there were faces watching but I'm not entirely sure – I think I imagined them.

My first instinct was to try and sit up. It wasn't easy because, jerking forward, there was nothing to lean against, only the gentle cushion of wind. It felt very cool against my skin and for a crazy moment I realised that I'd been granted my breakfast wish of floating with the gulls. This was a special moment and I stopped trying to sit up and started instead to look around at the buildings and the harbour and the hills and the sky beyond. The city was spread out like a poncho, chocolate-brown and gold in the evening sun, and the air was sweet. All over the town people were talking and laughing and sharing this moment in their own special way, engaged in acts so specific and necessary and intrinsic to living that their gracefulness would remain for ever obscure.

I wasn't falling: I was rising.

I opened my hands. I reached out. I reached out.

I hit a whole lot of things and finally the ground of the car park – I don't recall if I bounced – and lay there, dead.

III

23

At first, nobody came forward. A woman screamed. Then, slowly, a few pale faces gathered around. They looked and backed away, whispering behind their hands. The doorboy waved them back but didn't know what to do after that. They stood and waited, shuffling.

A police car pulled up. The younger of the two policemen stepped out and straightened his hat. He crossed the car park, his soles crunching the broken glass, and crouched down to touch my neck. The woman screamed again. The policeman asked if anyone had seen what happened and, while they blathered, looked up at the broken window on the eighth floor and then down at the crushed ferns in the front garden. He stood up and walked back to the car and spent several minutes talking on the radio.

The traffic was jamming as drivers slowed to look at what was happening. The other policeman opened the boot of the car. He took out a stack of big orange plastic cones and laid them across the entrance and exit of the hotel driveway. He took a roll of yellow plastic tape that read POLICE LINE DO NOT CROSS and tied it round the step railings in an ungainly bow. Then he walked backwards, unrolling the tape as he went. His heavy shoes mulched the forecourt garden as he tangled the tape in the shrubberies. He walked round the shrubs, the awning pillars and a stack of luggage trolleys until he had made an uneven yellow border beginning and ending at the Regent's front door. He tied it off and tore the tape with his teeth, smoothing down the sticky end with his palm. He knocked the dirt off his shoes and walked back to the car.

The young policeman stepped back inside the circle. He was carrying a flat notebook and a short cardboard box. He took off my watch and read out the time and sealed it in a plastic bag which he put in his pocket. Nice shoes, he said. Then he knelt again and carefully went through my jacket until he found my wallet. He checked all the cards and ID and noted down my name, then put them and the notebook to one side. Picking the box up by its edges, he prised open the lid. The box was packed with sticks of fresh, white school chalk. He drew a stick out with his fingernails, cupped it in his hand to blow off the loose dust, and then slowly began to trace the outline of my body on the asphalt. He started at my feet, bumping the soles of my shoes.

He stopped tracing along my left side, by my waist, when I coughed. The woman screamed again, and the policeman jumped back, scrabbling in the glass. I tried to sit up and tell him that I was alive but the effort was too great, and this time I finally did pass out.

I woke up in a white ward, cradled in the bed by a hard, complex harness. My neck was kept straight by a wide plastic collar that rubbed my chin. There was a thin tube hanging from the corner of my mouth. Something in my groin was intensely painful. I could not move, and lay listening to my breathing and the blood in my ears. My hands felt warm. Staring up at the cat's cradle of strings and weights spanning the ceiling, I could see my reflection in the stainless-steel pulleys: a white smear in a cotton web.

A surgeon came and spoke with me several times before I could catch his name or understand much of what he was saying. Dr Garbo was short and unshaven, and slopped around in sandals and a white coat. He spent a lot of time telling jokes and humorous stories about the nurses and hospital staff, sitting on the end of the bed balancing the clip chart on one knee. He explained that I was in traction, and my body was repairing itself, and reassured me constantly that I would be all right. 'A lot of cases like this come in to the spinal unit and don't come out,' he said, 'but you'll walk away. You're an incredibly lucky man.'

I couldn't reply. I was hampered by more than the tubes: there were so many words in my mouth, all trying to get out, but when they came even close, everything jammed and I was afraid and falling again. Dr Garbo stopped my struggle each time by grasping the unbandaged tips of my fingers. 'You'll be able to talk about it soon,' he promised. 'The drugs are making it difficult for now.' He smiled. 'Have I told you about the other doctor who comes in here?' And he told me the story, never letting go of my hand.

When I was strong enough to speak, he asked me how I had come to fall through the window and so, over the course of many hours, I told him about Palmer. It was a struggle covering all the details with such a clumsy jaw, but Garbo was happy to listen to my muffled account. He took notes, reviewing them as I spoke and confirming many different aspects of the events as I remembered them. Gradually he began to expand on what I'd told him, developing certain points and emphasising things here and there which I hadn't fully appreciated at the time. Although talking for such long periods was exhausting, it was a relief to unburden myself. That was how it felt in the beginning, anyway.

As I reached the end of my story, however, my relief gave way to something less secure. Garbo's questions became slightly confusing – annoying, almost – and I started to wonder what he was really after. He had spent an unusually long time sitting with me, and his jokes weren't that good, and now he was asking about a whole lot of things which weren't strictly relevant to Palmer and the events which had brought us together. His tone wasn't mocking, but he was straying unconcernedly from things he needed to know in order to understand fully. I became agitated in spite of the narcotics. I started to struggle in my casts until he reminded me to be calm, putting away his notes. He excused himself and slopped out of the ward, leaving me to fall into the slow warmth of sleep. My sleep in the hospital was unstirring. Waking came in flashes, regulated by the medication, and there was no variation in the depth of my slumber: each time, coming round, I couldn't judge how long I'd been out. I experienced no dreams because the medication prevented it: that's how I knew, when I saw Miranda Sunde standing above me, that she was real.

She looked the same as when I'd first seen her waiting for the taxi outside the Dilworth, and in the corner of the ramen bar. The long coat that had slipped between the Mardi Gras marchers hung worn and dappled with fresh rain. Strands of blonde hair hatched a forehead lined with concern. She tipped her head to one side, surveying my plastered length. She looked confused. She bit her bottom lip and I could see her dead tooth. Then she turned her head away again: she was presenting me with her profile. She wasn't examining me, but allowing me to look at her, to know every part of her face. I was her silent audience, my tongue dead with drugs.

I tried desperately to speak. I had to speak to her, ask her to stay, not to run this time. I blinked. My jaw was wired, frozen, my breathing thick. Right here, right in my face, inches away.

She looked on me with pity, and compassion. She put her hands on my forehead, stroking me, and leaned forward and kissed me on the mouth. She sat back on the bed. Tears were running down her face. She wiped them away, sniffing, and regarded me for a time. She tipped her head to one side in a day-dreamy way, stroking her hair. Then she carefully reached underneath her scalp, fingers inching like a spider, and pulled the blonde away in a tangled clump to reveal her short, black hair, bangs pinned back. 'I'm sorry, baby,' said Wilhemina, dropping the wig on the bed. 'It was me all along.'

My temples were drumming. Now, suddenly, I felt the cast and the harness and the fear of my restraint. I knew my helplessness and my inability to respond. I could not hold her and I could not shout. I could not use words, I couldn't kiss her. The wig was beyond my examination, the pockets of the raincoat out of sight. Her face remained in my line of vision for only as long as she sat there, leaning over me. I was desperate for her to stay, to explain, but I couldn't even beg. I could only wait, and hope. A second went past, and then another, and then a year. She wiped my face and then her own. I drew fugitive breaths.

'Have you ever imagined things, Ellie?' she sniffed. 'Ever had a dream you thought was real? Did you ever sit up at night wondering about things no-one else could see, hear voices no-one else could hear? Did you ever imagine phone calls, or read something from a blank page?'

I was choking. She slid her fingers round the collar, stroking my neck.

'Are you delusional, Ellerslie Penrose? Do you retreat from normal social situations, deny yourself human contact? Do you avoid other people because their version of reality doesn't tally with yours? Are you obsessive, hyperactive, paranoid? Are you sleepless? Do you have normal sleep patterns?' Her voice was shaking. 'Have you had suicidal thoughts? Have you ever attempted suicide by, say, jumping from a building?' Her cheeks were streaming with tears. 'Because Doctor Garbo wants to know,' she explained. 'He's been asking me lots of questions. They've checked you in as an attempted suicide, Ellie. They say you suffer from' – she looked up to count off each word – 'gradual-onset schizophrenia, and you've experienced an acute episode.' She looked back down at me. 'They say you're very sick.'

I sucked air. 'I'm not crazy.'

'Oh, I know,' she nodded. 'I know.' She took a deep breath.

'Palmer . . .' I gasped.

'He's gone. Packed and left,' she said. 'He was leaving when you . . . called. He probably walked past when you were lying outside. The doorboy said he got into a taxi, and the taxi drove away. And that was it.'

The shadows of my harness shifted across the ceiling. Wilhemina spoke with the nurses. I closed my eyes, I opened my eyes. She unbuttoned her coat and pushed it behind her to sit better on the edge of the bed. I asked her, a few words at a time, and she told me, stroking my hands as she talked.

'I got the job through one of the other girls.' She cleared her throat. 'I'd been down to the Cot Club and this girl told me there was work going if I wanted it. I was intrigued by it. I didn't say anything at the time.

'Sunde called me about a week later. She'd been watching me in the club. We never met: we only ever spoke on the phone. She told me I was special, and that she wanted someone who wasn't like the other girls, someone who could act.' Wilhemina smiled. 'She was a good talker – but then, you must know.' She brushed my fringe.

'She wanted me to pretend to be someone else and talk to this guy. Just talking: two hundred dollars an hour. So I said I'd try it.

'She couriered me a photograph of a blonde woman, and a package of clothes, this wig . . . Everything fitted – she'd measured one of my uniforms. There was a handwritten list of things I had to memorise: anecdotes about very specific places and events. I was playing a girl called Miranda and she was in love with a man named Palmer. There were some notes about her accent and I kind of clicked that Miranda was Madame Sunde, and that I was playing her. It was so specific – it was creepy. I didn't like it. I called her and bailed out. She was really upset. She told me the guy was ill, and she couldn't see him any more. This was the only way she could sort of speak to him, I guess. It was sad but I bailed anyway. And then I thought about it and felt bad. I called her back. She gave me more money.' Wilhemina shrugged.

'I put on this wig and the clothes, did my face exactly how she'd asked. Then I caught a taxi to the Regent. I was really shaking when I walked in but it was a different shift and I was wearing the wig and the clothes – nobody recognised me. It was strange: the moment I walked in I became somebody else. I didn't need to ask directions, I just went up to the room and knocked.

'I don't know what I was expecting – some guy in a wheelchair or something. When he opened the door I was still practising the accent under my breath.

'He was very tall and thin. He was wearing a funny suit, with a high-buttoned jacket. He had grey hair, in a ponytail. Long hands. His stare was very bright. He was almost smiling at me, and I smiled back. He called me Miranda and invited me inside. He sat on the bed, waiting, and I felt sick and then I thought, what the hell, I'll do it this once.

'So I started speaking in the voice, telling the stories Sunde had given me. I took off the coat like she'd said, and then,' – she waved her hand – 'the other stuff. I was talking a lot to cover myself up but then came this point when I was pretty much naked and I was thinking, God, this is really the pits – and then I looked up. He was just sitting there, looking sad.

'I wanted to say something but I'd blown all my lines. I'd gone through everything Sunde had given me. So I started asking him questions, you know, like, do you remember when we went to this restaurant, and so on. And he started talking, filling in the gaps. He remembered everything about me – her – all of it, but it wasn't in the past for him. It was really as if it had happened yesterday. He was really in love with her. *Still* in love with her, I mean, like I *was* her, like this was all happening now. I just thought, okay, this is an old guy, he's a bit senile, he's harmless. I stayed and talked to him till late, and then I got dressed, and left.

'The money was in the mailbox the next morning. Cash, nearly five hundred dollars. She rang me and asked me would I do it again, and I said yes. I told her I'd run out of things to say but she said that it didn't matter, just to go back and say the same things again. That night I finished my shift, walked to the gym, changed into Miranda's clothes and went straight back to the hotel.

'I saw him a couple of times a week, and each night it was the same. I'd undress and walk around and say all my lines, and he'd talk to me, and I'd get dressed and leave. It was like that for months – I made so much money, Ellie. I was so tired – I used to look forward to sleeping in your bed so much. I looked forward to you,' she sighed, 'and every time things didn't work out. But I put it out of my mind because I was earning and I would get away, and whatever was happening with us was just how it was. I just put it out of my head.

'And then one day, out of the blue, Sunde told me that a very good client of hers had died and she was distressed that she couldn't attend the funeral – she was too old and frail, she said, and the idea of being there just hurt too much. So I offered to attend the funeral – Tad Ash's funeral – in her place. As her representative. I didn't mind. I was used to being Miranda by then. I would catch taxis in the daytime and not worry if anyone saw me. I'd been playing her for so long by then that standing in the back row of a funeral was no stretch. She offered me money but I told her to forget it. Being her was on me.

'When I got to the funeral home and saw you – God, I was so angry, Ellie. You were there even when I was being someone else. Sticking your fingers in the parts of my life you didn't know about.

'I made sure I got out before you did. I went ahead to the cemetery and watched the service from a distance, like Madame Sunde had asked me to. And then I followed Tad's brother around. She hadn't told me to do that, but Miranda was thinking for herself by then. I saw Dede go into the ramen bar and I was hungry, and it was fun, all this spy stuff, so I went in and had a beer. And then you came in again. I was petrified. You walked past this close – inches away. You didn't look around, you were so intent on him. I watched you talking and I realised this man was part of what you'd been talking about – it was what you were working on. And that didn't feel good to me. It didn't give me a good feeling. When you finally turned round and saw me, it was like you were a different person. I got up and left.

'That night, when I came to see you, I'd been thinking a lot. I knew something wasn't right and I had to tell you what was happening. When you showed me the wallet, my blood just turned to ice. I realised that Tad Ash had been murdered and I had a terrible feeling that I'd been involved in that somehow. I wanted to tell you everything – and then you said you were calling Madame Sunde. I thought I was going to be sick. I couldn't stay in the room. I was too nervous – I just left. I'm sorry.

'Sunde called me the next day and asked a whole lot of questions about the funeral: who was there and so forth. She was alarmed when I told her the police had been there. She started talking about a diary – you'd been talking about a diary – and said she had to get it back, and if I ever heard anything about it I had to tell her, because there was some trouble about it, she didn't say what.

'The next time I saw Palmer things weren't so good. I mean, I went through the whole Miranda routine as usual, and Palmer said all the things he usually said, and nothing bad happened, nothing at all. But it was different. I knew it was his diary everyone was talking about, it had to be – this old man with all these memories. I started to think the brightness in his eyes wasn't a smile. It was as if his eyes were burning. He looked angry. I put my clothes on and said goodnight. I was really glad to get out of there.

'When you told me about the fire, when you rang me at work, my heart really jumped. I thought you were going to be – more than burned.' She winced. 'I was so glad to see you, and at the same time I knew what had happened. I knew Sunde was dead. I just held on to you all night, trying to think what to do and all I could think about was what Sunde had left behind. So I gave you the valium, and then got dressed as Miranda. Right there in the room, Ellie. You even opened your eyes and looked at me, and I just kissed you and told you it was a dream. You went back to sleep like a baby. I didn't want to leave you but I had to. I went back to the Cot Club and I collected up all Sunde's cats. It was the only thing I could think of. They were the only thing she really cared about. Those idiot girls would have let them stray. I took them back to my place – they're running round the flat now.

'I was afraid. I knew Palmer had started the fire. I knew he'd killed her. I had an appointment to see him that night and I had to go. If I didn't, he might come after me. This was the night of the Mardi Gras parade. I left work and changed and went back as Miranda and knocked. I waited in the corridor for a long time – it seemed like a long time, anyway – trying to imagine what he'd be going through. The more I thought about it, the more I thought I'd done the wrong thing by showing up. It was mad of me to be there. I don't know what I was doing. And then I got really afraid because he was taking so long and I thought maybe I should run – and that, of course, was when the door opened. And I thought, this is it.

'But then when I saw him, he was exactly the same as I remembered. He invited me in and we talked for a little while. I was looking for danger signs, I was ready to bolt at any moment, but it was all as normal as it had ever been. I took off my coat, and my dress, and talked about all the times we had spent together, places we had seen. He joined in, asked his questions. We swapped the same recollections, smiled at the same things that had always made us smile. And I walked around and he talked to me as if I was Miranda, as if we were both twenty-one and talking in the nightclub on that first night, wrapped in his leather coat. It was like the first night I'd come to see him.

'Nothing had changed in his life. He didn't think anything was real. That's how he could do what he did, Ellie. The only person he cared about was in the past. He couldn't understand the difference between the real Miranda Sunde and the fake, and so in a way, I guess, he never really killed her or those other people. But at the same time he never knew what he'd lost. I honestly felt sad for him when I said goodbye. Even I wasn't coming back.

'I waved at him from the street, from the middle of the parade, and then I went to go home. But then someone shouted at me, tried to grab me – I was hysterical, Ellie, I was so afraid it was him that I just ran. I didn't know it was you, and when I saw it was I was a mess and I couldn't explain. I wanted to get out of these clothes, just go home where it was safe. And besides' – she cupped my cheek – 'I had to feed the cats.'

She shut her eyes. She tipped her head back and breathed deeply. She raised her hands to her cheeks. Then she stood up and smoothed out the place on the bed where she had been sitting. She walked slowly round the bottom of the bed, slipping off her coat and the uniform jacket beneath. At the window she stopped and put her hand to her mouth, turning a fingernail. Her dead front tooth came away in her hand. She held it up: a square of grey paper, wet with saliva. She wadded it and flicked it out the open window. She didn't say any more. She stood with her arms folded and looked out.

The sun was sinking below the hills, tracing the city's outline. It was a shape that changed constantly, becoming taller, more tangled. The modern world was crowding the sunset, bringing night closer all the time.

As it concentrated on the silhouette, the light forgot the corners of the room and left it dim and warm. The discarded coat became an old woman's clothes. Wilhemina's skin turned olive, her hair tangled and soft. The window's sky discovered a wedge of moon, and somebody came and drew the curtains.

24

T angiers visited on a quiet afternoon. He waited for the nurses to
leave before he spoke. 'Heard about your accident,' he said.
'I'm sick of talking about it.'

He shrugged. 'The hospital will tell me anything I need to know.'
He eyed the wires and plaster and the drip's soft plastic bag. 'They've
really fitted you up there.' He squeezed the bag experimentally. 'We
got the guy.'

'I read the papers.'

'I assumed you would. You like to stay informed. That's a
respectable trait. Yes.' He sighed. 'The old man was killed by
his own dealer. There was money owed and things got nasty, as
they do. The killer stripped the body searching for cash and drugs,
then dumped what he thought was a dead body in the bin. Ash died
trying to claw his way out. The killer wasn't hard to track down, but
we took it carefully. Dotted the i's and crossed the t's. We want the
charges to stick on this one. And they will.

'Ash's brother was killed in a fire. You hear about that?' He
concentrated on the bag, careful not to look at me. 'Yeah. Fire in
the store. We found another body there: a Ms Sunde, local prostitute.
Fire department say it was started by electrical failure. The victims
received no warning because the alarm was disconnected. Street kids
break into places, cut the wires so they can shack up in there at night.
Sunde was procuring for both men from a brothel called the Cot
Club. Irony is, she was probably commiserating with Dede Ash in
some way. We haven't laid charges in relation to the fire. Coroner's
ruled accidental death. We have no problem with that.' He stared
at the bag, at the room hanging upside down in plasma.

'So there you go,' I said.

'That's right,' he said. 'We're still tracking down the girls who worked for Sunde, but it's difficult. All we can do is appeal to the public and hope someone comes forward. But nobody will. The victims were old. No family. People like that just slip away.' He sucked air between his teeth. 'End of story.'

'Is it?'

'I believe so,' he said firmly.

'So this is the official version?' I said.

'That's the one.'

'Nice story.'

'Great story.' He let go of the bag.

'Perfect.'

'It certainly is.' He leaned over so that his face was above mine, his eyes sharpened to little points. 'But I'll tell you some things we left out of the report. We visited your little friend Veale. Faggot didn't want to tell us anything but he did. We tickled him a little and it all came out. He said you'd been round. Asking questions regarding the dead man's estate. An unidentified Caucasian male was at the scene of the fire, your approximate height and build. You knew the parties involved. You were down at the Cot Club. You were associated with this case and you were meddling in it.'

'I found out some things.'

'And you're going to take them to your grave.'

'You know that dealer was not the killer.'

'Yeah?' The little smile was back.

'Tad was killed by a man called Palmer. Very old man.' The phlegm was tickling my throat. 'A long time ago, when he was a young man, he turned his back on the rules about living. He did it because he was afraid, because he wanted to survive. That survival was threatened when Tad found his diaries and threatened to circulate them. Palmer killed him to keep them secret.'

'Wow. This is interesting,' Tangiers said dryly. 'Maybe I'd better go ask this guy some questions.'

'You could try to track him down, but I don't believe you would succeed. People can be tracked because they are animals with life cycles and patterns of behaviour, but Palmer has none. He lives only for the moment. His faith has no centre. He is a wanderer. He searches for nothing except what is passing by, ignorant of the hour and the day and the year. He's barely a human being.'

'Can't hang a man for that.'

'That's right. He never really killed those people because he never really knew they were alive. I have that on authority.'

'Where's he from?'

'Eighteen seventy-five.'

Tangiers tipped his head at the drip. 'What have they got you on, exactly?'

'Morphine. Want some?'

'Oh, right.' He nodded slowly, smiling. 'I getcha.' He turned his finger on himself. 'You think I'm a stoner. You think I'm a little out of it? Yeah? Well, I'll tell you something. I solved this case,' he said. 'I'm the cop. You're incidental, a bit player. Darting around basing your beliefs on random, circumstantial evidence. I'm the one doing the hard slog, I'm the one going for it, trying to get to the bottom of this. My world is cogent and whole. If I investigate something, it's because it doesn't fit my rational view. But you' – he turned the finger on me – 'you stick your nose into things because you have no sense of the world. You don't know what it should be and you hope that whatever you find will explain it to you. Well, that won't happen. I look for answers. You're looking for truth: you won't find it.' He drew back.

'You're wrong.'

'When you have eliminated the impossible whatever remains, however improbable, must be the truth.' He stretched his neck so that the bones clicked. 'You're looking tired,' he said. 'You need your sleep.' He looked over the bed again. 'How are long are you going to be like that for?'

'A while.'

'Rather you than me.'

'There's lots to think about.'

He raised his eyebrows. 'Where there's no imagination, there's no horror. *Study in Scarlet.*'

He put his hands in his pockets. I looked at him and he waited, but we both knew it had finished. He had his answers. I wouldn't hear from Tangiers again.

Lying still for the next eight weeks didn't wash my responsibilities away, and I was determined to keep up. Wilhemina rang my answerphone for me, holding the receiver to my ear so I could hear the playback. She brought my courier parcels and mail and sat by the bed reading their contents aloud as I lay watching the sunlight track across the ceiling. Each day the things she recounted meant a little less than the sound of her voice or her fingers tearing open an envelope. I was in a world where there was no time, only sunlight and evening. I was relieved, drained, wiped and washed, indifferent to my physical progress. The re-ordering of braces and medication was a sign that my spine was healing. Soon I would be able to sit up in the real world. I began to stir in the white sheets, but my paralysis was far from cured. By the time I was out of traction and able to open the letters myself, their contents were meaningless. I had lost track of the markets. Phone numbers and personnel had changed. I couldn't remember what was in my bank account or how it had got there. Wilhemina pushed my wheelchair round the sunny hospital garden and discussed the flower beds. After the neck brace was removed I could rest my cheek against her warm grip on the handle.

The Tomaso turned up in Wellington on either side of a telephone pole. Kids got up some speed on one of those hills, apparently. I paid $250 to have it junked.

I leaned on my crutches in the elevator as it took us up to the fourth floor of the Dilworth. Wilhemina unlocked my office door and we stepped into a musty den filled with unread books, worthless piles of paper, records taped in cardboard boxes. The only picture on the wall was a city map busy with red tape. The place was too small and cluttered, but draughty at the same time, empty of anything warm. The bathroom was greasy with mould. The edges of the shower cabinet were black and rotten and the plug was blocked with hair. The kitchen bench was marked by cups and drinking glasses and the cupboards smelled of moth balls. The only view – from the windows that hadn't been sloppily blocked with paint – was of the shadowy street below, noisy with buses and road markings.

Wilhemina picked up the day's mail from under the front door. There was a letter from the building's landlord giving three months' notice of lease foreclosure and eviction from the premises. The Dilworth was being turned in to a block of luxury inner-city time-share apartments. As a current leaseholder I would have the privilege of making the first offer. I screwed up the letter and threw it away, shaking my head at their foolishness. I couldn't imagine why anyone would want to live here.

I heard from Tony that one of his customers had offered him a place on the west coast. The rents there were cheap now summer was over. Wilhemina drove us out to look. It was a low bach with chocolate-brown weather boards and white window sills, set back about two hundred yards from the beach. I took off my shoes and stood on the uneven lawn. Wilhemina dangled her legs from the veranda. The wind made everything sound the same. I saw a wave come in and then another wave. I got tired and sat down. There was sand in the grass.

It took a long time to move our things, to box them up and drive them out there. Two weeks after the eviction date I still had one more trip to make to the Dilworth. Pulling up outside, the first thing I saw was that Louise's store was closed. She was gone. She had left the empty black window shelves with a decorative display of a few choice titles, prices clearly marked. The curtain was still hanging over the back room.

The elevator had been torn out in lieu of a new machine. The shaft was padlocked and covered with safety warnings. I took the stairs. On every floor the legal firms had moved out their storage. The anonymous doors had been taken off their hinges and stacked in the end room. The spaces I had admired in pebbled silhouette were bald and white.

My office had also been stripped. Now it was divided by cheap aluminium frames that had yet to be fitted with walls. In the far corner where the bathroom had been, stood an imaginary side-room. Inside it were two men flicking through a big, hairy book of carpet samples. They looked up and then ignored me after I'd introduced myself. The papers I was looking for had been stuffed in a bin liner along with broken boards and paint-splattered ringlets of masking tape. I began picking them out of the rubbish and then stopped. I couldn't remember why I needed them any more. So I left the papers. I said goodbye to the carpet men on my way out. They didn't say anything, no doubt in anticipation being unable to hear through the walls that had yet to arrive.

I passed the elevator doors for the last time, my footsteps echoing down the empty shaft.

The last thing we packed were the cats. We got cages for Thufur, Apples, Sushi, Moonpie, Boy Cat and Travis – who was bigger now – and drove them out to the bach. We shut them inside so they'd get used to the smell. They scratched and meowed and hid in the cupboards and under the sofa. Wilhemina lay on her side on the floor and talked to them. Travis ventured out first, sniffing. By the time we left for the cemetery they were all out, climbing over the kitchen bench and complaining.

Dede Ash had been buried with Tad and, in accordance with somebody's wishes, Miranda had been buried with them. Their plot was the first in a new part of the cemetery, a low, unsheltered section adjacent to a creek and a tiny, artificial-looking lake with willows. The two plots were still freshly dug and without headstones. The ground felt damp.

'I don't know which one is her and which is the boys,' Wilhemina said, 'but I suppose it doesn't matter.' She crouched and shook out Miranda's coat and dress and shoes and laid them on the left grave, pressing the wig into the collar. The blonde curls shivered in the wind. 'Someone's going to think it's a joke, aren't they?' she squinted. She took my arm and pressed her face in my shoulder.

I took out Tad's wallet. It was warm from being in my pocket. I wanted to say something but I couldn't think of anything so I knelt, with some difficulty, and inserted it into the soil. It passed easily into the ground. I pressed it in until it was hidden, and smoothed over the hole. Then we stepped back and admired our handiwork, the real clues hidden, the disguise for everyone to see. It was all wrong. It was what they would have wanted.

We drove back with the radio on. The station played a Smokey Robinson song and then 'Baker Street', Phoebe Snow, 'Good Vibrations'. I leaned into the headrest and considered that it was a long time since I had perceived a melody. Listening to those songs was like waking up. My records were all in boxes, lying in the narrow crawl space underneath the house. I made Wilhemina stop at an ex-rental store and went inside and bought a working second-hand turntable. I rested it on my lap as she drove.

At the bach we opened the door and the cats ran out and scattered into the bushes. Wilhemina put their dishes out on the steps and filled them with food for when they returned. I wired up the turntable to her ghetto blaster, and then we crawled under the house and brought up the boxes.

They were unmarked: we opened them not knowing what we would find, choosing records to play at random. Then a song would remind us of another song and we'd go looking for it, checking through the piles, ripping open the unopened boxes. On the way to finding it, we'd come across something else and play that, and sometimes that discovery would change our minds about the song we'd first set out to find. Some songs made us play the whole album: others were a disappointment. But everything sounded fresh. The sun went down and left us sprawled on the floor surrounded by castles of records. The music carried along the beach and echoed off the hills.

And suddenly melody seemed important. The melody is the thing: everything else in the song either carries or distracts from it. It is the constant. At the end you can whistle it as if it's a simple thing but it's not simple at all: it's a beautiful construction, a fraction balanced by unseen proportions. We are inspired to lead lives with that purpose and lineage but it's not that easy. The more I look back, the more things are shaped only by retrospect, run together like beads on a string. We claim that it's reasoned but all we're really doing is linking things up. There's no point to any of it.

Wilhemina has nightmares that Palmer will come for her and that we ourselves will become a headline, bobbing face down in the surf. But I don't think that will happen. I'm not afraid of what might be out there in the dark – and the nights here on the coast are truly without light. I can't see the colour of her hair as I stroke it and she cannot tell my age. Each night could be our first, for all we can determine, and that is the lesson when you are away from the neon.

Loving her is a delicate science practised over many hours, many silences between breaking waves. When day breaks it finds her beautiful. She slumbers and smiles. Her footsteps break the salt crust of the sand. She exchanges kisses, rolls in the sheets, bares skin creased by their wrinkles. Her fragrances fade and are then replenished. She is amused and bored. She is a creature born of time, and its passing has come to matter.

Wilhemina is my remembered girl now, and I have stopped counting the minutes before these scenes cease to turn. I am as prepared for it as I can be. Everything we promise never to forget will be erased: last month's overtime, the sound of traffic, the cats' names. How we take coffee. Every word we have spoken.

There will be the last flash, a single note. A fluttering. These scenes will disassemble and fall, and words will drift downwards. She will follow them, supine, and her hair will spread out, and the earth which bore her will embrace her once again.

Don't pull it apart, Miranda says. Piece by piece it is a nightmare. Piece by piece we all are doomed. Look at me. Details: forget them. We are fighting the big currents now.

She takes a handful of the rice and black bugs and puts it in her mouth. She chews it and she swallows. It's food. Eat it.

Eventually the cats emerged from the scrub. They took the food that had been left for them and padded inside the unlit house. They stepped quietly between the ruptured boxes and stacks of records. The last disc was still spinning, the needle crackling in the groove. It was still warm enough on that first night to fall asleep on the floor. Wilhemina and I were spooned into each other's bodies like halves of a locket. The cats nestled against us, purring. The sea was breaking along the length of the bay. And the breeze said hush, hush and sleep.

I watch the sea a lot, now. I like to get up before dawn and leave her sleeping and go out and find a space in the dunes where I can wait for the sun to come up, the grasses moving in the wind. It's colder. Winter has rolled in, and summer will follow. You can see it all from here, the days peeling in one after another. Mostly that's what I watch for. I pull my raincoat round my ears and dig my bare feet into the sand. Dawn swimmers and fishermen steer clear in case I'm drunk or homeless, a needy itinerant. I guess they're half right. You don't spend all this time examining a place if it's truly your home.

Apart from looking, my concentration doesn't seem what it was. My body doesn't work so well after the fall. Something left me as I lay there on the ground. I've been depleted by it. One of my nine lives, Wilhemina said. I never told her about the four I used up on computer games. Past halfway now, I was thinking. Halfway to where we all will be. She's so beautiful, Wilhemina. Her beauty will last beyond that. It's a good reason for writing things down, although it's the one thing about her I can't really describe.

Slowly, I've been making plans to get my life back. I know most of it's lost, but I think some things can be salvaged. I'm going to do some things privately, things I won't tell her about straight away. The money she's saved won't last for ever: I'll have to do something. I'll draft a few letters, make a phone call here and there. I will get back to it eventually. Nothing major, not at first. I'll work my way up. And instead of telling you about it, I'm going to keep it for myself, and it will be part of my life, private and beyond analysis. I'm going to start clawing my way back.

It will take a long time, but I think it's possible. I know no-one else can do it, that it has to be me – but the difference is, now I think I can. The decks are clear. There's space to think. I could fill it with more words and notes . . . but I don't want to do that. If Wilhemina joins me later, comes out and finds me in the dunes, we might discuss breakfast or the colour of the clouds as they are turning out that particular day, but we're through with the thing that brought us here. The papers are sitting in box files under the house, exposed to the rats and the salt air. The cold has emptied the beach of passers-by. We stopped reading the papers, and the hills make television reception difficult. So there is nothing to prompt memories. Any lingering they do is of their own accord.

In the meantime, this is where I have landed. My fall has ended on the soft sand, in my bare feet, the wind turning my lips blue. The city is a long way away, and I like it there. I know it is reaching out with thickening arteries for places such as these. I know that yesterday's monuments are coming down to make way for our own. It's not disapproval, you understand, nor is it mourning. My sadness is a kind of engine because it is driven by the knowledge that it will some day stop, that we will all end, all be gone. That concerns me, day in, day out. It's hard to say why. Impossible almost. People ask: why do you do it? And you can't answer.

We hug memories because they are where we've been: always better than where we are going. There's no point, I sometimes think, to what I do, no aim in the task other than its completion. All I know is that I have to do it, and it will re-emerge soon. I can't leave it alone. I've tried and I can't. In the end, nothing else works and nothing else makes me happy. It will come back to me and make me itch. I do mean that, I really do. At another time – night, probably – I could put it in a more convincing way. For now it all rolls too easily off the tongue: this is nice, but, you know, I'm devoted to my work. I reach for new thoughts and find only stale water. But I keep going, keep going, running my fingers along each fragment and chipping away until it comes free, because only when all the pieces are gathered will a total form emerge. In my life this is the only thing that rings true and I know, no matter where I am now, that I will return to it, and it will return to me. It has to: it is my only belief, as close as I can come to faith. And where this faith comes from, I couldn't begin to say. Sometimes, late at night, lying between the sheets, I can find the words to explain: mellifluous phrases, slick, able things, and I can paint what I do as part of some larger logic or philosophy, maybe even belief. But in daylight people

The cold freezes the water in the pipes and they burst. A stranger makes remedy with a copper ring and a pale blue flame. Hammering, jocular, he introduces me to anecdotes of his family and a photograph of the child: round face, striped pants, red trolley. I pay him in cash.

It is a bastard lineage from which I spring, a crooked and unnatural tree. I harbour no hopes for a son. I am given, however, to ramblings: who knows what my travels have spawned? Miranda as his mother, his own spouse in her likeness . . . These projections are selfish, shaped by burdens relieved only by his existence, this imaginary son. I crave a redeemer, proof of my purpose. Not one of the bright, stupid things in the world . . . I yearn for an arrest, a full stop. And certainly, while I concede a despairing aspect of the birthright, of dread and anxieties which have driven me great distances. I would gift him the treasure of everything I have learned. The delight that I have known would be his, the errors his caution.

Alas, it is impossible. I fear a child could only be acquired by the perverse methods which have served me thus far. His inheritance would be as unwelcome to him as mine was to me. He would declare his father fathomless and strange. He would abandon me, or be abandoned. Nonetheless, I sit, and I wonder what form he would take, where life would find him. I sit and I wonder and I talk . . . Are you listening?

I sit, and I wonder.